WHEN A GANGSTA WANTS YOU

AN URBAN FICTION LOVE STORY

JADE JONES

ABOUT THE AUTHOR

Jade Jones discovered her passion for creative writing in elementary school. Born in 1989, she began writing short stories and poetry as an outlet. Later on, as a teen, she led a troubled life which later resulted in her becoming a ward of the court. Jade fell in love with the art and used storytelling as a means of venting during her tumultuous times.

Aging out of the system two years later, she was thrust into the dismal world of homelessness. Desperate, and with limited income, Jade began dancing full time at the tender age of eighteen. It wasn't until Fall of 2008 when she finally caught her break after being accepted into Cleveland State University. There, Jade lived on campus and majored in Film and Television. Now, six years later, she flourishes from her childhood dream of becoming a bestselling author. Since then she has written the best-selling "Cameron" series.

Quite suitably, she uses her life's experiences to create captivating characters and story lines. Jade currently resides in Atlanta, Georgia. With no children, she spends her leisure shopping and traveling. She says that seeing new faces, meeting new people, and experiencing diMaster cultures fuels her creativity. The stories are generated in her heart, the craft is practiced in her mind, and she expresses her passion through ink.

JOIN THE FAM

SIGN UP FOR OUR NEWSLETTER

CLICK HERE

MOVIES STREAMING ON TUBI

"FANATIC" is now streaming on Tubi
CLICK HERE to watch

"CAMERON" is now streaming on Tubi
CLICK HERE to watch

SYNOPSIS

**A STANDALONE URBAN FICTION ROMANCE FROM
BESTSELLING AUTHOR, JADE JONES**

Nova isn't your typical around-the-way girl. Far from it. Her life has been an uphill battle from the start, raised by crack-addict parents who dealt her a bad hand. She's had to hustle and scheme to survive, even if it meant getting into trouble along the way. Young and headstrong as ever, Nova is determined to stand by her boyfriend, Sensation—a jack boy who ended up behind bars after being caught with stolen goods.

Blinded by love and loyalty, Nova swears to hold Sensation down through thick and thin. But everything changes when Sensation's older brother, Master, steps into the picture. At 38, Master is everything Sensation wishes he could be: powerful, respected, and the undisputed boss of H-town. Nova can't resist Master's charms and falls for him hard and fast, leaving Sensation forgotten in the past.

Master's presence throws everything into chaos. Sensation idolizes his older brother, but what happens when he gets out of prison and finds Nova in Master's arms? Will he still want to follow in Master's footsteps, or will betrayal ignite a desire for vengeance? And can Nova find a way to turn her life around and break free from her troubled past?

Find out in this standalone novel packed with love, passion, betrayal and reckoning.

*** *This book is a re-release, previously called "Zoe and Verse"* ***

1

NOVA

"How you doin', ma?"

"I'm good," I said, batting my long, curly lashes.

"Shit, I can look at you and tell you good," he said, spinning me around. "Come dance for a nigga," he told me with a look of approval.

"Alright," I smiled, following him to his section.

I didn't even like table dances, but the only reason I agreed to one was because he had mad stacks of cash on his table. If he was gonna spend that kind of money on anyone, he might as well spend it on me. The bills were practically begging to be plucked from the table and stuffed into someone's pocket, and I figured it might as well be mine. So, with a deep breath and a confident smile, I walked over, ready to claim my share of the fortune.

However, two songs in, I noticed he was focused on everything *but* me making my ass clap. "Wassup, baby?" I was throwing my shit so hard, it felt like my ass might fall off my back. "You don't like what you see?" I asked, masking my annoyance. I was dancing like my life depended on it, but he wasn't the least bit interested.

It didn't matter though. He was nothing more than an easy mark to me.

I'm finna juug the fuck out of this nigga, I thought sinisterly.

At only 20, I knew how to stick and move. I'd been robbing niggas with my boyfriend for years. Shit, I knew everything there was to know about robbing. Hell, I wrote the fucking book. It wasn't like I had much of a choice, though. You see, as a child, I had to steal to survive since I was raised by crack addicts.

Before I was of legal age, I used to rob men that I met in the mall, on Tinder, Instagram or just out and about. But when I turned 18, my boyfriend convinced me to start stripping. That's when the licks really came in abundance since I met all of my marks in clubs. Schemin' on these horny ass niggas was like taking candy from a baby. It was just too easy.

"C'mon now, ma. I *love* what I see." The guy I was dancing for smiled, showing off his gold grill. He rubbed my thigh where my scar was for reassurance. "Nigga just keepin' an eagle eye out for somebody, that's all," he explained.

He was actually a cute guy, in addition to being quiet and mysterious. Although he was skinny as hell, he had these big, pretty eyes, thick ass lips, and pearly white teeth. Dressed head to toe in all black—black hoodie, black jeans, and black Air Maxes—he exuded a kind of effortless cool that was hard to ignore. His skin was so dark it felt like I was dancing for my shadow, a beautiful, living silhouette. Every time I looked at him, I couldn't help but think of Ralph Angel from Queen Sugar, with that same brooding intensity and quiet charm.

"Who you lookin' for, if you don't mind me asking? I may know her," I said.

I assumed he was waiting for one of the other dancers and

just grabbed me to pass the time. It wasn't unusual for regulars to have their favorites, especially with the kind of women who danced at Tops & Bottoms. The club was known for its lineup of real lookers, and I was definitely one of them. The competition was fierce, but I knew how to hold my own. With a confident sway of my hips and a seductive smile, I could captivate any audience.

Standing at a mere 5'1", I was sometimes overlooked until men saw the booty dragging behind me. Despite my height, I was built like a stallion. My body was a mesmerizing mix of strength and curves: a small bosom, a flat tummy, a tiny waist, thick thighs, and a perfectly round derrière. My skin had the rich, warm tone of roasted pecans, and my light brown eyes always sparkled with a hint of mischief. A pair of dimples framed my smile, capable of bringing any man to his knees. If I weren't so short, I would have pursued a modeling career, but the streets got to me well before any modeling agent could. The call of fast money and the adrenaline of the nightlife had lured me in, making the neon lights of the club my runway.

"It's cool. You ain't gotta bother yaself wit' all dat. Just keep doin' ya thing, ma," he said, squeezing my ass. He sounded like he was from up top. Maybe New York or New Jersey, possibly even Philly. Wherever he was from, them niggas *had* to be freaks, because he kept pulling my thong to the side and spreading my cheeks just to look at my asshole as I performed.

I think I liked him better when he wasn't paying me any mind.

Speaking of attention, a familiar face emerged in the thick of the crowd, capturing my gaze instantly. He wasn't hard to spot. At 6'5" and 265 lbs. of solid muscle, Master commanded a presence that was unmatched by anyone else. Whenever he walked into a room, it was like a tidal wave of raw power and confidence followed him. His enormous height and physique made him stand out like a titan among mere mortals. I always said he was like a monster among men, his build reminiscent of a professional bodybuilder. His broad shoulders and powerful chest seemed to fill the space around him, and his biceps were so defined they looked like they could crush steel. In the dim, pulsating lights of the club, he looked even more formidable, a living, breathing sculpture of strength and dominance. The mere sight of him sent a thrill down my spine, reminding me why he was impossible to ignore.

From the VIP section, I watched as he stalked through the packed club, moving both silently and threateningly. Despite his massive size, he had the nerve to be surrounded by a pack of cutthroat hitters from New Orleans. You would've thought he was a celebrity with his entourage of hardened men acting as his security detail. It was crazy to witness; he was built like a linebacker, exuding a physical presence that was impossible to ignore. Hell, he was so big, you could've easily mistaken him for a bodyguard himself. But in reality, Master was one of the biggest bosses Houston, Texas, had ever seen—both literally and figuratively. His reputation preceded him, a blend of raw muscle and ruthless ambition that made him a force to be reckoned with. As he navigated the sea of people, it was clear that he was in complete control, every step he took reaffirming his dominance and authority. The air seemed to crackle with tension and respect, and I couldn't help but be drawn to the sheer power he exuded, a living legend moving through the shadows.

Hmph.

I was surprised his ratchet ass wife wasn't accompanying him, too. Any time I saw the nigga, she was practically joined at his hip. I guess she thought if she left his side, another bitch would go after him. And if that was the case, she wasn't wrong in her assumption. Master was a hood heavyweight so all the bitches flocked to him any time he pulled up to a spot. He had money and he was an animal in the streets, and all of the thirsty, dry ass bitches knew it.

"Out of all the strip clubs he could go to, he just *had* to come here," I mumbled under my breath. I was so happy that the nigga behind me had stopped doing that weird ass shit. It was already embarrassing enough having Master under the same roof as me. Up until now, he didn't even know that I was a stripper.

Master's younger brother, Sensation, was my boyfriend, and currently serving federal time. Two years ago, he got pulled over by the cops and was found with a couple of kilos in the trunk. Given the quantity, the charges were severe, and he was initially staring down a 40-year sentence. It was only after Master finessed the judge, using every bit of his influence, that they managed to shave off 25 years, leaving Sensation with a 15-year stretch.

As silly as it sounded, I had promised to hold him down while he served his bid. We had been together for eight years, and he was my first love. The bond we shared was unbreakable, a deep connection that had weathered many storms. I couldn't see myself moving on from him, not now, not ever. Even with him behind bars, Sensation still had me head over heels, my heart tied to his in a way that made distance and time seem irrelevant.

I often replayed our memories together, the laughter, the late-night talks, the dreams we shared. He was the first man who saw me for who I truly was, and that kind of love didn't just disappear. Despite his absence, his presence was felt in every aspect of my life. His letters, his phone calls, and the rare visits we managed to arrange kept our connection alive. I wore his love like an invisible armor, a constant reminder of the man

I was waiting for, the man who still held my heart captive even from behind prison walls.

Suddenly, I looked behind me and saw that the guy I was dancing for had his eyes on Master too. Apparently, Master was just the nigga he'd been waiting on to show up. *I wonder what business the two of them have with each other,* I thought.

Suddenly, Master and I locked gazes, and in that fleeting moment, it felt as though time itself had come to a standstill. Master, nearing 40 years old, hadn't laid eyes on me since I was a mere 16 or 17. Our encounters had been rare, shrouded in the lingering tension between him and my man, Sensation. Despite their blood connection, the two didn't really fuck with each other, and I often found myself caught in the crossfire of their unresolved conflicts.

I hadn't spent much time around Master; he and Sensation kept their distance from each other, and I was naturally drawn to Sensation's side. But the divide between the brothers ran deep, fueled by Sensation's simmering jealousy of his older brother's success. And who could blame him? Sensation, with all his swagger and street smarts, was the epitome of a screwup, leaving a trail of broken promises and missed opportunities in his wake. In contrast, Master was a figure of authority and respect, a man who had managed to rise above the chaos of their upbringing and carve out a life for himself that commanded admiration.

As Master and I stood there, our eyes locked in a silent exchange, I couldn't help but feel a surge of conflicting emotions. There was a complexity to him that intrigued me, a sense of mystery that begged to be unraveled. Despite the animosity between him and Sensation, there was an undeniable pull that drew me to him, a magnetic force that defied explanation.

Ever since I could remember, Master had been *that* nigga.

He was the first guy I had ever seen pull up to the hood in a big body coupe. For twenty-something years, he had the streets of H-Town on lock. Everyone respected Master as an OG because he stood up for the city and always made sure his hood ate. All the ladies loved him and all the fellas wanted to fuck with him. He was a real, genuine, magnanimous type of cat. He even bailed his brother out of jail whenever he found himself locked up—which was quite often. Unfortunately, he couldn't get Sensation off the hook for his last screw up.

I knew it was a dangerous game to play, but I couldn't deny the magnetic pull I felt towards Master. He exuded a raw masculinity that was impossible to ignore. Standing tall with a muscular physique that seemed chiseled from stone, he commanded attention wherever he went. His presence was imposing, yet there was a quiet strength in his demeanor that spoke volumes. In many ways, he was a larger-than-life version of Sensation, with the same rugged charm and commanding presence, but without the signature dreads that framed his brother's face.

It was hard not to be drawn to him, to the way his muscles flexed beneath his clothes, hinting at the power coiled within. He moved with a grace that belied his size, every step deliberate and purposeful. And while I knew I should keep my distance, I couldn't help but feel a flutter of excitement whenever he was near.

Regardless of Master being a Texas legend and sexy as fuck, I still couldn't stand his ass. I refused to respect a man that wouldn't put his own brother on. He had all of these people working up under him but couldn't even spare a single position for his own family member. Sure, Sensation was a wild card and often reckless, but he was still his baby brother at the end of the day.

Hell, Master was the reason me and Sensation were even

on this stick-up shit. If Master had just given his brother a spot in his so-called cartel, Sensation would've never gotten knocked because of that stolen work and he damn sure wouldn't be serving a bid. I knew it wasn't right but I blamed Master, wholeheartedly, for that shit.

Speaking of Master, I watched as his eyes roamed across the vastness of my coke-bottle figure. It was his first time seeing my fully developed frame. Hell, it was his first time seeing me half-naked, period. As much as I hated to admit it, I was peeping him out, too. To be damn near 40, he didn't look a day over 25.

That nigga had a whole lot of order about himself and he always pulled up flexing in designer shit and jewelry. Master was killin' the game in a Dapper Don Gucci fit. He had so much icy jewelry on, he looked like a human glacier. On his feet was a pair of Gucci sneakers with the sparkling emblem. His shoe game was always proper, ole flamboyant ass.

He and Sensation had different mothers so they barely favored each other. The only thing they had in common was their caramel skin and slanted eyes. His mother had died before we even met. He said that she was Haitian and that I reminded him a lot of her. Despite their ages and different personalities, Master and Sensation were clearly brothers.

In spite of knowing that, I still found myself checking out Master. He licked his lips and nodded his head a little, as if he, too, was giving me a look of approval. Or perhaps, it was an innocent and meaningless gesture, but that's still the way I took it. Before I got any ideas in my head, he looked away and then, and only then, did time seem to resume.

"Yo, you tryin' to get up outta here?" the guy I was dancing for asked.

I looked back at him and smiled. Now, we were on the same page. "If I'm making some money, hell yeah."

"C'mon, ma, you know I got'chu." He slapped my ass. "I'm tryin' to eat this booty like groceries...if it's clean," he added.

"That's it? Just the booty?" I laughed. "You might as well lick the whole damn grocery store."

"Baby, I'mma lick you from front to back," he said.

"Mmm. Sounds good. Let me get dressed and tip out," I told him. "Then after, I'm all yours."

He looked at my ass and licked his lips. "I'll be right here," he said, grabbing hold of his dick.

As I headed to the dressing room to change, I smiled to myself because his silly ass was about to get jacked and he didn't even know it. Besides, I had promised my baby that I'd put some money on his books, plus rent was past due. I couldn't ask my sister for the money because I still owed her for the last favor. A bitch had no choice but to get it how she lived, at any and all costs.

Halfway to the dressing room, I noticed that Master was still watching me like I was Sunday night football or some shit. I didn't know why he was all of a sudden fixated on me. But I knew that if we kept exchanging these lingering stares, then something was bound to pop off.

2

MASTER

I'd just taken a seat in VIP when I spotted the baddest bitch on earth. I did an automatic double take when I recognized who she was. I shouldn't have been staring her down so tough, but it was hard for a nigga to keep his eyes to himself. Nova had filled out something crazy.

As she walked past, I stole a quick glance at her ass. That thing was movin' like crazy. I almost couldn't believe it was her, and I had to check her left hand just to make sure that it was. The back of it had been burned as well as her thigh. But scars and all, she was still a bad muthafucka.

"Damn..." I said under my breath. I was amazed at her visual.

Nova wasn't a girl anymore. She was all woman and then some. Shit, truthfully, this was my first time really *seeing* her lil' ass. I mean, she was just a kid the last time we brushed shoulders, so I wasn't checking for her at all. But now...I couldn't even deny it. Baby girl was looking like a whole snack aisle, cookies and all.

"Say, bro. Ain't that Sensation's piece?" Dru asked, leaning in. Her voice was rusty and masculine as fuck. She had a double cup in her hand filled with purple Texas Tea.

Dru was my right hand, my shooter, my A1 day1. She was also a stud, who looked so much like a nigga people often mistook her for one. At 36, she'd been ridin' for me ever since I was a mid-level dealer. She'd saw me get it out the mud. Watched me scrape and claw my way to big boy status and was there for me the entire time. In exchange for her loyalty, I made her lieutenant. She was also my operations chief in charge of money, murder, and logistics. Sensation was *still* salty as fuck about me not giving him that position. He felt like it was owed to him because we were family, but shit didn't work like that.

Trill recognized trill.

Dru had earned her spot, and all Sensation earned was a trip to the muthafuckin' slammer. I ain't have time for that bozo shit.

Nobody knew that the dope he had gotten caught with was actually mine. If it wasn't for us being blood, I would've killed his bitch ass. Instead of waiting his turn, he took the coward's way out and skated off with the work. It was pure coincidence that nine pulled his ass over. But like I always say, *if you do wrong, wrong will follow.*

To be real, I never did like how Sensation moved. That's why I didn't want him representing my brand. Hell, I barely wanted him representing me but we were family. Sensation was a live wire. He'd do anything at any time. He was just too reckless with his shit and in life, recklessness was always a recipe for disaster.

"Yeah, mayne, that's that ratchet ass hoe. All she missin' is a bag of Takis," I said, frowning my mouth up in disgust. I swear, that bitch made my balls itch.

"I don't know about all that. But that hoe lookin' real hittable these days," Dru said, licking her dark purple lips. "On moms, I'd clap dem cheeks on sight. Sensation better keep a leash on his girl, 'cuz if she even looks my way, I'm bussin' in dem guts," she cackled. Dru was always talking shit like she had a dick, and because she acted like one of the homies, I often forgot that she didn't.

"You don't want them guts," I said.

"Man, speak for yaself. I'm tryin' to feel that cake. That shit lookin' right," she laughed like a horny ass man. She couldn't take her eyes off Nova. "All that ass."

I just shook my head at her. I knew all about Nova hitting licks on niggas and I didn't approve of it one bit. "It's like my grandma used to say. He that lieth down with dogs shall rise up with fleas."

"Nah..." Dru said in denial. "The bitch crazy like that?"

"Crazier than a bat with rabies flying around in the day time," I said. To be real, I never understood what Sensation saw in her. She was pretty as fuck, but she portrayed herself to be very ignorant and one-dimensional. Honestly, every bitch that dealt with Sensation was.

"Mayne, hol' up...So you wouldn't clip that?" Dru asked, giving me a sideways look.

"Fuck nah. Boy, dat bitch dirtier than that Sprite you drinkin'. Straight up," I laughed.

Dru broke out laughing too. "Boy, you wildin'."

"Shit, I just got rid of my own headache. Nigga don't need another," I said, sipping my deuce. I'd recently separated from my wife of 21 years. However, neither of us had gotten around to filing for divorce.

"I feel that. All I'm sayin' is some headaches might be worth it," Dru laughed. "We all know pussy is the medicine."

I couldn't help but chuckle too as I looked back at Nova. My mouth was saying one thing, but inside I was screaming "I need that."

"Master!" Profit, the club manager, stepped into our section and dapped me up. He was a white boy but hood as fuck at heart. Even though he acted black, he was as straight-laced as they came. His haircut was so sharp and crisp you just knew he had an 815 credit score or higher. "Wuz happenin' wit'cha, mayne?"

I smiled at him with a $30,000 grill in my mouth straight from Johnny Dang. "Shit. Out here movin' and groovin'. Gettin' this muthafuckin' money. Tryin' to keep shit rollin'," I told him. "Say mayne, what the fuck is this shit, though?" I asked in regards to the song playing.

"What? This shit?" He pointed back at the speakers. "Super Slimey. Young Thug's newest joint. The shit bump hard as fuck in Atlanta."

I knew my ass was getting old. I'd never heard of Super Slimey or a muthafuckin' Young Thug. "Well, this ain't gay ass Atlanta. This Terror Town. Tell the DJ to throw on some bangers. You finna run all our clients outta here wit' dis."

"No cap," Dru agreed.

Profit laughed and raised his hand to the DJ, signaling for him to play my shit. Seconds later, Z-Ro's *Mo City Don* poured through the speakers and the whole club was shockin' and rockin'. That shit was a classic in H-Town. If you ain't know the words, you weren't from Houston.

"Anything else, Boss Man?" Profit asked me.

"Yeah...the joint that just walked in the dressing room—"

"Who? Nova?"

"Yeah...I don't want her ass back up in here," I told him.

"Damn, shawty only been here a week. But if you don't want her here, I got no choice but to respect it," Profit said. He was the manager, but I was the owner of Tops & Bottoms, so he understood that my word was law. And I didn't want that bitch in my club, robbing niggas and making my shit hot.

"Cool, cool. You ready to make that play then?" I asked.

"I'm always ready."

Dru and I stood from our seats and Profit followed us to the lot in the back, where only the elitist of clientele could park. Since it was valet only, the lot was empty which made it the perfect place to do a drug transaction. Tops & Bottoms was one of my first business ventures and, as of today, my most lucrative. I hired Profit to manage the spot and oMastere sales and revenue. In order to keep the Feds and IRS off my ass, I used a sophisticated laundering system to hide the money trail.

Once we reached my '73 Chevy Impala, I popped the trunk, revealing two big ass Goyard bags full of dope. It was some new shit I got straight from the Mexican Cartel. I learned early on that creating alliances was the key to success, and it was that very thing that helped me establish one of the biggest drug empires in the South.

See, you had to be special to even get the trust of the Mexican Cartel. When they saw how fast I sold off the work they fronted me 15 years ago, they agreed to supply me with some of the purest cocaine that money could buy. Because of that, I dealt with nothing but top-paying customers like rappers, athletes and Hollywood A-listers. Shit, I was so major out here, I was even invited to all of the red-carpet events. After all, cocaine was one of the biggest glamour drugs in the world, and the demand for it had only skyrocketed over the years.

With them as my source, I built a billion-dollar empire brick by brick. I had niggas on my payroll that could've easily made these coke runs for me, but I opted to do them personally. With so much money at stake, I couldn't risk taking any chances. "This that *real* super slimey," I smiled, unzipping one of the bags. "Go 'head. Try it out before we bring it in," I said, handing Profit a pocket-knife. I already knew I had the best filth out here but a nigga just wanted reassurance.

Profit took the knife and sliced into one of the bricks, a little too eagerly if you ask me. Scooping out a small portion, he snorted it up his nostrils. "Gotdamn!" he choked out. He started gagging and his face went numb. That's how good my shit was. "This here gone sell like Jordans on release day!"

"I know it is," I said arrogantly. I had an ego twice the size of the moon. Yours would be too if you owned half the city.

"You wanna bring it in now? Or you wanna wait till all of the old shit's gone?" Profit asked. He still had some leftover "merchandise" from the last shipment.

"Fuck all that waitin' shit. This ain't a mufuckin' restaurant, this the streets. Plus, we maximize profits by doubling output," I schooled him.

"Already," Profit smiled, grabbing the duffel bags.

Suddenly, Nova and her little fuck boy walked out of the club. The fact that he'd parked in the back too meant he was a top-paying customer. Knowing her, he was probably 'bout to get his pockets ran.

We locked eyes for a prolonged beat and she sorta grinned at me like she was rubbing it in my face. She knew I wasn't with all that robbing shit. That was one of the main reasons why I didn't fuck with Sensation.

"Bro, we bet not ever hear you playin' that weak ass shit again," Dru laughed, breaking into my thoughts.

I quickly tore my eyes off of Nova and looked over at Profit. "Yeah, tell the DJ to burn them mixtapes," I joked.

"Man, whatever. Ya'll old asses better get to this new shit," Profit laughed.

***

After making the play, I left Dru at the club with the rest of my hittaz, since she claimed she wanted to stay a bit longer.

Half the time, they were just for show anyway; I had no problem migrating alone. Solo, and with nothing better to do, I somehow found myself following Nova and her fuck boy to wherever they were headed.

Fat Pat's *"So Real"* poured through the subwoofers as I sipped my lean and smoked a Backwoods. I drank promethazine from time to time, but I didn't get too leaned out to where I couldn't take care of business. Houston was a big, sprawling, slow, hot city, so drinking it was just part of the culture.

Sipping syrup made a nigga feel warm inside, like there was a veil between me and the world. A lot of niggas nowadays were dying from the shit, but only 'cause they failed to do it in moderation. I usually only did it whenever I needed to feel relaxed. Niggas watched a couple rap videos then went wild with that shit.

"Man, where dis bitch goin'?" I asked as we neared a 'hood known as Gunspoint. One of my traps had been hit there some years back. But like they say, *if you don't have enemies, you don't have character.* That was the first and only time I'd ever been robbed, and best believe I made examples out of their asses.

Popping the glove compartment, I checked my piece to make sure the magazine was full. Even though my shooter was gone, I still kept it on me with 30 in the clip. You never did know when some shit might pop off. And knowing Nova, some shit was *bound* to go down.

As I tailed them, I thought about how Nova's parents tried to sell her to me when I first got on. This was before she even met my brother and she wasn't even old enough to remember. Hell, she couldn't have been more than 4 or 5 years old. Nova didn't know it, but her parents were one of my biggest buyers. At that time, I was servin' nothing but stepped on coke. Of course, I turned their crazy, cracked out asses down. But it was sad to see a couple willing to sell their own daughter just for some dirt. I couldn't say I was too surprised Nova went down the path that she did. At the end of the day, she was merely a product of her own environment.

Moments later, Nova and her fuck boy eased into the parking lot of a ran down motel. I thought about parking too but realized how creepy I must've looked following them this far. I doubted that they'd noticed me but it still gave me a fucked up feeling. It wasn't like me to follow a bitch around, least of all, one that belonged to my brother. *Does Sensation know about her late night rendezvouses*, I thought.

From my old school, I watched as Nova climbed out of his whip and grabbed her suitcase from the backseat. He jumped out too, then looped his arm around her shoulders possessively. I don't know why, but the shit left a bad taste in my muthafuckin' mouth.

Man, that bitch knows what she's getting herself into, I reasoned. *She can hold her own in these streets.*

Switching gears, I pulled out of the parking lot and headed home. "Not my pussy. Not my problem," I told myself.

3
NOVA

"So...do you take all the dancers you meet here? Or am I just one of the lucky ones?" I asked, tone laced with sarcasm. I looked around the cruddy motel room as I waited for a response.

"We don't need some fancy suite to have a good time," he said plainly. "Besides, I don't like fancy shit. I'm a simple nigga. What'chu see is what'chu get."

Well, I *seen* them racks on the table and I'm trying to *get* all that, is what I wanted to say. Instead, I kept my thoughts to myself. "Simple is cool," I said. "But the real question is, are you generous? 'Cuz my time ain't cheap," I added.

"I told you, I got'chu shorty."

Yeah, he was definitely from up top.

"So...how long you been living in the South?" I asked, making idle conversation. "I can tell you're a long way from home."

"Is it that obvious?" he smiled.

"Yeah. Your accent's thicker than me," I laughed.

"That's sayin' a lot then," he chuckled. "But nah, I been

here for 'bout four or five years now. But I'm always in and out for work."

"Oh yeah? What do you do?"

"I'm a freelancer," he said, vaguely.

"Really? What type of freelance work you do?"

"Yo, you ask a lot of questions, Ma. Do you interview all the niggas you meet? Or am I just one of the lucky ones?"

I laughed at him for hitting me with my own game. He was smooth as fuck. "I don't know. Maybe I'm tryin' to get to know you on some personal shit." I was an excellent shit-talker, who played the role of a con with ease.

"Word?" he said, grabbing his crotch. "This dick tryin' to get to know you too."

"I'm a good girl," I lied. "You got me in here cuttin' up."

"You can cut up for me," he said, licking his lips.

"I never even got your name," I said, feigning shyness as I smiled innocently, knowing damn well I was the furthest thing from it.

"Syan...but niggas call me Shoota."

"Shoota," I smiled and licked my lips. "I like that."

"And I like you." He started stroking his dick through his jeans harder. "Now come here. I'm tryin' to slide this stick in that ass." He took a seat on the edge of the bed. "Quit actin' shy and come up outta them clothes."

"I will. As soon as you come up off that cash..."

Shoota shook his head at me and grabbed his MCM backpack. "You ain't gotta twist my arm, Ma. I get it," he said. "Business before pleasure, right?"

"Always."

"I feel it." He pulled out a stack and handed it to me. "That's a banjo right there. We good?" he asked.

"Yes. Thank you," I said, accepting the cash. Kneeling

down, I unzipped my suitcase and tossed it inside. "Now I need the rest," I demanded.

Shoota took one look at the submachine gun in my hand and froze. "Really? So that's how you comin'?" he asked, shaking his head.

"That's *exactly* how I'm coming. Now toss the rest of the cash in here, with your cheap, skinny, black ass. Lookin' like a closed umbrella." I nudged my suitcase over towards him with my foot, making sure to keep a firm grip on the gun. "You real fucking funny, my nigga. A measly fucking stack, though?? That's all your funky dawg ass was gonna give me?" I asked, talking shit for the fuck of it.

"Right now, I can think of givin' you somethin' else," he retorted. "For example, a closed casket service."

"Oh, you think I'm playing?! You think this shit is a game???" I screamed. "Give me the muthafuckin' money, before I blow your muthafuckin' head open!" I tightened my grip on the submachine gun, but Shoota just looked at me and laughed. "Dookie-dick ass nigga, wipe that shit-eating grin off your muthafuckin' face!" I yelled.

But he didn't. He only continued to laugh harder.

"What the fuck is so damn funny?!" I hollered, losing my patience.

"Yo clowned out ass," he chuckled. "You wanna know why they call me Shoota?" He stood to his feet and bravely grabbed the barrel of my gun. "'Cuz I got a gun game that you wouldn't believe and enough sense to know this shit ain't real."

"Oh yeah? You wanna try me?" I challenged. "Go ahead. You gone fuck around and get your ass wiped off the map!!!"

WHAP!

Shoota punched the shit out of my ass, drawing blood instantly. Falling to the floor, I grabbed my nose in agony. For a bitch who'd been doing this shit for years, I had never felt more like an amateur till now.

"You ain't gone do shit, bitch," he said, tossing the useless weapon at my feet.

It was actually an airsoft gun, a mere replica of the ARES FMG, that I found on eBay for the low. I didn't have enough bread to cop a real one because I was always paying bills, lawyer fees and putting money on my boyfriend's books. After he got knocked, I bought the gun online and had been using it for stick-ups ever since. Usually when people saw it, they emptied their pockets on sight...but I'd finally come across a nigga who recognized it as a fake.

My ass should've known better.

This game was nothing to play with, and unfortunately, I had to learn that shit the hard way.

"I—I'm sorry! I'm so sorry!" I said, backing away in fear as I felt the blood drain from me. I was fucking scared shitless. "I'm sorry!" It was all I could think to say to keep him from whoopin' my little ass. "*I'm so, so sorry!*"

"Dick-sucking bitch, you gone be sorry," he said in a menacing tone. "You gone be real fuckin' sorry when I'm through with you!" He balled his fists and cracked his knuckles at the same time. "You obviously don't know who you fuckin' wit'...But you finna find out real soon..."

This was the first time I ever got caught slipping and I didn't know what the fuck to do. All I knew was that I saw my life flash before my eyes in that heated moment. "Please!!! Please, Shoota, don't hit me again," I begged as blood seeped into my mouth. "I was just tryin' to eat! My rent is past due, I got eviction and shut off notices all over my damn door! I was only trying to make some extra money," I told him, voice trembling with fear. "On my mama, I had no intentions of hurting you! I swear!"

Shoota grabbed me up by a fistful of my hair and threw me onto the bed. My head hit the headboard hard as fuck, leaving me slightly dazed from the blow. "I wish I could say the same," he said, unfastening his jeans. "But I plan on hurting you so fuckin' bad, you gone be *beggin'* me to kill you." He grabbed my legs and snatched me towards the edge of the bed where he was standing. I just knew he was about to rape me and I started freaking the fuck out.

"GET THE FUCK OFF ME!" I tried to swing on him but he grabbed my arms so hard, I thought my shit would break.

WHAP!

Shoota punched me in the mouth with a closed fist, busting my shit wide open.

"NO! PLEASE! I'M SORRY!" I cried, voice muffled due to my swollen nose. "Don't do this! Please!"

He had just snatched my jeans down my legs when the door to the room flew off the hinges.

BOOM!

Master stormed the room like SWAT and dived on Shoota. His scary ass tried to grab his MCM bag, where his gun presumably was, but Master beat him to the punch. Grabbing the nigga like a rag doll, he launched his ass into a nearby wall.

WHAM!

Shoota crashed face first into the wall, denting the surface upon impact. Master had damn near thrown his ass into the next room over; that's how strong he was. Shoota crumpled to the floor, head split and leg twisted at an awkward angle. I would've thought his ass was dead if it wasn't for the steady twitching of his fingers. Master had rocked that nigga to sleep without even breaking a sweat.

Damn, he pressed his shit.

Sensation told me about Master strong-arming niggas in the hood who owed him money. He'd always claim that he had this herculean type of strength. I figured he was just talking shit but that was before I saw Master in action. The nigga was certainly nothing to play with. After tonight, I knew I would never ever try him.

"I see you still out here fuckin' with these fuck niggas," he said.

I didn't say anything as I sat on the bed looking dumbstruck.

"Get yo shit and breakout," he told me in an irritated tone. He sounded like he didn't want to be bothered, and the fact that he hadn't even made eye contact with me let me know he didn't want to look at me either. He probably had more pressing shit to do than to come to my rescue, but I appreciated it all the same. Lord knows if he wasn't here, Shoota would've broken his foot off in my ass.

Scurrying off the mattress, I pulled my pants up, grabbed my suitcase, fake gun *and* Shoota's MCM bag. I was about to leave the room but something told me to flip through the bills. Much to my dismay, all them shits were counterfeit. "Mutha-fucka!" I hollered in anger.

"What the fuck is you doin', mayne? Didn't I just tell yo ass to bounce?"

"The move didn't go down like I thought it would. This nigga still owes me for wasting my time. And I'm not a bitch who's fond of wastefulness in any capacity," I said, kneeling beside Shoota's unconscious body. "If not for him, I'd be at the club still waiting to push up on something!"

Master sucked his teeth. "Man, you stay doin' this slime shit."

"You call it slime shit. I call it surviving."

Master shook his head as he watched me relieve Shoota of his Rolex, chain and rings. Since the money was counterfeit, there was a high probability that his jewelry was too...but I'd let the pawn shop determine all that.

"Broke, bitch ass nigga!" I said, kicking him around like he was a garbage bag. "Now who's the one hurting?"

"Easy now, killa," Master said sarcastically. He was being a smart ass since my kicks were doing little next to no damage.

I spat on Shoota's fake, flexin' ass just because. "I ain't like the way the fuck nigga was talking. Plus, he put his hands on me! Look at my muthafuckin' face!" I kicked him again.

"You done now?" Master asked. He didn't seem to care the least bit about my injuries.

I kicked Shoota one last time, then tossed the jewelry in my purse, wiped the blood off my chin and smiled. "Now I am."

4
MASTER

I just knew this bitch was gonna find herself in some shit. To be honest, dude seemed like a funny guy. His vibe was off, and judging from the scene I walked in on, I was right. Still, I was mad as fuck that I even had to come and help this hoe. If she hadn't tried to line the nigga in the first place, none of this shit would've gone down. She'd made her own bed.

After leaving the fuck nigga sprawled out in the room, I wiped my prints and left the motel as quickly as I had come. With everything I had going on, I couldn't risk being tied to this shit. I didn't know his face, and I wasn't trying to be around when the laws put an ID on him. I thought about calling Dru and having her put that murda game down, but I figured the nigga wasn't on shit. At the end of the day, he was only a victim. Like Nova said, if it wasn't him, it'd be some other unsuspecting sucker.

Now if he ended up being an issue later on, I'd have to send the mob after his ass. That nigga ain't want them problems. I kept soldiers on deck. Speaking of Nova, I found her troublesome ass in the parking lot leaning up against my car. "Get'cho big ass off my ride 'fore you dent my shit."

She moved forward and I saw that the damage was already done.

Damn. I had *just* gotten my shit repainted, too.

Swear this lil' bitch is like a bad omen, I thought.

"Fuck is you doin' out here still?" I asked, instead of addressing the dent.

"My car's in the shop," she said pointedly. "I need a ride home."

"That's what Uber is for," I said dismissively.

"Can't." She held up her iPhone. "My shit just died."

I sighed dramatically, fatigued from her constant nuisance. I was all tapped out of tolerance when it came to dealing with Nova and my veteran instincts told me not to fuck with her. Like Sensation, she stayed in some shit. "Gone get in the fuckin' car," I said, biting the bullet. Nova hopped in and I started the engine, but instead of pulling off, I sat there for a second. "You a fuckin' crash dummy. You know dat? Always putting yaself in these dangerous ass situations with no consideration of strategy, tactics or self-preservation. Look before you leap."

"Huh?!"

I shook my head at her. "I'm responsible for what I say. Not for what you understand."

"Whatever," she waved me off.

I really pitied this girl. "You stay on that path you on, you gone fuck around and end up like ya lil' boyfriend...or worse, end up in the dirt. I'm only tellin' you this shit 'cuz I know how much Sensation cares about you. You gotta switch ya ways up, mayne."

Nova sucked her teeth. "I'll take my chances," she said snidely. "Now are you gonna take me home? Or do you plan on lecturing me for another twenty minutes? 'Cuz I got shit to do in the morning, starting with hitting the pawn shop."

"Fuck you talkin' to? Who you talkin' to like that?" I asked angrily. Usually, people were too scared to disrespect me but not her. She'd never seen that homicidal side of me before, so she enjoyed pushing my buttons.

Nova shrugged her shoulders.

"Yo smart-mouthed ass is never at a loss for words, are you?" I said bitterly.

Nova just looked out of her window. "How can you be rich *and* mean?" she mumbled.

I never understood how my brother put up with her ass. Shaking my head, I switched gears and pulled out of the motel. To be so young and smart, she was so damn lost and misguided. I wasn't like that at her age. Every move I made was carefully thought out and executed. Niggas played checkers while I played chess, and I was always a step ahead of the game. Now I was living in a world full of entitled, young, stupid people. They didn't think before doing shit, they just did it. Created their own storms, then got mad when it rained.

That's what's wrong with this new generation.

Suddenly, my Fat Pat CD ended and an old DJ Screw mixtape started playing. I was old school and so was most of the shit I listened to. No matter how hard I tried, I just couldn't get with this new shit. That was another thing wrong with this new generation. The music was ass.

Hopping on the nearest interstate, I headed towards Nova's crib which was on the opposite side of town. She and Sensation shared an apartment in the South Park neighborhood of Houston. I'd offered to move him up outta the hood countless times but he always declined, citing that the hood was his home. Who the hell was I to argue?

From the corner of my eye, I peeped Nova running her

hand down her thigh. The back of it was completely burned, fingers and all, but in my eyes, it only made her more distinct and special.

I tried my best to keep my eyes on the road and not on those thick ass legs of hers. But the harder I tried to ignore her, the more I thought about how she looked half-naked. Shawty was curvier than a backroad in West Virginia. She had that cum-fast body, and that booty...don't even get me started. All I could think about was sticking my dick in that horse ass of hers. Before I knew it, I had a whole hard on, balls tight enough to explode. I hadn't fucked anyone in almost 2 years, partly due to my work load but mainly 'cuz me and wifey were no longer on good terms.

I still didn't understand her reasons for wanting a divorce. I mean, I was far from being husband of the year, but I was still a good nigga at the end of the day. Even when we were going through our shit, I never cheated on Maloni. Not even after I found out that she couldn't have kids due to abnormal cervical mucus. The mucus made it difficult for my sperm to penetrate her eggs.

Despite her shortcomings, I had a canine sense of loyalty and a one-woman-man mentality. Hell, I made enough money to knock a new bitch every night. I could easily stick and lick a broad every second of the day, but I wasn't on that type of time. Hell, I'd been owning strip clubs for years and never hit any of those broads. I was strictly dedicated to my wife, and other than stepping out on our marriage once, I was as faithful as they came. And even *that* one hiccup was many, many years ago.

Maloni and I had just gotten married, I was 18 at the time, fresh out of high school, and having way too much fun at my bachelor's party. I ended up getting throwed and wound up sleeping with one of the dancers. It took some time but Maloni forgave me. She held me down while I served in the military for four years. I promised her that something like that would never happen again and I kept my word for the most part.

Maloni and I married young to take advantage of perks on the taxpayer's dime. If you were married in the military, you could easily make tens of thousands of more dollars than a single soldier, plus you were given better benefits. I hopped on that shit, then after my brief stint in the military, turned to the streets. Like the devoted wife she was, Maloni continued to hold me down. She had my left and I had her right, and we were a match made in heaven.

We grew up in the same hood, our parents played dominoes and bust cards together, and she was something like a homie. Shit, we'd dated throughout our high school years, so popping the question wasn't hard at all. She did everything a wife should do. She cooked, she cleaned. She had morals, principals, and she respected herself. All the niggas in the hood told me to, "wife it bro, she a trophy." So I did.

Maloni was perfect for the first 16 years. But the last five had been pure and utter turmoil for the both of us. Regardless, I still never gave up on my wife. Ultimately, it was *her* decision to end the marriage and after 20-something years, I was all out of fight, so I agreed.

Suddenly, Nova reached over and turned up the volume to DJ Screw's "*After I Die.*" I smiled 'cuz her young ass wasn't even alive when this shit dropped.

"What'chu know 'bout dat? That's some real deal playa shit," I told her.

"I know a lil' somethin' somethin'," she grinned.

"Oh yeah? What'chu know?"

"I know DJ Watts bit the fuck out that nigga's style. DJ Screw paved the way for these cats. Nobody was choppin' and screwin' shit till he came along and started doing it. Don't get me wrong. I like Swisha House but I love me some Screw. I think my favorite album from him is All Screwed Up, Volume two. Straight vintage shit," she said.

I nodded my head in agreement. Nova, surprisingly, was up on her hip-hop facts. Needless to say, I was impressed. "So, you *do* know a lil' somethin' somethin'."

"I know a lot," she challenged.

"Oh really? Like what?"

"I know your dick's been hard ever since I got in this car," she boldly said.

Sliding my eyes off the road, I looked over at Nova and saw her looking right at my shit, licking those full lips of hers. We were, surprisingly, on the same token and our eyes met in perfect accord, like we were reading each other's minds. Without thinking, I pulled over to the emergency stopping lane and switched the gears into park. Nova was in my lap before I could even get the seatbelt off.

Like a dog in heat, she crushed her lips against mine as I roughly tore off her top. There was some dried blood on her face that slid across my taste buds but not enough to stop me from devouring her lil' ass—and I definitely wasn't the type to be kissing everybody. Tongues exploring one another, we kissed sloppily yet passionately. Like the world was ending and we only had ten minutes to fuck. "Master," she moaned against my lips. "This seems so wrong..."

I helped her out of her jeans, moved my chain out of the way, then started kissing down her neck and shoulder. "Yeah... But it feels so fuckin' right," I whispered.

Reaching around, I unhooked her bra and let it fall, exposing her little, perky tits. Grabbing hold of one of her breasts, I slid my other hand onto her panty covered mound and pressed two fingers into her slit, rubbing her soft pussy lips through the thin material. She was unbelievably wet as fuck.

"Damn, Nova," I groaned as she unbuttoned my jeans.

Running my fingers over the scar on her thigh, I leaned in and started placing gentle kisses on her small yet firm breasts, taking time to circle each nipple with my tongue and lips. While doing this, I eased two fingers inside her soft and wet walls. Nova moaned a little as I gradually slid them in and out of her, while teasing her clit with my thumb. She got wetter and wetter with each stroke and within a matter of minutes, she started shaking and whimpering; she was already cumming. Her juices flowed down my hand and I could smell her delicious scent rising up in the front seat of the car.

"I need it, baby," she moaned. "I need you to fuck the shit out of me, right here."

I forgot about everything I'd said earlier as Nova pulled my dick out and started massaging it in her hands. It was an impressive 10 inches in length and 3 inches in girth, a bead of precum rested on the tip. Sliding it between her pussy lips, she braced herself for my entrance.

I chuckled softly as she struggled to put it inside of her. Her tightness coupled with my size had her needing some assistance. "I got'chu, baby," I whispered.

Grabbing hold of my python, I pressed the tip into her and began slowly thrusting from underneath. Nova moaned in ecstasy before falling helplessly against my chest. She was so small in my lap that I just held her there, wrapped my arms around her tiny form and fucked her. Her pussy was every bit of tight and hot as I imagined.

Thrusting myself into her warm and welcoming opening, I leaned forward and kissed her hard on the mouth.

"Shit...this pussy, girl...shit..." It was all I could think to say as I slid in and out of her creamy, slippery folds. I pounded into her willing body with rough strokes that made her nails dig into my back. I hadn't even stuck my dick all the way in her, and I was already 'bout to cum.

"Master! Oh my God!" she cried out. "Don't stop! Shit, baby! Please, don't stop!"

"Damn...I'm finna nut..." Before I could fully get the words out, I was shooting like an Uzi into her womb. I swear, I'd never come so hard in my life as I caged her in my arms, savoring the way her pussy tightened around me. Whether she knew it or not, her ass belonged to me now.

"You done?" Nova asked with a look of disappointment.

I was kinda embarrassed, but what could I say? A 2-year drought and some good ass pussy had a nigga nutting prematurely. I softly laughed to mask my humiliation. "Yeah...This old man is done," I said defeated.

Nova climbed off me and slid her jeans back on and neither of us said a word as I eased back into traffic. When I finally reached her crib twenty minutes later, I parked outside of her building and hit the automatic door unlock. I was about to grab her suitcase for her, but Nova beat me to the punch. After collecting her shit, she slammed the door with an attitude and stormed off. She didn't even stop to say thank you once.

A slice of humble pie wouldn't hurt her, I thought.

Regardless of her temper tantrum, I knew that I had to have her.

5
NOVA

Storming into my apartment, I slammed the door behind me, tears streaming down my face. I couldn't bear the thought of Master seeing me like this, so I ran off, desperate to hide my anguish. Once inside, the weight of my actions crashed over me like a tidal wave. Overwhelmed with regret, I collapsed onto the floor, sobbing wretchedly. The betrayal I had committed gnawed at my soul, and I was consumed by the shame and sorrow of my own doing. I'd been with Sensation for 8 years; fell in love with his ass at the age of 12. He was the first and only man I'd ever kissed, touched or fucked.

I might've ran down on niggas but I never slept with any of them. I always robbed them before they could even try to get me out of my clothes. I'd been nothing short of faithful to Sensation and somehow, I'd slipped up and fucked his brother —of all people. I just couldn't help myself. When I spotted his dick print, I let go of all my inhibitions. At the time, all I could think about was sitting on his cock.

"If Sensation ever finds out about this shit, he'll kill me," I whispered to myself, consoling my feelings as best as I could.

Sensation's ass was crazy as fuck and he rolled with nothing but young killers with baby faces. Some of the most notorious killers in the city They were in a street gang, known as Terror Squad and responsible for 50% of the deaths in Houston. Even behind prison walls, Sensation could still reach them niggas if need be, and it wouldn't take much to put a hit out on me.

"He'll never find out," I convinced myself. "What he don't know won't hurt him. Besides...it's not all my fault. I'm only a woman at the end of the day. I haven't had any in two years. That shit just happened." I planned on taking this secret to my grave, and I was sure that Master would do the same. "It was just a one-time, stupid ass mistake. It ain't like I'll ever fuck him again."

If you could even call that fucking...

Master had cum so fast, it felt more like a sample than actual sex. The dick was superb, it was just short-lived. I wanted more, more of him, more of that toe-curling sensational feeling he was giving me.

With all the hoes throwing pussy at him 24/7, you'd think he'd be able to last a bit longer. If I didn't know any better, I'd assume he hadn't fucked anyone in ages. But I knew that couldn't be true, 'cuz there were too many bitches on him.

Wiping my tears, I kicked off my shoes and trudged over to the media console. I walked past the cluttered table piled high with bills and shut-off notices, the physical reminders of my life's chaos. My gaze fell on a framed picture of Sensation and me in Miami, and a small smile tugged at my lips. I picked up the photo, my fingers tracing the edges as I admired how genuinely happy we looked. In that snapshot, we were carefree, basking in the sunlight and each other's company, a stark contrast to the turmoil I felt now. For a moment, the memory of that blissful day lifted my spirits, offering a brief respite from my overwhelming regret.

Sensation wasn't your typical boyfriend. He wasn't romantic at all, and he never told me that he loved me; not once. He didn't believe in licking pussy and he never took me out on a date. His definition of a sentimental weekend was watching Netflix and eating popcorn. My sister didn't understand what I saw in him. I guess I just loved his thuggish ways. He was short and scrawny as fuck but wouldn't hesitate to slap the shit out of a nigga twice his size.

His mother was Haitian, so he spoke French fluently and he had a subtle accent. On the real, that shit was a major turn on and it always made my pussy wet. It was also one of the reasons I fell for him as hard as I did. I loved when he spoke another language while fucking the shit out of me. He had all the hoes in high school going crazy, and I'd fought half of them just to keep them at bay. Still, he cheated on me so much you would've thought I gave him an unlimited pass. He was only 19, so I knew he was just young, dumb and full of cum...but that still didn't stop me from expecting loyalty from him. I mean, what was so hard about keeping your dick in your pants? Now that we were older, nothing much had really changed. He was still a whore, and at this point, prison was the only thing keeping him from cheating.

Shaking my head, I ran my fingers over Sensation's face in the photo. His long dreads were always tied up in a ponytail on top of his head, the front ones cascading down into his face while the shorter ones stayed in the back. He had this peculiar obsession with Asian culture, always sporting a white and red headband emblazoned with Chinese characters. Everything he wore had to feature some kind of Asian symbol, from his shirts to his sneakers. Above the mantle in our living room hung two

Chinese dragon swords, testament to his fascination. Sensation was just different, with a unique swag that set him apart. In a land of 10,000 wannabes, he was an original, unapologetically himself. His individuality was one of the many things that drew me to him, and even now, thinking about his quirks brought a bittersweet smile to my face.

Sensation's mom died when he was young, leaving him to be raised by his maternal grandmother. She was far too old to keep up with his wild energy and rebellious streak. Lacking the guidance he needed, Sensation fell in with the wrong crowd, quickly getting sucked into the world of gang-banging and hitting licks. Despite the chaos and danger that surrounded him, Sensation had a sharp mind. He somehow managed to graduate from high school with a 3.0 GPA, a testament to his intelligence and resilience. Universities across the country offered him opportunities, but college was the furthest thing from his mind. Sensation was addicted to the rush of the fast life, the thrill of danger, and the allure of easy money. He idolized his older brother, Master, yearning to one day reach his level of street status and power. Sensation's dreams were not of degrees and stable careers, but of commanding respect and fear in the underworld, carving out a name for himself that would echo through the streets.

Speaking of Master, my legs turned to jelly when I thought about what we'd just done. Our time together may've been short, but it was the best few pumps of my life. Before him, all I'd ever known was Sensation...and then he came along.

"That shit will never happen again. It was just a one-time, stupid ass mistake," I said. Placing the picture back on the console, I padded to the bathroom and ran a hot shower. The whole time I was underneath the spray I thought about Master.

Why was he kissing me like that?

Why was he holding me like that?

Why did he have to be so passionate?

Why did he have to kiss me like that?

My head was all fucked up by the time I climbed out of the shower. "Jesus, be a fence."

I was about to roll a blunt when I heard a knock at my door. I didn't live in the safest area and I thought about grabbing my airsoft gun. Then I remembered how useless it was since it shot out nothing but rubber pellets.

Ambling to the door, I stood on my tiptoes and peered through the peephole. *Oh my God.* Much to my surprise, it was Master. *What the hell is he doing here?*

Against my better judgment, I unbolted and opened the door. "Why did you come back here?" I asked, awestruck.

Master walked inside without invitation and kicked the door closed behind him. "You know what the fuck I came here for," he said, lifting me off of my feet. Master had the body of a prisoner dedicated to pumping iron, so picking me up was like lifting a feather. He was so big and strong and I loved how he took control of me.

Wrapping my legs around his waist, I started kissing him despite my earlier protests. Master carried me through the apartment in search of my room and when he finally found it, he tossed me on the mattress. I eagerly unwrapped my towel and spread my legs, pussy quivering in heated anticipation. But instead of climbing onto the bed, Master walked over towards my closet. Next, he did something that I didn't, at all, expect. He opened the closet door, looked inside to make sure the coast was clear and closed it.

What the hell was that, I wondered. *Does he really think I will set him up?*

"What are you looking for?" I laughed.

"I'm lookin' to make you cream," he said, crawling onto the bed.

I anxiously helped him out of his clothes—and that's when I saw the unsightly scar on his stomach. It was 6-inches long with small staple scars surrounding it. He'd obviously gotten stitches and the skin was somewhat dented in, which meant that he may've had skin-grafting done too.

I wonder what happened.

I didn't get a chance to ask him as he grabbed my legs and pushed them far apart. His hot lips created a trail of kisses along the inside of my thigh. I stifled a moan when he reached my center. I had never been licked down there so I didn't know what to expect.

What am I talking about?

He may not even eat pussy, like Sensation.

Just 'cuz his head is down there doesn't mean he's about to lick it.

Master blew his warm breath onto my bare pussy and I damn near lost my mind. Using his thumb and forefinger, he spread my pussy lips, exposing my engorged clitoris and causing my inner labia to spread. This was the closest any man's face had ever been to my lady parts and it felt like he was looking inside of me. Leaning in, he started nuzzling his nose against my slit, inhaling and stimulating me at the same time. The tiny hairs from his neatly trimmed beard tickled my skin, further exciting me to the point of near climax.

"I love the way this pussy smell," he whispered into my mound.

His heavy breath on my hot pussy had me shaking and shivering in delight. Cupping my butt cheeks in his massive hands, he pulled me forward and ran his tongue up the crack of my ass to my tingling clit. I cried out in ecstasy; it was the most sensational thing I'd ever experienced. He was tenderizing my young ass.

"*Mmm*...I love the way this pussy taste, too," Master whispered.

Face pressed into my pelvis, he slowly moved my hips up and down to match the rhythm of his tongue. It felt incredible and it was so unexpected, which made it all the more sensual.

Suddenly, he slipped two fingers in me, while pushing lightly on my lower abdomen. Out of nowhere, I started crying and shaking uncontrollably. I'd never felt this wondrous feeling before and I didn't know what was happening. On the real, it actually scared me!

"V—Master," I stuttered, alarmed.

"That's it, baby...Cum for me," he whispered into my pussy, while continuously licking my clit. "Cum for Daddy."

My legs shivered and my eyes rolled to the back of my head. So, this was what cumming really felt like...Well, what the hell had I been doing with Sensation all these years? Because we damn sure weren't fucking like this. Master was a whole different type of animal in the bedroom. After today, I knew that I'd forever be addicted to him.

"Yeah...that's it," he moaned. "Cum all over my tongue, baby...."

"Shit, Master..." I breathed. "That feels so fucking incredible..."

He merely chuckled at my reaction. There was a proud yet arrogant look on his face as he continued to lick me dry. "I wanna eat this pussy like this every day for the rest of our lives," he said. "You gon' let me do that?"

"Yes, baby!" I screamed out. He was licking my shit so good, I would damn near say anything. "You can do whatever you want to me, Daddy! I'm yours!"

Master smiled sexily, not once breaking his task. My toes

curled in pleasure as his tongue flicked feverishly across my clit. It was moving at the speed of light, and so were his fingers as they slid in and out of me. He had me squirming and squirting all over the place as he sucked and licked on my clit. Before today, I didn't even know that shit was possible. Sensation had never made me squirt. Hell, he'd never even come close to it.

A jolt of pleasure shot through my body as I felt myself about to cum. His tongue darted in and out of my pussy hole a few times before going back to work on my clit. I couldn't believe how amazing Master was at eating pussy. And I really couldn't believe that I'd hated his ass for as long as I did.

Sensation always had me watching lesbian porn with him and that's exactly what Master reminded me of. A lesbian. He was so in tune to a woman's wants and needs, so knowledge-able of the female anatomy He knew my body better than I knew myself. He was way older than me so he'd obviously gotten a lot of practice. He had a seasoned-ness about him. He was a vet when it came to oral sex.

"Damn, Master! I think I love you!" I cried out as I came a third time.

Master laughed haughtily before placing a kiss on my outer lips. Climbing on top of me, he wiped his cum-soaked fingers across my lips and kissed me. I hated to admit it, but his ass was turning me out.

"That shit sounds good." He kissed the back of my hand again. "But you gone fuck around and get a war started, you keep talkin' like that."

"Well, we fuckin' now, so the shit's already begun," I said, climbing on top of him.

I couldn't ride him in the car, so I didn't know what made me think I could ride him in bed, but a girl could still dream. After several failed attempts at trying to mount him, Master flipped me over onto my back and eased between my legs. Neither of us mentioned a rubber as he pressed the tip against my slit.

"*Ooooohhhh*," I whimpered. "Shit, Master, you're filling me up," I moaned as he slid deep inside of me. This time he put it all the way in and taking him on was like birthing a baby. He was so big, and I was so tight, young and inexperienced. "I feel like I'm going to explode."

"Don't worry, baby." He kissed my chin, then the side of my neck, then the back of my hand where I'd been burned in a house fire. "I'mma take my time with this pussy." He grabbed my throat and kissed me softly.

A scream of delight erupted from my mouth as he pulled out halfway, then drove his dick deep inside of me. Master didn't care to silence me as he fucked me harder and faster. *He had totally lied*! He wasn't taking his time at all. As a matter of fact, he was flat out punishing me. Maybe he was still mad at me for denting his car, so he was taking it out on my pussy.

"Damn...bay...bee...slow...down," I panted.

Master pinned my ankles behind my ears and went balls deep. His speed increased and before I knew it, our pelvises were slapping into each other. I was so damn wet, that I had his entire dick coated in cream. The headboard pounded into the wall as my pussy clenched and twitched with sporadic convulsions.

"You a big girl. You can take this dick," he growled, plowing into me. His hips were pumping nonstop, pistoning his dick into me while kissing me at the same time.

Damn.

I could fuck him forever.

I could survive on fucking him.

I could wake up and go to sleep fucking him.

Master's sex was so good. It was like he was pulling the

orgasms out of me, demanding that my body obey him. His dick had me feeling like I was getting the best massage of my life. I'm talking Tempur-Pedic dick. He was pumping the shit out of my little ass.

"Oh my God, Master! I'm 'bout to cum again!" I bellowed.

"Oh shit, I love you, baby! I fucking love your ass!"

He gave me that arrogant laugh of his and kissed me. "Yeah...Cum all over this dick. I won't let yo ass leave me without cumming again. Cum on this dick as many times as you want."

A mind-numbing orgasm rocked my body and sent my eyes rolling to the back of my head. Seconds later, I felt his seeds fill me up. We came together in a whirlwind of lust and then after we kissed for what felt forever. Master was a good ass kisser, too. So good that he made me feel amateurish, but once I found his rhythm I quickly fell into it. Sensation didn't like to kiss, so I guess I'd never gotten that much practice. But Master... Master was the very essence of intimacy.

"I can't believe we just did that," I said once he rolled over.

"You took the words right outta my mouth," he said. "Call me fucked up, but I don't regret that we did."

"You don't?" I asked, firing up a blunt. Marijuana was the only thing I fucked with. After seeing what drugs did to my parents, I promised to stay far as fuck from it.

"Nah...you shouldn't either..." he said.

I passed him the blunt and he took it. "How'd that happen?" I asked, pointing to his scar.

Master took a hard pull on the blunt, then blew the smoke through his nose. "How'd *that* happen?" he asked, pointing to my hand.

"You can't answer a question with a question," I said, laughing at his pettiness.

"I was shot...some years back. No big deal. Nigga still breathin'."

"Why were you shot?"

Master pulled me close to him and kissed me. "Let's not talk about that shit," he said. "I wanna enjoy this moment."

"Oh, you wanna enjoy this moment, huh?" I repeated. "Well, you better enjoy the fuck out of it 'cuz we ain't doing this shit again."

Master just laughed. "Yeah, we'll see about that."

6

SENSATION

While everyone was enjoying their rec time, I was busy swiping through pictures on Tinder. I tried to like the profiles of as many unattractive women as I possibly could before final count was called. If you were cute, I swiped left. If you looked like you could turn Medusa to stone, I swiped right. The shit was as simple as that, and it'd been my lil' gig during my time in prison. One thing about ya boy, a nigga knew how to cake up.

Six months into my sentence, I fucked one of the female guards to get this burnout phone. There was a limited number of minutes on it, so I never used it to call Nova or any of my homeboys. It was strictly for making plays.

All day long, I'd finesse these fat ass, lonely bitches into sneaking in contraband and putting money on my books. I even fucked a few of them in the closet during visitation. Of course, I had to pay the COs, but it was worth every penny since I was locked the fuck up.

All my life, I'd been pimping bitches like it ran in my DNA.

And I ain't never fucked with a bitch I couldn't go back and fuck. When I was a kid, I used to sweet talk little girls into carrying my school books. Then, as I got older, I got more conniving and my demands became worse. At only 19, I kept a roster in rotation. I had these hoes praising me like the Pope. These bitches would do anything that I asked. I had these hoes smuggling in dope, weed, pornos and whatever else these niggas in here were willing to pay me just to get their hands on.

I made a nice lil' check off that, and if I kept this shit up, I'd be ballin' by the time I got out. And with the things I had planned, I would definitely need some paper to make it all possible. Luckily, I'd been stacking my bread. Plus, Nova was still putting money on my books.

I had that hoe housetrained, and she was far too dumb and naïve to realize I'd been pimping her duck ass the longest. Hell, I'd never even told the hoe that I loved her and she was down to do anything. Nowadays, bitches were so untrustworthy, I had no choice but to stick and slime 'em. A pimp was a master of love, never a slave to it.

I wasn't too worried about Nova replacing me while I was up the river. I knew I had that shit on lock. Her ass wasn't going anywhere—and if I *did* find out about her fucking around, I wouldn't hesitate to put a bounty on her head. All I had to do was say the word and my young boys would leave her somewhere stankin' in a ditch.

Only thirteen more years of this shit, I thought to myself.

I didn't bitch or complain about it too much 'cuz some of these cats were facing life. At least, I was a little over a decade away from tasting freedom again. Plus, time seemed to fly in this bitch, especially when you were stackin' whores and blue faces.

In my downtime, I studied accounting and business and even took a few correspondence classes. I needed to polish up on my education. A nigga was slowly masterminding a strategy to take over the game and my mind needed to be up to par with my plan.

By the time I was released, Master would be in his 50s, well past his prime and ready to step down. And if he wasn't ready to step down, I had no problem knocking his ass down. He should've been grateful I ain't have my young niggas blow at him. If it wasn't for him being my father, I would've been gave them niggas the greenlight.

Master had been lying to everyone about me being his brother for so many years, I think he started believing the shit himself. But the truth was, he'd knocked up my mother at 18, back when she used to strip at the old Onyx.

I was 5 when he found out about me so he just passed me off as his baby brother. His pops was a rolling stone anyway, a well-known pimp who was heavy in the game in his heyday. It wasn't hard, at all, for people to believe that he'd knocked up some young bitch. The nigga was 60, had 20 something kids and was *still* pulling hoes to this day. I guess that's where I got my pimp mentality from.

For the longest, I never understood why Master didn't wanna claim me as his son. But that was before I found out he was married to a bitch who couldn't have kids. He must've figured she'd up and leave his ass after finding out about me. And the blow would've been twice as devastating since Maloni couldn't have kids of her own. So, for 19 years, Master told the world that I was his baby brother.

He still looked out for me whenever I needed it, but his riches couldn't fill the void that not having a father left. You'd think the least this nigga could do was put me on to some bread. I was out here tryin' to get it just like him. He wasn't starvin'. He wasn't missing any meals. But he fed everyone else at his table, then gave me the fucking scraps. I was his son, his flesh and blood. Why the fuck couldn't I have been his lieutenant instead of that dyke ass bitch, Dru? I had never once seen a brick and my father was the king of cocaine. Yet I was out here hustlin' 8 balls and shit, like some small-time corner boy.

I ain't even gone front. That shit had a nigga feeling some type of way.

I felt unwanted, unloved and most of all, abandoned. And then when my mama died, I just knew he'd step up to the plate and be a man...but he didn't. He just continued to lie about me being his brother and treating me like some outcast. I was denied my right as the sole heir to his empire and that shit really pissed me off. It was also the reason why I joined a gang in the first fucking place.

That shit made a nigga feel like he had a family, a family who wanted me. And since my mom died when I was young, I used bitches to fill that hole in my heart. Nova was the closest thing I found to my mother, and because of that, I knew I could never let her go. I might not have loved her, but she was something special to me and I cherished her.

"FINAL CALL!" a male CO shouted throughout the pod.

After swiping one last profile, I closed the app and powered off my cell before stuffing it under my pillow. I wasn't worried about anyone stealing it since I didn't have a Bunkie. I paid a lot of money to keep them from sticking someone in my cell. I didn't like a lot of niggas, other than the ones in my street gang. Hopping off the bed, I walked over to my calendar and crossed off the current day with a red marker.

Only thirteen more years of this shit, I thought miserably.

Stepping out of my cell, I waited for my name to be called off. Prison was hell, but at least I had a solid plan for when this shit was all over. I was determined to take Master's spot on his throne. And if he didn't willingly hand down his crown, I had no problem taking the shit from his ass and killing him. I didn't give a fuck about him being my father. A nigga could still get spent.

7
MASTER

The sun had barely peaked over the horizon when I crept out of Nova's crib that morning. I made sure to leave some money for her on the table next to her collection of bills and shut off notices. She was still asleep, fatigued from hours of fucking, so I didn't bother to wake her. Truthfully, I wouldn't have known what to say if I did. Regret was already gnawing at my conscience and I couldn't believe that I'd fucked her.

What type of nigga slept with his son's bitch? It was already bad enough that I didn't claim Sensation, and now I was layin' wood to his woman. The shit was beyond fucked up —even for a nigga of my caliber. I'd done a lot of bad things to get to where I was, but none was as bad as this. I honestly didn't know what had come over me and if I could, I'd take it all back.

"I should've just taken her muthafuckin' ass home," I said, starting up my car. "I should've never went there wit' her ass."

I'd just eased out of Nova's apartment building when my cellphone suddenly rang. It was Dru and I answered immediately. "Aye jack, say jack? Where you at?" she asked in a some-what urgent tone.

"Wuz good? Everything cool?" I asked, momentarily alarmed. I just knew she had bad news.

"Yeah, bro. I'm at the warehouse. The one we supposed to be closing the deal on. Everyone's here, waitin' to sign the papers and do the exchange, but we can't without the man of the hour."

"Damn, my bad. Nigga fucked around and overslept," I lied. "But I'm headed that way now."

"Nigga, you ain't overslept. What bitch got you distracted? 'Cuz yo ass is always on point."

"Bro...you won't believe me if I told you."

"Try me..."

I shook my head in disbelief. "Nova," I admitted sheepishly.

"*Sensation's piece*?????!" Dru asked shocked. "Hell nah! The one from the club last night??? Nah, bro. You ain't clap that," she said in denial.

"Oh, I clapped it...and I'm not proud of that shit either," I added.

"Damn, I can't wait to hear how that shit went down. I guess I'll see you when you get here."

"One hunnid," I said, hanging up.

After signing off on the new warehouse, Dru and I went to *The Breakfast Klub* and I filled her in on everything that went down between Nova and I, sparing no details even when it came to the bomb ass sex. I had to tell someone because the shit was eating me alive.

"So, she just hopped on ya shit?" Dru asked before eating a forkful of eggs.

"Like a cowboy on an Appaloosa," I confirmed. "And when

she did it, I just rocked wit' it. Shit, I ain't know what else to do."

"Other than to fuck her," Dru added. "So...on the cool though, how was it?" she asked.

"Man..." I sighed and ran a hand over my brush waves. "I'mma keep it a buck with you. Shit was gucci...She had that splash."

Dru cackled a little then composed herself; she was spitting food all over the fucking place. "So, is this a one-time thing or you cuffin' it?"

"Man, I don't know what we doin'," I said exasperated. "All I know is that I can't shake this bitch for shit."

"*Daaammmnnnn*. Shawty must got all the juice, huh? Bitch had that fire in the hole," Dru laughed. "She put it on you, bro, 'cuz yo ass was speakin' mighty different yesterday."

"It ain't even just that," I told her. "She got potential. I see it in her swag."

"What type of potential?" Dru asked skeptically. "Please enlighten me. 'Cuz at this point, I think yo dick's doin' all the talkin' for you."

I chuckled and shook my head. "I don't know, man. She's lowkey smart for her age...and somewhat street savvy..."

Dru gave me a sideways look. "Just 'cuz you fuck her don't mean you know her."

"I know enough to know all she needs is proper guidance."

"And you the nigga to guide her?" she asked pointedly.

I leaned back in my seat and frowned at Dru. "I ain't say all dat."

"But you thinkin' it."

I couldn't even argue with her there because I was. Ever since I stuck my dick in Nova, I'd been thinking all type of shit.

"*Broooo*, I can't 'een believe yo ass," Dru chuckled. "You hulled out."

"Mayne, hol' up. Weren't you the one just sayin' you'd knock her walls loose if given the chance."

"Yeah, but I was talkin' shit. No way in hell I'd fuck that crazy ass bitch. You better hope Sensation don't find out. Or else he gone continue being a pain in yo ass."

"You let me worry about Sensation," I told her.

Dru just smiled at me and shook her head before biting into her pancakes. Even though she didn't judge me for sleeping with Nova, I still ended up judging myself. It wasn't like me to let my feelings dictate my actions. I knew better than to stick my dick in that young bitch and I still fucked around and did it.

After breakfast, I went to cop a deuce and a pack of 'Woods and headed home. A nigga needed to get throwed. I *had* to take my mind off of Nova. My thoughts were consumed by everything that'd happened between us. I was trying hard to shake her, but the scent and taste of her body stayed with me.

I hated to admit it, but that young bitch had my head spinnin'.

When I walked inside of my crib, the first thing I did was check the closets. Once I made sure shit was good, I cracked the seal to the Sprite, poured a decent amount in a cup and dropped a deuce in it. I planned on being on some slow-motion shit for the rest of the day. I had a lot to think about, starting with how to handle this "situation".

After rolling a fat ass blunt, I got comfortable on the sectional and placed my choppa on the coffee table in front of me. Now that I was single, I lived in a high-rise penthouse near the Gallo. I also liked the small space since it was easy to keep in order. Unfortunately, I no longer had a wife to clean up after my ass.

Prior to our separation, Maloni and I lived in a $30,000,000 secluded mansion on the outskirts of the city.

However, I refused to stay in that big ass house without her there. She'd already moved her shit out months ago, so I ended up putting the bitch on the market. Honestly, I didn't care to keep the memories. I'd given her ass some of the best years of my life, but now, I simply wanted to move on. I needed a fresh start and relocating was the first step.

Damn.

Nova, Nova, Nova.

My mind drifted back to that feisty ass 20-year old. She'd been preoccupying my thoughts ever since I left her place. I'd only hit a couple times, and she already had a nigga sweatin' her.

"I can't believe I went sushi in that bitch," I thought, puffing on a Backwood. I kept telling myself I should've worn a rubber. But every time I thought about skinny dipping in her, my dick got hard. I needed to feel her walls gripping my shit again.

As old as my ass was, I think this young bitch had me whipped. Twenty-four hours ago, I was ready to write her off and now I was ready to write my vows. She had an OG unfolding, whether she knew it or not.

I looked at my phone and considered calling Nova. I wanted to see what was poppin' with her but thought better of it. "Damn, big dawg. What the fuck have you got yourself into?"

8

MALONI

"Well, well, well. Look what the cat dragged in," I said as Shoota walked his sorry ass into the kitchen of our apartment. We lived in a cozy 2-bedroom in Clear Lake City. I took one look at his busted up face and knew that the plan hadn't gone accordingly. His forehead was cut open like someone had run a cheese grater over his shit.

"Yo, don't start with me, 'Loni," he said exasperated. "Nigga already had a fucked up night."

I went to the bathroom to get the medical kit and returned. "If you weren't tryin' to get your dick wet, it wouldn't have been fucked up!"

Shoota scoffed and shook his head at me. "So, you were followin' a nigga?" he concluded.

I opened the kit and pulled out alcohol pads and a Band-Aid. "Apart of me felt like I had to."

"Well, a part of me feels like you can do this shit yaself!"

In spite of his attitude, he allowed me to clean and dress his wounds. "You know that I can't kill Master," I said, sounding vulnerable. Not only did he move with precision, he was my husband and I didn't have the balls to kill him. Sure, I wanted his ass dead. I just couldn't handle being the one to pull the trigger. That's what I had Shoota for, the finest murder-for-hire in these streets.

We'd been fucking with each other off and on for several years. He tried to kill Master in the past but shit didn't go accordingly then, either. Master and I had just laid down for the night when Shoota popped out of the bedroom closet as planned. He hit Master at point blank range with a 12-guage shotgun. Despite taking a dozen bullets to the gut, Master still managed to grab his piece and started busting back at Shoota.

I could still remember how Master's entrails were pouring out of his body. I saw his intestines and everything; the shit was fucking horrific. Thankfully, Shoota made it out alive, only suffering a minor graze to the back of his leg. I needed him to survive so that we could try our hand again.

No one knew it, but that's why Master had this weird ass peculiarity about checking the closets. Luckily for me, he never found out about my involvement, or that I'd been trying to get him killed for the past few years.

Don't get me wrong, Master was a good man and his sex was off the hook. He spoiled me and did right by me for the most part, but I just wanted more from our marriage. I was also angry about him keeping his side baby a secret for damn near 20 years. For the longest, I'd always thought that Sensation was his half-brother. But one night I overheard them arguing on the phone. This was right after Sensation had been arrested. He blamed Master for not being a father to him and for forcing his hand. He was yelling so loud at Master that I heard him through the bathroom door and he wasn't even on speaker. When I found that shit out, I was hurt, upset and stunned...and it only fueled my intent to kill him.

Not only that, but I was tired of coming second to the streets and those long hours without Master made me feel empty inside. Eventually, I started to crave someone else. I lost the love I had for my husband and started falling for another. Someone that would see to it that his estate became mine once he was gone. That's why I hadn't gone through with the divorce yet. I knew that if I did, I wouldn't be entitled to half of his riches because of the prenuptial agreement.

"Well, since you can't kill his ass, I suggest you shut the fuck up and let me do what I do," Shoota said.

I smacked a Band-Aid on his head hard as fuck. "Nigga, I'm sick of you comin' at me flaw! Disrespect me again and I'mma fuck around and kill *you*!" I threatened.

Shoota just laughed. He loved when I talked that crazy shit.

"Keep talkin', I'mma kill that pussy," he said, licking his lips.

"Nigga, I don't know what all your triflin' ass was doing in that strip club, or who's pussy you was doing it with. Don't think I ain't see that lil' bitch you walked in the motel with."

He held his hand up like a soldier, pledging to the army. "Man, I wasn't 'bout to fuck that bitch. On moms, I just paid her to polish me off."

"You shouldn't have been paying any fucking body! You should've been keeping your dick in your pants and your eyes on the muthafuckin' prize!"

Shoota frowned. "Yeah, well that nigga was keepin' his eyes on me, seeing as how he snuck me. I would've handled his shit at the club but there were too many eyes on him. A nigga couldn't make a move even if I wanted to."

I crossed my arms and pinned him with a shrewd glance. "I take it you had no idea he followed you from the club."

"Hell nah. If I'd known that, I would've been gave that nigga the whole clip."

"I think he was trying to help that bitch you were with. The fact that you were in there with her obviously had his ass hot." I sucked my teeth in envy.

"Ole sucka for love ass nigga," Shoota huffed. "Captain-Save-A-Hoe ass mufucka."

Master had been that way for as long as I could remember. He loved helping people and his brother was his biggest charity case. He was always getting his ass out of trouble and we fought about that shit all the time. Master never listened to me, though. He was always riding for everybody *but* his bitch. That's the reason we were in this predicament now.

"Wait a minute...if you were there all that time, why didn't you come and check on a nigga? Bitch, I been passed out in that muthafuckin' motel room for hours!" Shoota complained.

"Fuck outta here. You shouldn't have been trying to pay a bitch to suck your stinking ass dick."

"You ain't gone suck it," he reminded me.

Shoota was right. The only man's penis that had ever graced these lips was Master's. He was my first, my everything, but shit changed when he started selling drugs. I probably could've forgiven him for lying about Sensation all those years, but he started paying less attention to me and more attention to the streets. I got lonely and resentful, and before I knew it, I started fucking with someone else. Someone who wanted to see Master in a grave just as bad as I did.

In addition to being a murder-for-hire, Shoota also fucked with the plastic and funny money. Being from New York, he put me on to all sorts of scams and ways to make extra cash. At 25, he was thirteen years younger than me but I kinda liked that shit. I needed to feel in control after being with Master for so long.

Shoota made a bitch feel young again. As I started to get older, I began to feel less and less attractive—especially with all of the young hoes constantly at my husband's neck. Don't get it twisted, I knew I was good-looking. With milk chocolate skin, gray eyes and naturally long hair, I was often told that I looked like Naomi Campbell. And while I agreed for the most part, I knew I couldn't hold a candle to some of the women attracted to Master. Luckily, Shoota came along and restored my sense of confidence. He was a hood nigga at heart, but still sweet in a sense, and he always told me that I was beautiful.

Not only that, but Shoota turned me out to getting fucked in the ass and I'd been addicted to that shit like drugs ever since. I promised him that when he killed Master, we'd get married, take the money and live in South America. I always wanted to live on the beach in an exotic, Spanish speaking, subcontinent.

"I just hope you learned your lesson," I said, wagging a finger at him.

Shoota was young so I gave him a pass on some shit. I saw the potential in him and I knew with the right amount of grooming, he could be the perfect husband.

"I'mma learn *you* a fuckin' lesson," he said, bending me over the kitchen counter.

In one swift motion, he snatched my panties down and pressed the tip of his dick against my opening. I thought he was about to go in my pussy, till he moved it up and pushed the tip into my asshole. My booty hole walls got wet and creamy and I started shaking like a muthafucka. This young ass boy had turned me out and I couldn't get enough of him.

"Don't fuck up the next time," I panted as he hit it from behind.

"I got'chu, baby," he promised. "That nigga Master is as good as dead."

9
NOVA

When I rolled over and touched the other side of my bed, I was surprised to find Master's spot empty. I didn't even hear him creep out that morning and I was somewhat disappointed by his absence. I really couldn't blame him, though. What the fuck would we possibly say to each other after everything that happened last night?

Reaching over, I grabbed my phone off the nightstand and looked at the time. Damn. It was a quarter after noon. "I can't believe I slept this late," I told myself. *I guess good dick will do it to you.*

Smiling at last night's memories, I placed my phone down and looked at my hand that had been burned badly in a house fire. I thought about the way Master had kissed it and it made me feel warm and fuzzy inside. Sensation hated my scars. Whenever we got into a fight, he would always throw that shit up in my face. He knew I was self-conscious about it...but the way Master kissed them last night made me want to embrace my imperfections.

Rolling over in bed, I rubbed the spot where Master had been as I allowed my mind to return to the night of the house fire.

I was 10 at the time and my sister, A'shaunie, was 12. After eating bologna sandwiches on some stale ass bread, we were put to bed early so that our parents could get high while we slept. A'shaunie and I always knew that our mom and dad were drug addicts. Hell, the whole 'hood knew and kids at our school often teased us about it. We lived in a shoddy, little trailer home in the 3rd Ward slums—one of Houston's roughest and most dangerous areas.

Our parents were so hooked on that shit that they hardly even took care of us. A'shaunie and I shared clothes, panties and school supplies. We had no toys and we treated the roaches and rats like they were our pets just to get a sense of what 'fun' felt like. Sometimes, when our parents went on dope binges, we stole from the corner store just to put food on our stomachs.

One night, after returning from a drug binge that lasted a whole week, our parents came home, fed us, then put us to sleep. But instead of going to bed, A'shaunie and I stayed up to count the stars in the sky. Not even an hour into the objectiveless game, we heard the sound of a window breaking in the living room.

KSSSSHHHHHHHHHH!!!!

"What was that?" A'shaunie asked, a frown of concern on her face.

Before I could answer, our mother screamed and we heard her yell at our father. "MAX!!! MAX, WAKE UP!!! WAKE THE FUCK UP, MAX!! THE HOUSE IS ON FIRE!!!! THOSE FUCKERS JUST TORCHED OUR HOUSE!!!! MAX??!! GET UP!!!!"

Suddenly, A'shaunie and I smelled smoke and shortly after, my mom barged in our room. "Girls, let's go! We have to get the fuck out of here!" she said frantically, covering her nose.

She grabbed me by the hand and A'shaunie ran after us into the living room. By then, a third of the trailer was already engulfed in flames. A'shaunie started coughing and I quickly became light-headed, and in the midst of everything happening, our father was still passed out on the sofa, a needle dangling out of his forearm.

"MAX!!!" Our mother ran over and smacked the shit out of him. "MAX, WAKE UP! WAKE THE FUCK UP, MAX!!! THE FUCKING HOUSE IS ON F—"

Out of nowhere, a Molotov cocktail came sailing through the shattered window. It hit my mother in the chest, knocking the wind out of her, and instantly setting her clothes ablaze. "AAAAHHHH-HH!!!!! AAAAAGGGGGGHHHH!!!! MAAAXXXXXXXXX!"

Her bloodcurdling screams sent chills down my spine. I would never forget the way her skin crinkled and turned black like burning paper. Nor would I forget the way her melting flesh smelled, or how the fire from her clothes quickly crept onto mine. After all, she was still holding my hand, even while she was on fire.

"Mommmmmmmyyyyy!!! Owwwwwwwwww!!!! MOMMY!!! It hurts!!!!"

A'shaunie backed away in tears, terrified by what she saw.

I was on my way to being burned alive before my father grabbed me and put a blanket around my body, extinguishing the flames. My mother dropped to the ground and started rolling around like a dog. Snatching the blanket off me, he rushed to douse the flames. When he pulled the blanket off of her, pieces of her skin were stuck to it. Most of her hair had been burned off, and she looked like a naked mole rat fried in acid. There was blood, exposed muscles and patches of her flesh covered in pus and white gunk. I almost didn't recognize her and the horrific sight had me ready to faint.

Suddenly, that's exactly what A'shaunie did. I wasn't sure it was from the smoke fumes or from seeing our mother get burned like a marshmallow at a camp fire. Either way, my father grabbed her and tossed her over his shoulder. Lifting my mother to her feet, he carried them towards the door and I anxiously followed suit. We could already hear the ambulance coming by the time we made it out of the burning mobile home.

My mother was unable to move as he laid her seared body on the front lawn. "I...told you...we shouldn't...have done it..." she struggled to say through the pain. "This...is all...your fucking fault, Max. I told you we shouldn't have done it! This is all your fucking fault!"

Our neighbors rushed out of their homes as the ambulance pulled into our trailer park. The EMTs had just hopped out of the truck with stretchers when our father took off running. I never understood why he ran off like that. Maybe the guilt of what happened was too much for him to bare. Regardless, we never saw him again after that night. Our mother miraculously managed to survive, but she'd have to live the rest of her life covered in 3rd degree burns on over 75% of her body. She never touched a single drug after the horrific incident, and A'shaunie and I never found out why our house was torched in the first place.

Rolling over in bed, I sat up and swung my legs over the edge of the mattress. My life was so damn crazy, I could write a fucking book. I guess, that's another reason why I fell for Sensation the way that I did. I didn't have much growing up, so to me, he was way out of my league. Everyone else saw me as a bum with crack addicts for parents, but he saw me for who I really was. Then when we got together in high school, he upgraded me and I'd been smitten by his ass ever since.

Sighing deeply, I thought about how he'd react if he found out I'd fucked his brother. *That crazy ass nigga will kill me,* I told myself.

Climbing out of bed, I headed to the kitchen but stopped mid-stride when I saw the money Master had left me. So much for going to the pawn shop. It was just enough to cover this month's rent, plus all of my utilities and even a lil' extra to have fun with. I smiled at his generosity. Even though the lick didn't go as planned, he still came through. A bitch couldn't have been happier. Whether he knew it or not, he was a huge blessing to me.

Maybe Master wasn't as bad as I thought he was.

10

MASTER

The following day, I went to check on my trap in Northside. I'd just left a meeting with my lawyers to ensure my stocks and investments were being handled properly, and I found out that profits had, surprisingly, tripled. To keep the DEA off my ass, I poured my revenue into stocks, bonds, CDs and legit businesses.

Lil Keke's *"Southside"* poured through the custom speakers of my souped-up '73 Impala. After getting some ass, I was feeling like the man, ridin' slab through the hood with the rear of my car leaning to the ground. There were kids jump-roping on the sidewalks, pit bulls on chains, niggas flossin' their candy paint Cadillacs, and Mexicans on horses in cowboy boots.

Just another day in Hustle-town.

I didn't bother stopping home first to change into my street clothes, and I was still rocking a Burberry suit and Tom Ford Gators. I wanted to tap into the hotspot before I called it a day. I usually hit the trap every week to make sure production was going smoothly and niggas weren't slacking off. I had my young boys holding shit down and oftentimes, they got distracted. If they weren't fucking bitches, they were playing Fortnite or too busy getting leaned out. I thought about using seasoned vets, but I liked the idea of giving some of these young niggas out here a shot. I refused to overlook the lil' homies. Besides, they were nowhere near as reckless as Sensation.

When I walked in the trap, I quickly realized that hiring their asses might've been a big mistake. No one was manning the dope or the safe, and they had niggas in there that weren't even on my payroll. At least, this time, they didn't have a bunch of hoes here, too. They were notorious for that shit and I stayed in their asses about it. They knew better than to bring outsiders to my trap.

Shaking my head at their unproductivity, I asked myself if I really wanted to continue paying these niggas. They should've been movin' work, but instead, they were huddled in the living room, watching some old ass wrestling match. Pimp C's "*Hogg in the Game*" was pouring from the stereo system. Too bad them niggas didn't know the first thing about the game.

"See, look! Right there! That muthafucka's tooth went straight through his lip into his nose!"

"Mayne, that shit's faker than my baby mom's tits."

"Man, on hood, that shit real as fuck!"

"If you believe that, you dumber than the niggas in the audience. That shit ain't real. Everyone knows wrestling is a middle-finger to boxing."

"My nigga, so you tellin' me you ain't just see the Undertaker knock that nigga's fronts out."

"The shit is staged, my nigga! That's a fact."

"Yeah, it's staged, but some of 'em really get fucked up in the ring. Google it, bro."

"Fuck Google. That shit is fake, too."

"Fuck you, man. *You* fake. At the end of the day, Foley's the GOAT. I don't wanna hear na'an nigga say otherwise."

This was a prime example of broke nigga activity. "You niggas got the laws fucked up," I said. They all turned around in surprise at the sound of my voice. None of them even heard me walk in, which meant that none of them would hear an intruder. "Nobody's manning the work. Nobody's manning the safe. You niggas must not want a fuckin' job," I said in a calm and measured tone. "I don't pay you muthafuckas to waste time. I pay you muthafuckas to work."

"Man, cut yo bullshit. It was slow in the streets so we chilled."

I quickly cut my eyes at the kid sitting to my left with a face full of tats. "Nigga, if you value yo life, you won't be so quick to lose it," I warned him. "Watch how you speak when you speak to me."

He snorted and waved me off, further adding to his disrespect.

Without warning, I grabbed his ass and snatched him over the back of the sofa. Lifting him off his feet like the fuck nigga he was, I held him in mid-air with one arm. I could've snapped his bitch ass in two and not even break a fucking sweat.

"Nigga, you must've forgot who the fuck I was. Don't let the corporate suit fool you."

"My bad, Master!" he cried, feet dangling like a child in a high chair. "On my mama, that shit won't happen again!"

Only a man as menacing as me could demand such respect and fear. Tossing his ass to the floor like a ragdoll, I caused him to land on his funny bone. "You damn right it won't. Now get the fuck off ya'll sorry asses and get to the money. And don't let me catch you muthafuckas lackin' again. Stay on point. Keep this shit black and white, not red and black. You understand what I'm sayin?"

I looked down at the kid sniveling at my feet. "You got it, Boss," he said. You could hear the fear in his tone.

One of the young niggas rushed to the back of the trap to fetch the duffel bag and when he handed it to me, I shook it a couple times and frowned. "Why the fuck this shit feel so light?"

"Like Tevin said, shit's been slow, Boss."

"Well, it probably wouldn't be if you niggas weren't in here jackin' each other off. When shit get to movin', shit get to happenin'," I told them. "Get on the block and get this mutha-fuckin' money on rotation."

Half of them left the trap to hold down the block while the rest stayed back to cook and cut the dope. I was a tough-as-nails leader and hard on them at times, but it was only because they needed it. Most of them had no fathers growing up so they didn't know the first thing about responsibility. Grooming them was a process, but in return, I would have loyal and hard-working soldiers. After all, success comes from delegating, risk-taking, and having a good team.

***

"Pops! You in here?" I asked, letting myself in my father's apartment.

He lived in the heart of the River Oaks area of Houston in a luxury senior living community. He hated me for putting him there but it was one of the nicest buildings in the city. Hell, even flyer than my own shit. From the outside, you wouldn't have known that it was a home for senior citizens. It looked like a regular high-rise and I had him on the top floor, granting him sweeping views of the city skyline.

I also loved how they encouraged independence, mental wellness and social involvement. Every Friday, they had bingo and my pops stayed mackin' on the female employees. He was a pimp back in the day, and some things would never change.

"Aye, pops!" I called out.

"I'm old, not dead," my father said, shuffling out of the back of the apartment. He must've been taking a shit, which was why he couldn't get to the door.

At 6 feet even, he was slender in frame with caramel skin, slanted hazel eyes, and curly gray hair. He was strikingly handsome for a man his age and all of the females loved him. He was full of charisma, wisdom and charm.

"Nigga had to make sure," I chuckled.

"Where the hell you comin' from, all dressed up like that?" he asked, firing up a cigarette.

"Pops, c'mon. You know I don't like you smokin' them cancer sticks."

"And I don't like seein' you dressed like you just left somebody's funeral." He was also a wise ass.

"Aye, mayne, what's wrong with a suit and tie?" I chuckled. "'Good grooming is integral. If you don't look the part, no one will want to give you time or money.' You taught me that."

"Can't argue with you there," he said, firing up the cigarette anyway. My father was a stubborn man, and Sensation had, obviously, inherited that trait. "So, what the fuck you been on lately?" he asked.

"Shit, not much," I lied.

"Bullshit. Mayne, you ain't seen me in months."

"Aww, pops. My bad 'bout that. Nigga just hate to put his burdens on you when shit's goin' south in my life. You always told me that a man holds his own in the face of adversity."

"Yeah, but I also told you to be strong enough to stand alone, but smart enough to know when you need help." My father took a seat on his armoire. "Talk to me, mayne. What's been goin' on wit'cha?"

"Well...for starters...Maloni wants a fuckin' divorce."

"Good," he said. "I never liked her ass anyway, no disrespect. You know I operate by the old law. Can't no hoe sit back and watch me hunt and kill the cattle. In my day, I had—"

"Bitches on the stroll and payroll, I know pops," I said, finishing for him. "But you know I loved taking care of my woman. I never wanted her to want for anything. Never even wanted her to lift a finger."

My father scoffed and shook his head. "Yeah, well, you see where that shit got you."

I was silent, unable to say anything in my defense. My pops was right. I'd tried to do right by Maloni for years and it still wasn't enough to keep this divorce from happening.

"Mayne, I can look at you and tell you miss her. But if you want my advice, you better off without her," he said. "For twenty-something years, I watched you build a billion-dollar business from the ground up with your bare hands. You understand what I'm sayin'? You don't need some broad sittin' back enjoyin' the fruits of your labor, then bitchin' when you gotta go out to water the seeds. You need a humble, selfless, hardworking woman to compliment your hustle. You dig?"

"So, essentially, I need a hoe," I teased.

"Lemme tell you somethin', behind every strong man is an even stronger woman. And behind that woman is a hoe," he laughed.

I walked over to my dad and plucked the cigarette from his lips while he was chuckling. Next, I dug in the top drawer of his kitchen counter and grabbed the pack of Marlboros. He'd been stashing them there for as long as I could remember, and no matter how many times I confiscated them, he never sought a different hiding spot.

"Shit, son. You worse than the muthafuckas here," he complained. "Say, if you won't let me smoke my squares, then at least toss me an eighth." He smiled devilishly. "I hear you've got the best shit in the streets."

"You heard right. Shit so good, it might fuck around and kill you," I laughed. Instead, I tossed his ass a seventh of bud. He could smoke that shit all he wanted. I wouldn't be held responsible for my dad overdosing on some good ass dope.

"My boy," he smiled, sniffing the contents.

I handed him a pack of High Hemp rolling papers and a lighter.

"So, how's the bachelor life been treatin' you?" he asked.

"Been too busy to enjoy it," I told him. "But I have, uh, recently taken interest in a young woman."

"Oh yeah? And who's the lucky lady? An old flame, I presume."

I paused as I debated on whether or not to tell him. "I'm kinda iffy on sayin'. Right now, shit's complicated."

"Life is complicated, son."

"Shit. Tell me about it." I ran a hand over my brush waves.

"So wuz good?" my pops asked, waiting for me to spill the tea. "Talk to me."

"Man...I done snagged Sensation's bitch," I finally admitted. "And ever since, I can't get this broad off my mind."

My father stopped breaking down the weed to look at me. "Now that, son, *is* complicated," he laughed. "You done hoe-jacked ya own son." He shook his head in amusement.

"On some real nigga shit, it just happened. It wasn't planned or no shit like that."

"Our biggest mistakes are the ones unplanned," he said. "So...have you told him?"

"Right now, I'm keepin' the cards close to my chest in order to see how the chips fall."

"So, you not gone tell him?"

"Man...I'm not even sure. You know me and that lil' nigga don't rock like that..."

"And who's fault is that?"

"Aww, pops, c'mon. Don't start with that shit."

"I'm just sayin'. I never denied you or any of my other kids, no matter the circumstances."

"Yeah, well our circumstances were different, pops. I wasn't pimpin' out a bunch of bitches. I was married, and I did what I thought was best for my marriage at the time."

"But what about your son, Master? Did you ever stop to think about what was best for him?"

Suddenly, my phone chirped with a text message—and it was just in the nick of time. Things were really heating up. Talking about Sensation was always a sore topic for me. "I gotta shake back to the city, pops. But I'mma be back soon so we can finish choppin' game."

My dad just looked at me and shook his head. "All our dirt catches up to us one way or another," he said.

I knew he would never respect my reasons for doing what I did, and I didn't expect him to.

11

NOVA

My Steve Madden heels clicked against the tile as I walked through the Federal Correctional Institution in Beaumont, Texas. Since most drug arrests were made by local police, anyone arrested for any drug offense ended up in the federal system because it was considered as both a state and federal crime. Luckily, the facility wasn't too far from where I lived. Depending on traffic, it was about an hour and a half from Houston.

Sliding my hands down the front of my slutty, fuck-me dress, I made sure there wasn't a wrinkle in sight. I needed to look immaculate for when my baby saw me. I went the extra mile and got my hair and makeup done with some of the money Master had left me. I was even able to get my car out of the shop. Afterwards, I hit the Galleria. I wanted to wear the sexiest, tightest dress I could find on the sale rack. One that I knew Sensation would love. I wanted him to think about me when he rubbed one out that night, so a bitch *had* to leave a lasting impression.

When I finally walked in the visitation room and saw him,

my stomach muscles clenched and I felt giddy inside. I was like a girl with a schoolboy crush and Sensation was the bad boy all the girls wanted. *How the fuck does this nigga still give me butterflies*, I wondered.

"Hey, baby," I smiled.

"Hey yourself, sexy," he said, standing to his feet. Pulling me close, he tongued me down while grabbing on my hips and ass. Surprisingly, the COs didn't trip. It was a medium-security facility and touching during visitation was strictly prohibited. At the time, I didn't know he was paying them. "You look good enough for a poke," he said, pressing his hard dick into me.

"Too bad you can't give me one," I winked. "So, how you been holding up in here?"

"You know how it go. Tryin' to stay busy."

"You been staying out of trouble?" I asked him.

"Always. Have *you* been stayin' out of trouble?" he countered. "You ain't been givin' my shit away to these fuck niggas, have you?"

My heart instantly went into overdrive. "N—no," I stuttered. "What would make you ask that?"

Did Master tell him about us?

Did one of Sensation's homeboys see Master walk in my crib last night?

Does Sensation know?

So many thoughts ran through my mind as I waited on a response.

Sensation just smiled and pinched my cheek. "Nigga gotta ask," he said. "Maybe bein' here is makin' me paranoid."

"Well, you have nothing to worry about. I'm on yo team baby. Always."

"Facts. No other way to be," he smiled. "I know you mine. And you know I'll cut a nigga down about you."

I blushed like a fool in love. "I know you will."

We took our seats. "So, you got that for me, baby?" Sensation asked.

"Yeah..." Making sure to be discreet, I rolled my panties down my legs, balled them up and handed them to him. He had my ass so brainwashed, I'd do anything for him.

"That's my girl," he smiled.

I figured he was gonna use them to rub one out tonight. "So...what do you need them for?" I asked out of curiosity, just in case my assumption was wrong.

"Yo ass don't need to know all dat," he said, insulted.

I frowned and sucked my teeth at him. "You're gonna sell them, aren't you? Nigga, I should've known you had some slick shit up your sleeve!"

"Hey, hey," he said in a hushed tone. "Bring it down a fuckin' notch. You makin' shit hot." He looked around to make sure no one was ear-hustling. "Fuck you trippin' for anyway? They just panties. You even know how much niggas is payin' just to get they hands on this? A whole helluva lot," he answered for me. "A nigga just tryin' to eat. It's nasty out here, bay, and my back's against the wall."

I rolled my eyes and shook my head at him.

He combed his fingers through his dreads and then looked at me, studying me almost. "Bay, I got thirteen years left in this bitch," he reminded me. "You gotta be a nigga peace of mind in this crazy ass world. I got enough problems," he said.

"I don't wanna be a problem," I said in my defense.

"It's all good. Life can do a whole 180. Once I'm free, I'mma be able to give you the moon and stars. We ain't gone be strugglin'. You ain't gone be in some club. We gone have it all. The whole world at our fingertips. *Pour moi, tu vaux tout l'or du monde.*"

Hearing him speak French gave me chills.

"I'mma put this shit all the way right," he said. "Everything gone be on track the way we want it to be, trust me. Just fuck wit' me. You know you my baby. All I need you to do is stay down. That's all you gotta do. Don't worry 'bout shit else. I got us, bay."

My heart melted and my face took on a sympathetic expression. "I want that too, Sensation," I told him. "And I have been holdin' you down. And when you make it to the top, don't change up on me."

He took my hands in his. "Never that, babe. I already changed *for* you."

I smiled at him. He always knew the right thing to say and the shit worked every time.

"We gotta bright future ahead," he said, rubbing my knuckles. "We're gonna take over the world."

"Now that, I do believe."

"So...were you able to come up on somethin'?" he asked, changing the subject.

I thought about the money Master had given me. I almost slipped up and told him about it. "I was...but I have to pay bills tomorrow."

"Man, fuck them bills. I need that shit on my books, like pronto."

"Nigga, I've got eviction and shut off notices everywhere—"

"Man, you can go catch somethin' tonight," he said. "You still at Tops and Bottoms, right?"

"Yeah, I'm still dancing there."

"A'ight then. You can make that shit back in one night."

I shook my head and sighed in surrender. "Fine," I agreed. "I'll give you the money. But if I end up getting put out, your ass better make room for me in your cell."

***

That evening, I put my big girl pants on and went right back to Tops & Bottoms like I hadn't just tried to rob a nigga that I met there last night. I thought about going to some other club but I had niggas looking for me left and right for setting them up. I'd done so much foul shit that I couldn't just dance anywhere. Sensation had me living a very fast, very dangerous life. One where I had to watch my back 24/7.

As soon I approached the entrance doors of the club, I was stopped by security. "Sorry, lil' Ma. Profit says you can't come back."

"What??? Nigga, I'll believe it when I hear it from the horse's mouth. Go get Profit," I demanded.

The security sighed in frustration but walked inside the club to fetch him. Shortly after, he returned with the manager of the club—who was, ironically, A'shaunie's baby daddy. I never understood what she saw in him. He was decent looking for the most part but as white as the coke in the corner of his nostrils. I didn't care how sweet she claimed he was, I just couldn't get down with the swirl.

"What the fuck is this shit? Nigga just told me I can't come back in. What the fuck is he talkin' 'bout?" I asked Profit.

"You done here," he said.

"Says who???"

"Says me. The muthafucka that runs this bitch."

"Well, right now you runnin' yo mouth like you in a damn marathon. You stopping me from doing what I need to do."

"You gone have to do it elsewhere. Yo ass is no longer welcome here."

"Where the fuck is this shit even coming from?" I asked angrily.

"It's comin' from a higher power. The man who signs my paychecks. He told me not to let you back in. I've got no choice but to respect his wishes."

"And who the hell is this *higher power?*" I demanded to know. I desperately wanted to speak with him. I was trying to catch a lick tonight and I was pissed that he was stopping me.

"Yo ass don't need to know."

"Profit, are you serious right now? My nigga, you know my situation. You know I'm on my knuckles. I just gave all the money I had to Sensation. I have to pay my fucking rent tomorrow or else I'll be out on my ass!"

"You should've told Sensation that shit. Besides, a real man wouldn't wanna see his girl down and out anyway."

His words cut like a razor and stung like he'd poured salt into those cuts. "Fuck you and your white ass mama with a horse dick!" I yelled. "Cock ridin' ass nigga! Let me in this bitch, or I'm telling A'shaunie you fucked Cherry!" My sister had no idea that her man was having an affair with one of the dancers.

Profit just laughed. "You burnt out bum bitch. Yo sister won't believe shit that comes out of yo lyin', dick-suckin' lips."

I was just about to slap that coke out his nose when I heard a deep ass voice behind me. "Now P, that ain't no way to talk to a lady."

It was like the voices of Vin Diesel and James Earl Jones had blended somehow just for the sole purpose of making me turn around. When I did, I saw Master and some butch-looking bitch standing there. She was almost as big as him with burgundy dreads pulled into a bun.

"My fault you had to hear that shit," Profit said, apologizing to Master instead of me. Shit, I was the one he'd offended. Not Master. Profit was doing a lot of cock-biting since Master was his boss. "I was just relaying to her what you told me."

"So, it was *you?!*" I rounded on Master. "*You* told him not to let me back in?!"

"I did," he said unflinchingly.

"Nigga, I don't give a fuck who you are, or what club you own! Don't ever get in the way of me making my muthafuckin' money!" Pushing past him, I stormed towards my car in tears. I'd put every fucking dollar I had on Sensation's books. Now I had to come up with a way to pay my rent before I ended up on a cot in a fucking women's shelter somewhere.

12

NOVA

Tears blinded my vision as I made my way home. To say that I was furious was an understatement. Where the fuck did Master get off telling me that I couldn't come back to his club? I should've smacked that smug ass grin off his face. He had some damn nerve! If there was one thing I hated, it was someone standing in the way of me getting a bag.

I was grateful when I finally stopped at a red light. I used that moment to wipe my tears. "I should've never given Sensation that fucking money, knowing I was down to my last! UGHHHHHH!" I screamed. "This nigga got me so fucking stupid for him!"

Only Sensation could convince me to do such dumb, irresponsible shit. Hell, he was the reason I was even on this stick-up shit. At 16, I let him talk me into hitting licks and ever since, I'd been depending on that lifestyle to eat. Back then, it wasn't so bad 'cuz I had him by my side. But now he was locked up and I was all alone in this fucked up world just trying to get it.

Suddenly, a green drop top with elbows and peanut butter guts pulled alongside me. It was leaning from right to left and

"Murder" by UGK was blasting from the speakers. I did an automatic double take when I saw who the driver was.

"Shit!" I felt the blood drain from me as my face went pale with fear.

It was Marcus, one of the niggas I'd robbed a while back at my old strip club. He looked up at me with red eyes, staring in disbelief. He was a mid-level dealer who sold weed and pills. He reminded me of a young Slim Thug with his braids and beads on the end. He must've recognized me too, because he immediately popped the trunk on the boulevard. Slamming my foot on the accelerator, I peeled off in my little Honda before he could grab his burner. My worst nightmare had finally come true.

I was halfway up the street when Marcus's crazy ass shot out my rear window! "AAGGHHHHHH!" I screamed, swerving lanes and ducking for cover. I'd damn near ran over a homeless man while avoiding being hit. Luckily, the guy jumped to his feet and scurried off.

POP!

POP!

POP!

"THIEVING ASS HOE! BITCH, I'MMA FUCKIN' KILL YO ASS!!!" He hollered over the gunfire.

POP!

POP!

Marcus continued to let off rounds. I just knew his ass was about to kill me. And if he didn't, I was surely going to kill myself driving with my head ducked down. I could hardly see the road, but I was afraid to lift my head for fear of being shot.

Well this Bun-B bitch and I'm the king...

I'm movin' chickens got 'em finger lickin'...

Stickin' nigga's dat be trippin'...

You need a swift kickin', yo azz is right for the pickin'...

I could hear the music pouring from his subwoofers as his car quickly approached mine.

POP!

POP!

He let off two more shots, blowing out my back tire and causing my car to veer out of control. I ran smack into the curb but was, miraculously, able to get out of that pickle and quick. Eyes darting around for something to protect myself with, I found nothing but my suitcase in the backseat. Rushing to unzip the front compartment, I snatched out my airsoft gun, pointed my arm out of the window and aimed at his top.

He took one look at the submachine gun and swiftly changed directions. Unlike Shoota, he thought it was real. Using the distraction to my advantage, I pulled into a nearby alley and waited two hours before getting back on the road. Luckily, the guy I'd robbed was nowhere to be found. I couldn't believe how close I was to dying. I was *this* close to getting my ticket punched and I had no one but myself to blame. If only I'd gotten a legit J-O-B, then none of this would've happened. Sadly, I couldn't see myself working some crusty 9 to 5. Once you got a taste of the underworld, it was hard to get out.

Counting my blessings, I drove home with a flat tire—and was surprised to see Master's car parked in front of my building. *Has this nigga been waiting for me a whole two hours?* "Damn...as if my night could get any worse," I complained. He was the last nigga I wanted to see, and he'd costed me whatever money I could've potentially made tonight.

Fuck him.

Master climbed out of his old school the minute he saw my busted ass Honda. It was a miracle that I even made it home with the left back tire blown out. Climbing out of my car, I grabbed my suitcase and headed to my unit without even stopping to speak to him. In my opinion, this was all his fucking fault.

"The fuck happened to yo ride?" he asked, sounding worried.

"None of your fucking business!" I spat with an attitude.

He grabbed my elbow and whirled me around to face him. "You are my fuckin' business."

I snatched my arm away from him. "Just 'cuz we fucked don't make me your business," I said, stepping inside my apartment.

Master walked in too, then slammed the door behind him. "I won't even combat ignorance with ignorance," he said.

"Whatever," I waved him off. "Then don't." I didn't care how childish I looked or sounded, I was pissed at his ass.

"You might as well tell me what happened. Shit, I'mma find out either way," he said.

"What happened was *you!*" I yelled. There was a simmering storm of hatred and rage inside of me. And beneath all that was sadness "If I'd been at the fucking club, then none of this shit would've happened!"

"Trouble seems to follow yo ass wherever you go. That shit has nothin' to do with me," he argued.

"What the fuck is you talkin' 'bout?! It has *everything* to do with you!" I screamed. "Why couldn't you just give Sensation a shot?! Why couldn't he work for you??? Nigga, I wouldn't even be out here like this if he was making some decent paper!!! Look how the fuck we livin'!" I said, pointing to our surroundings. "But yet you call this nigga your family!" I shook my head at him. "You act like you're the man, like you're some big-time hot shot, but in reality, you ain't shit! You're nothing but a selfish, self-absorbed, fucked up cocktail of a human being! Just another loser in a long list of poor choices I've made."

Master approached me and I slowly backed up. I just knew

he was about to slap me...but he did no such thing. "Cut it out. You know you don't feel that damn way, girl." I was surprised at his level of calmness after my breathless and disrespectful rant. Master definitely wasn't the nigga to try, but that still didn't stop me from going off.

"That's exactly how I feel. Now get the fuck out of my house," I said stubbornly, knowing damn well I didn't want him to leave.

"Cut it out, Z," he smiled sexily. "I don't wanna hear dat shit 'cuz I *know* you don't mean it. You wanna know how I know?" he asked, sarcastically but with a tone of honest intent. He was so close that he was towering over me like a skyscraper. It didn't make any sense how tall he was. He was the very embodiment of raw manliness. "When I hold you in my arms, it feels natural," he admitted. "I know you feel it too. Hell, you feelin' it right now," he said. "A nigga need that, Nova. I been missin' that shit so much in my life." There was adoration and desperation in his hazel, soulful eyes.

Before I knew it, I was once again melting from his stare. "But Master...you're married," I reminded him. "And have you forgotten that I'm with Sensation." For a moment, I felt a pang of guilt shoot through me.

"Fuck that nigga. You wit' me now," he said, possessively.

All of my guilt vanished when he took hold of my body and kissed me. I felt so weak I thought I was going to faint and my knees started to buckle. A jolt of blinding pleasure rocked through my body at the sensation of his mouth on mine. The fact he was handsome as fuck only amplified that sensation.

My eyes shut and I crumbled underneath the pressure of his touch and before I knew it my lips had parted for his tongue. Although his passion caught me off guard, I welcomed it because I'd been waiting for this moment.

Master's lips went to my neck as he placed a trail of kisses.

He had me feeling a little tingle in my chest and the sensation traveled to my clit when he reached my spot. "Just 'cuz we fucked don't make you my business, huh?" he repeated in an arrogant tone.

"*Mmm*," I mumbled softly as his lips roamed to my ear. I gasped when his tongue found its way in. That shit instantly drove me crazy.

"Yo ass is mine now," he whispered. "I can't give you up."

I whimpered as he slid a hand down the front of my panties. With his other hand he pulled my face to look up at him, but my eyes were still closed.

"Look at me, Z," he said sternly.

I defiantly kept my eyes shut, ignoring him.

"Now," he said, pulling me close against his body. "I want'chu to know somethin'."

I shyly looked up into his hazel eyes. The tone of his voice brought me back to the first time I'd seen him as a child.

I was only 12 when I saw him pull up to the hood in a Monte Carlo with everything decked out. He was the first nigga to ever come to the hood in a big body. If anyone else tried that shit, they would've been robbed. But not Master. He had too much respect in the streets as a hood legend.

A'shaunie and I were outside playing when all the neighbors stopped to marvel at him. In our neighborhood, the only thing we were used to seeing pull up was junkies on bicycles. Master's car had high ass rims and leather and wood interior. Devin the Dude was pouring from the speakers. His wife was in the passenger's seat looking like America's Next Top Model.

"Who's that?" I asked my older sister in awe.

She had this dreamy look in her eyes as she watched him climb out of his car. He had on a red Houston Rockets jersey, baggy jeans and Timberland boots. Both of his hands were shining in jewelry and we could see the diamonds in his grill from way across the street.

That's how much they were sparkling. Everything about him screamed 'money' and just the sight of him made my little clit twitch.

"That's Master. I hear he's a Texas legend," A'shaunie explained. "All the boys in my class wanna be him and all the girls wanna be with him once they get older."

"Do you wanna be with him?" I asked, giving her the side eye.

"Eww, no. Gross," she said. "He's way too old for me. Besides, I've got my sights set on his brother, Sensation. He's in your grade, though, but I don't care. By the time he's Master's age, we'll be married and rich as fuck!"

"What makes you think he'll marry you?" I asked A'shaunie. "Every girl at our school likes him."

"Yeah, well, I'm not those girls," she said, batting her long, curly lashes.

Secretly, I envied her because she didn't have any scars like me. She was so pretty and perfect.

"Fine...you can have the brother. I'll take the Boss," I said, looking back over at Master as he dapped up one of the corner boys. I was too young to care about him being married. "And we're gonna be waaaayyyy richer."

"A nigga feel good when he wit'chu," Master whispered, bringing me back to reality.

It was funny how A'shaunie went on to meet Profit, while I ended up getting with Sensation a few months after Master came to my hood. Life could be so ironic...We had no idea, at the time, that our child-like dreams would someday come to fruition.

"I feel good when I'm with you, too," I admitted.

Lifting me off my feet, Master carried me bridal style to the bedroom. "I'll make you feel even better once I put this dick in you," he said.

The mattress creaked beneath our weight as he placed me

onto the bed. I eagerly helped him out of his clothes, then started kissing on his perfect pecs and chiseled six pack. When I reached the scar on his stomach, I paused and pressed my lips against it. Master ran his fingers through my hair as I continued to kiss his body in a downward motion. He'd made me feel so good the last time we were together. All I could think about was returning the favor.

Taking hold of his python, I stuffed as much as I could fit of him in my mouth. Master groaned as he watched me struggle to suck his cock. Gagging, I worked the fat member between my lips, pushing it to the back of my mouth until it was poking at the entrance of my throat. Enjoying the taste of him, I started moving my head up and down. I wasn't a beast at giving head, and Sensation wasn't shy about letting me know that. Still, I continued to slowly bob up and down, trying my best to please Master like he'd pleased me last night.

I heard his breathing become strained as I ran the tip of my tongue over the head of his cock and through the slit which caused his precum to leak out. "Damn, Nova..." he moaned.

The fact that he seemed to enjoy it made me wanna show out, so I started pumping my mouth faster, really getting into it. He groaned in pleasure and I moaned with him from the pleasure I was inflicting. I enjoyed making him feel good.

He took my head in both hands and began to assault my throat as he face-fucked me. The fact that his dick was huge was the only thing keeping him from sliding into my esophagus. I was drooling and gagging in rapid succession, my saliva coating my chin and his balls. I just knew he was about to nut, but suddenly, he popped his dick out of my mouth.

"Why'd you stop me? I have a job to finish down here," I smiled at him.

I tried to grab his dick but he pulled it away from my

hungry lips. "Trust me, the last thing I want is for you to stop... but we gotta get some shit straight," he said.

"Like what?" I asked, lowering my mouth onto his dick.

"Like if you keep suckin' my dick like this, I'mma have to put a ring on you."

I chuckled as I continued to do my thing. I didn't really like giving Sensation oral sex. He fucked around with too many other hoes, and it was obvious from the way his dick smelled half the time. But with Master, it was different. Something about him made me love giving head, and he really seemed to appreciate my effort.

Massaging his balls, I slowly worked him in and out of my mouth. I was enjoying it so much that I wanted to take my time. "I wanna deep-throat you but you're so big," I moaned.

"Stick yo tongue out," he whispered. "I'mma show you how to really suck this dick."

Obeying his request, I stuck my tongue out and he, miraculously, pushed more of his dick down my throat. Apparently, sticking my tongue out made more room and helped with my gag reflex. "I've never used that trick before," I laughed. "You're showing me something new ..."

"Stick with me, kid. I'll show you a whole lot of shit..."

"Like what?" I teased, licking the head of his dick.

Master grabbed me and flipped me onto my back. Seizing my legs, he pushed my thighs apart. My pussy was tingling and already moist; I don't think I'd ever been more turned on than when I was with Master.

"Like this," he said, easing his middle finger into my pussy.

I moaned in ecstasy as he slid in another. "Yessss...That feels so fucking good!"

He curled his index finger and rubbed my g-spot, making me squirm and squirt from the pleasure. Master worked his fingers deep into me, exploring every inch of my pink fortress.

Leaning forward, he inhaled the erotic aroma of my pussy. He then dropped his head and began dragging his tongue over my pussy.

I gasped and squealed as he licked and sucked on my clit like candy. I was so damn wet, I had the sheets beneath me soaked. Digging my nails into his scalp, I watched as he worked his tongue between my folds, licking me from the top of my pussy down to my asshole.

"Master!" I cried out as his tongue snaked into my hole. He was turning me the fuck out and his ass knew it.

"This shit mine now," he groaned, tongue-fucking me till I couldn't breathe. "This shit mine and I'mma taste every fuckin' part of you."

"Oh my God, Master!" I whimpered.

He slowly came up, grabbed my breast and started sucking my nipple, flicking it with his tongue. While he did that, he continued to rub my clit furiously with his other hand.

"Shit, baby, I want you!" I said, reaching for his anaconda.

"Not yet," he whispered, climbing back down at my waist. He pushed two fingers back in my pussy, then sucked my meaty lips into his mouth. Sliding his tongue between my folds, he seized my clit and started suctioning it, making my toes curl in ecstasy. Before long, I was cumming over and over with intense orgasms coursing through my body.

Master moved up and took my small breasts in his hands. Caressing them ever so gently, he sucked my nipples into his mouth, inciting smaller orgasms just from the sensation.

"Baby, what are you doing to me?" I whispered.

Master grabbed my body and pulled me into a sitting position. Holding onto my shoulders, he eased me onto his lap like I was his daughter and he was my daddy. With my back facing his chest, his dick stuck up between my thighs and rested against my pussy lips and stomach.

The sensation of his erection pressing into my clit, caused me to squirm in his hold. I was so sensitive still, but Master just wrapped a massive arm around my body and held me tightly in place.

"Put it in," he whispered.

When I struggled to mount him properly, he grabbed his dick and guided it to where he wanted it. Biting my lip, I stifled a moan as he lowered my body onto his footlong. I grabbed his thigh as he pushed me down; his dick was so much to take all at once.

"Oh my God! I love you!" I cried out.

He kissed the back of my shoulder. "I love you, too."

His dick filled me up like nothing I'd ever felt before. Bouncing me in his lap, he fucked me from the bottom while playing with my clit. The pain quickly subsided to pleasure as he stretched me to accommodate his girth.

My juices soaked his dick and inner thighs as he thrusted into me hard and fast. My body went limp in his arms and my mind melted from the pleasure he was giving me. Eventually, all I could do was lay there as he pounded into my hole.

Suddenly, I let out a shrill scream as I came. My pussy clamped down on his dick and he shot his load deep inside of me. I shrieked and jerked in his arms as my body was racked with the strongest orgasm of my young life. My pussy spasmed and clenched his dick as he emptied his seeds in me. Once again, a condom was the furthest thing on our minds.

Climbing off of him, I collapsed onto the mattress, ignoring the warm semen as it ran down my inner leg. Master got up, checked the closet, then laid down beside me. I thought about asking why he did that shit, but instead found myself curious about something else.

"So, what happened with you and your wife?" I asked,

daring to get a little personal. "I'm assuming ya'll aren't together."

"Your assumption is right," he said plainly.

I didn't press the issue. Instead, I laid my head on his muscular chest and played with a few of his hairs. "Did you mean what you said...about me being yours?" I asked in a small voice.

He chuckled. "If I slap you with my left hand even though I'm right handed, did you still get slapped?" he asked. "Of course, I meant that shit. Yo ass is mine now, Z."

"But what about Sens—"

"What about him?" Master said. "You can't miss what you can't measure."

13
MASTER

"Wake up, baby." I brushed a kiss over Nova's forehead, where there were baby hairs lining her edges.

Sunlight pierced through the open windows, creating a golden hue against her cocoa skin. She looked like she'd been dipped in chocolate. Makeup or no makeup, she was still everything. I kissed her temple. She looked so pretty and peaceful as she slept. Or maybe she looked peaceful because she wasn't running her fucking mouth. Grabbing her hand, I kissed her scar.

No.

I can't let myself drown in this moment.

She's Sensation's girl.

What the hell am I doing?

I tried to talk some morality into myself, but the truth was, I was falling for this girl at the speed of light. Suddenly, I heard Dru's voice in the back of my mind. *"At this point, I think your dick's doin' all the talkin' for you."*

Fuck it.

At least we spoke the same language.

Trailing my thumb over Nova's baby hairs, I leaned down and pressed my lips against hers. She stirred softly in her sleep. "*Mmm.* Don't kiss me," she whined. "I haven't brushed my teeth yet."

"I know," I chuckled. "That breath on kick ass."

"Fuck you," Nova laughed.

"I don't give a fuck, though. C'mere." Pulling her close to me, I tongued her down, morning breath and all. "No sleepin' in today," I told her. "I wanna take you condo shoppin'."

"What?!" she asked in disbelief.

"Right after I taste this pussy..."

"Master!" she yelped as I disappeared under the sheets. "I didn't even shower first!"

"I don't give a fuck," I said, inhaling her musky fragrance. I could wake up every day eating her pussy. That's how good her shit was. "I like it."

I kissed her thick lips and curved a middle finger before slipping it in her pussy. I groaned at the feeling of her warm wetness. She was already soaked and primed. Nova let out a deep moan as I rubbed her g-spot.

"Tell me again that it's all mine," I whispered.

"*Mmm.* It's all yours," she moaned.

I slowly began wiggling my fingers inside of her, opening her up as I slipped in a second. She was still slightly swollen from the pounding she took last night.

"Oh my God, Master, you're getting me wet," she said, pinching her own nipples.

Sucking her clit in my mouth, I began pumping my fingers in and out of her tight hole. I was visibly churning the honey out of her pussy. She plucked and writhed her nipples as she squirmed underneath me.

"Aaaahhh, fuck! Oh, yes! Oh, God! Ooooohhhh!" Her hips

lifted off the bed as she grinded into my face. I was finger-fucking the shit out of her gooey, wet cunt.

"Yeah...that's it, baby," I moaned into her pussy. "Flood my mouth with your cum."

"Shit, Master!" she squirmed and squealed under my fantastic tongue.

She tried to run, but I locked my arms around her and ran my tongue up her slit, then used the tip of it to feverishly tickle her clit. She tugged on my ears while I sucked on that fat button of hers.

"Aaaahhh! Fuck yes! Don't stop! I'm gonna cum!" she bellowed.

Her words spurred me on as I devoured her like breakfast. Quickening my pace, I licked her harder and faster, and within seconds she was spraying cum onto my chin. Like a parched animal, I greedily lapped it all up before grabbing her throat and kissing her. When I pulled back, her lips were sparkling with juice.

I spanked her ass. "C'mon. Get yo ass up and get showered. We got moves to make," I told her.

***

After showering and dressing, we stopped at my spot so I could do the same. The whole time there, Nova wandered aimlessly through my crib, admiring photos on the wall of me and my top-paying celebrity clients.

"How do you know all these famous people?" she called out to me.

I'd just stepped under the shower spray. "Fuck you mean? I'mma famous nigga," I teased and Nova just laughed. "Hell, I'm the reason the world didn't end in 2012, no cap." Seconds later, she snatched the shower curtain back and joined me.

"You talk a lot of shit, you know that?" she smiled.

I pinned her against the wall. "That's 'cuz I can back it up."

We fucked in the shower like it was our first time.

After we got out, I threw on some street clothes and took her to *Snooze, an A.M. Eatery*. We had pineapple upside down pancakes and egg scrambles with hash browns. "Oh my God," she laughed after a chive dropped into her lap. "I'm sorry you have to see me eat like a Neanderthal. But this shit is *too* fucking good." She was tearing her food up like she hadn't ate a decent meal in years.

"You ain't been here before?" I asked, cutting into my pancakes. With all the junk I consumed on the regular, it was mandatory to stay in the gym. I had a pretty strict work-out regimen. I hit the weights and treadmill three times a week.

"No. Never. Honestly, I've never even heard of this place before."

"Sensation never brought you here?" I asked curiously. *Snooze* was a staple in Houston and by far one of the best restaurants.

Nova rolled her eyes. "Please. Sensation feeds me frozen Jimmy Dean sandwiches for breakfast."

I had to cover my mouth to keep from laughing and spitting food all over the place. That sounded like some shit Sensation would do. The nigga was hood. "Damn, bay...that's all bad. Don't worry. We gone change all that shit."

"What's your favorite food?" she asked, out of nowhere.

"Um..." I rubbed my chin and thought about it. "To be real, I don't even think I have one. All I know is you the best thing I've eaten so far," I said, licking my lips.

Nova just looked at me and shook her head. "Real clever. So, you don't have a favorite food?"

"I like all foods. I always say I'd rather eat well than sleep well," I laughed.

"So not a one?" she pressed.

"I do enjoy sushi."

"Really? Never had it before," she said.

"I see a nigga gone have to introduce you to some culture."

"Blame your brother," she smiled. "Besides, I don't have the money to be eating all fancy like you," she shot back.

"Aye, as long as I got it, you got it," I told her. "You my baby. We locked and loaded."

Nova blushed and looked down at her food.

"So, I noticed you like old school cars," she said. "Is the Impala the only one you have?"

"Nah, but it's my favorite," I said. "I also got a 'Lac, a Mustang and a Buick CSX."

"What year is the Buick?" she asked. "My daddy loved Buicks."

"A seventy-one," I told her. "So, ya pops is into muscle cars too?"

"Oh yeah. Big time. He didn't own any, though." She laughed and there was a faraway look in her eyes as she reminisced. "One time...he made me and my sister go to the store with him. Told me to act like I fell and hurt myself so the employees could stop what they were doing to check on me. While they were distracted, he stole every Hot Rod and Mopar magazine he could get his hands on."

I couldn't help but laugh. "That's some wild shit right there."

"Oh, it gets worse," she said. "One time, this guy parked his Buick at a gas station in the hood. It was one of those fancy ones with the drop top. My dad told me that only a handful of 'em were built. Said that he *had* to get his hands on it. Anyway, when the guy went in to pay for the gas, my dad hotwired his shit and yelled at us to jump in. He drove that damn car two miles before the laws pulled us over—and they only did because he'd ran a fucking stop sign," she laughed. "He ended up spending six months in jail. When he got out, my mom asked him if it was worth it."

"And what did he say?"

"That he would've happily served a year just to joyride for two more miles," she laughed.

I chuckled. "Pops sounds like he was a savage."

"He is. Well, he was...I haven't seen him since I was a little girl." Nova's smile disappeared. "My family is fucking crazy. I actually feel embarrassed telling you these stories."

"Trust me, there's somethin' with everyone's family. No need to be embarrassed with me. Man, my pops is just as wild."

"Oh yeah? What's he like?" she asked. "Sensation doesn't talk about his father at all."

"Well...he's kinda stubborn, like Sensation," I added. "He used to be a pimp back in the day..."

Nova's eyes got big. "Oh really?" she laughed. "So, are *you* a pimp?" She looked at me sideways. "Pretending to be a gentleman but really just some greazy ass nigga."

"What do you think?"

Nova shrugged. "I don't think you are. But I don't think you aren't, either."

I was hoping she hit me with something smooth. And she hit the nail on head. "Aye, mayne. I'm the same way on all four sides, you dig what I'm sayin?"

"Yeah, yeah...I hear you..."

"Aye, man, I'm just a humble ass, low key ass, chase a bag ass nigga."

Nova took a sip of her mimosa. "*Mmmhmm,*" she said with narrowed eyes.

"So, were you close to yo folks growin' up?" I asked, taking the focus off of myself.

"Not really. My parents were strung the fuck out. I was close to my sister, though. She's two years older than me."

"She out here in Houston?"

"Yeah. She and her baby daddy live in the 'burbs. As a matter of fact, you know her baby daddy. He manages your club."

"Real shit? I ain't know Profit was your sister's baby's father. It's a small ass world, ain't it."

"Yeah, well, I didn't know that you knew him. Hell, I didn't even know you owned a club till the other night."

There's a lot about me you don't know, is what I wanted to say. Instead, I kept my thoughts to myself.

Once we got our filling there, I hit up my realtor to let her know that I'd be looking at some properties today. As soon as we reached the parking lot, I tossed Nova my keys. "You drivin', I'm too full," I said, patting my abs.

"I've never driven an old school before."

"Aye, there's a first for everything."

We climbed in and fastened our seats and Nova stuck the key in the ignition. She started laughing as the car revved up and leaned from right to left. "What in the sittin' sideways shit is this?"

"You ridin' slab now, baby," I laughed, grabbing my cup of lean.

"What the hell is that?" she asked, looking at the lavender liquid.

"Don't focus on my cup, youngin'. Focus on the road," I said, sounding more like a father than a friend. I couldn't help it.

Nova switched the gears and eased out of the parking lot. This was the first time she didn't say some smart-ass shit in return. Slowly but surely, I was breaking down her barriers.

***

It was a quarter after 2 p.m. when we arrived at the first condo in Upper Kirby, an upscale district in Houston, Texas containing many businesses and restaurants. Lydia was waiting for me in the lobby in a black pantsuit and a bun on her head. She was wearing glasses and all she was missing was two-chopsticks in her hair. She was black but had every feature of an Asian woman, thanks to her Filipino father. She'd also helped me close the deal on the mansion I once shared with Maloni.

"Master! So good to see you! How are you?" she asked, hugging me.

"Mayne, no complaints. Out here maintaining, tryin' to stay above water."

"I hear you. So, who's your friend?" she asked with a curious smile. Nova was shyly standing behind me. Any other time, she was the mouth of the south. But being in the presence of an educated, professional black woman had obviously humbled her lil' ass.

I slowly stepped to the side. "This here's my woman, Nova. Nova, Lydia," I introduced the two of them.

Nova looked stunned by the fact that I'd addressed her as my woman. But after the night we had, I didn't know what the fuck else to call her. My woman was the most natural thing to come to mind. At the end of the day, it was something for me to work towards. I wanted to wake up next to her pretty ass every day, so that I could slide inside her body and be reminded how glad I was to be her man.

Lydia extended her hand, but Nova seemed afraid to shake it. "Hi. Nice to meet you," she said shyly.

"The pleasure's all mine. It's not often Master brings beautiful women around me," Lydia smiled, licking her pink lipstick-coated lips.

Lydia loved pussy, so I immediately pressed pause on her shit. I didn't play dem type games. "Paws off now, mayne. This one's all me," I laughed.

Lydia held her hands up in mock surrender. "I hear you loud and clear, Boss Man. So, you ready to look at the place?"

"Been ready."

"Right this way then. And watch your step. They're still doing some minor construction." Lydia led us through the posh lobby with 20-foot ceilings and glass chandeliers. Nova looked like a kid in Disneyland as we followed her to the elevator. "The building is brand new. Everything is key-accessed," she said, holding up a key fob. "So, security is top of the line. Not only that, but there's gated entry and 24-hour concierge, as well as on-sight officers. In addition, every unit comes with sweeping panoramic views of the city, a state-of-the-art gym, dry cleaning and 5-star amenities," she rattled off. "This building was voted #4 in the top living communities of Houston."

I took Nova's hand in mine, snapping her out of her stupor. She didn't seem the least bit concerned with what Lydia was saying. She was too busy admiring the place. "You good?" I asked her.

Nova smiled nervously and nodded her head.

The unit Lydia had in mind was a 3-bedroom on the 30th floor. The condo was sleek and modern with updated appliances and new floors. "Spare me the spill," I said after realizing Nova was in a world of her own. Lydia would only waste her breath explaining the apartment's features. "Let's cut to the costs."

"The asking price for this unit is nine thousand dollars per month," Lydia said. "That's not including parking, trash and common area fees."

I turned to Nova. "You like it?"

"I love it. But nine grand seems a bit steep, don't you think."

"No expense is too high if I'm spendin' it on my baby," I said smoothly.

Nova cut her eyes at me and grinned. "Oh, you doing it like that, huh?"

"Should I give you two lovebirds a minute to discuss the details?" Lydia asked, looking from me to Nova.

"Nah," I said, making the decision for Nova. "We'll take it."

Because of who I was, we were able to secure the apartment that day. Nova got the keys in her hand and I even put the place in her name to let her know it was real.

"Why are you doing this for me?" Nova asked as we walked through the empty condo. Lydia was downstairs filling out the necessary paperwork for us. "Your ass couldn't stand me two weeks ago," she reminded me.

"Shit, I couldn't stand you two *days* ago," I laughed.

"I couldn't stand your ass, either, nigga! Fuck you!" She playfully hit my shoulder and I grabbed her elbow and pulled her towards me. She felt so good in my arms; I could've held her for the rest of my life. *Can't believe this young broad got me soft on her already*, I thought to myself. I was like putty in her hands. It wasn't like me to fall this fast for anyone. Not even Maloni.

"Once we get you some new furniture, I will," I smiled.

"Slow down, low down. You still ain't tell me why you doing this for me," she said. "Is it because of the shit I said last night?"

I thought about telling her that I wanted to move Sensation out of the hood a long time ago, and that he claimed he liked it there. I didn't wanna throw him under the bus, though. I just hated the picture she'd painted of me in her head. I knew she was only going on what he had told her, but I wasn't the bad guy he made me out to be. Then again, I wasn't the good guy either.

"I just wanted to," I said vaguely. "A blessing gone keep on blessing."

Nova looked up into my eyes. "You don't just *want to do* shit like this for people. There's always a motive behind it."

"Nah, the world don't work like dat. You talkin' to a real nigga, not some lil' punk ass boy. If I wanna do somethin' out of the kindness of my heart, I'mma do it. That don't mean I'm expectin' some shit in return."

"Oh, you're expecting something," she said acerbically. "So, tell me, Master. What do you expect from *me*, besides good pussy?" she added with a smirk.

"I already had that." I tapped her chest, where her heart was. "Now...I want this..." She had my nose so wide open and she didn't even know it.

"Master...you know I still love Sensation..."

"I'm not askin' you to stop lovin' him," I said. "All I'm sayin' is, whatever you dealin' with wit' boy, you ain't gotta move like that wit' me."

14
MALONI

I was getting my pussy licked by Shoota when my phone started ringing on the nightstand. Reaching over, I grabbed it and looked at the caller ID. It was my home girl, Lydia.

"You gone get that?" he asked, kissing and sucking on my clit.

"*Mmm*," I moaned.

"Huh?" he probed my pussy hole with his tongue. "You gone get that shit?"

"I might have to," I said. "But don't stop..."

Shoota grabbed my hips and continued to feast on me.

"Hello?" I answered, trying my best to sound like I wasn't getting the shit licked out of me.

"Bitch, guess who the fuck I just closed the deal on a condo for?"

Lydia was my husband's realtor, but also a good friend of mine. Master didn't know we were cool. We got close after bumping into each other in a gay bar one night. I was drunk as fuck at the time and ended up pouring my heart out to her about everything that went wrong in my marriage. She listened without judging me and ever since we'd been tight.

"Who?" I asked, sitting up on my elbows.

Shoota grabbed my ass cheeks and pushed his tongue even deeper into my pussy.

"Master!" Lydia said. "And you won't believe this shit, but the condo wasn't even for him! It was for some young bitch, who looked like she hadn't even gotten her first period yet!"

Suddenly, I pushed Shoota off of me in anger. "WHAT?!" I hollered into the receiver.

"I'm telling you, the bitch couldn't have been older than nineteen or twenty," Lydia said. "And he had the nerve to introduce her as *his woman*."

"Are you serious?!" I was consumed by rage and jealousy. In all the years I'd known Master, he'd only ever referred to me as his woman. I was the one there throughout his military stint. I was the one there when he started climbing ranks in the streets. Hell, I was there even after I found out that Sensation was his son. Who the fuck did he think he was staking his claim on some other bitch?

Now I *really* wanted to see this muthafucka go down!

"I'm as serious as a heart-attack," Lydia said. "Put her up in a nine-thousand dollar condo and everything. I stopped by that morning to drop off a spare key and a copy of her lease, and the whole place was decked out in expensive ass furniture. She wasn't there, though. Probably somewhere laid up with the nigga," she instigated.

"What fucking condo did he put her in?!" I demanded to know.

"The Huntington House."

"What???" I snatched the sheets off and hopped out of the bed. "THIS NIGGA GOT THIS BITCH LIVING IN UPPER

KIRBY???" I hollered. That was one of the wealthiest, most prestigious neighborhoods in Houston.

"Apartment 3015," Lydia said.

"Good lookin'," I told her, ready to pop up on their asses.

"You my girl. You know I had to come through with the tea."

"I'll hit you later and let you know what's up," I said before hanging up.

Shoota just stared at me incredulously from the bed while I dressed. "Fuck is you goin'?" he asked.

"Where the fuck do you think, nigga? I'm finna get this ball rollin'!" I told him.

I thought about the bitch I'd saw him enter the motel with. She, obviously, knew Master since he came to her rescue, and she *did* look young as fuck. I wasn't sure if they were the same woman or not.

Regardless, I planned on canceling her *and* my triflin' ass husband! She didn't know it but she was a dead woman walking. And I was a dynamite waiting to explode on a bitch!

15
NOVA

After I was given the keys to the condo, Master took me furniture shopping at *High Fashion Home*, a massive showroom stocking upscale, modern and eclectic pieces, fabrics, and beddings. He let me pick out whatever I wanted and I ended up choosing an emerald tufted sofa and two swivel chairs that matched. For the bedroom, I picked out a wood-finished queen bed and a matching dresser and nightstand.

Afterwards, we swung by Best Buy and grabbed 2 curved Smart TVs and a couple DVD players. Since Bed, Bath and Beyond was in the same plaza, I ran inside to get all of the bathroom décor. When it was all said and done, he spent close to $15,000 just furnishing my brand new apartment.

Once he made sure that I had everything I needed, he fucked the shit out of me in my new bed until I couldn't breathe, then left me alone, claiming that he had to hit the streets. I didn't mind because the D put me to sleep like Zzzquil.

The following morning, I woke up in a new condo with a

new outlook on life. Now that Master was taking care of me, he gave me a lot of inspiration to get my shit together. I didn't have to rob guys anymore, shit, I didn't even have to step foot in a strip club. I could find something I was good at, then maybe start my own business. I could go back to school or maybe get a decent job. Anything was better than lining niggas.

I was tired of that lifestyle. Tired of having to look over my shoulder 24/7. Now that I didn't have to pay bills, perhaps I could work on paying back everyone that I'd ever wronged.

Since Master didn't hit my line that morning, I decided to reach out to A'shaunie. I could start by paying her back the money she'd lent me 6 months ago. "What the fuck do you want, Z? I don't have no money to give your ass," she answered with an attitude.

"I don't need any money."

"That's a first," she snorted. "So, what the fuck do you want then?"

Me and A'shaunie used to be close as kids, but when we reached womanhood we developed a strained relationship. She went on to nursing school and graduated and even though she got with a drug dealer and had a kid young, she still managed to make something of her life. I, on the other hand, was a complete and utter fuck up.

"I wanna see Shawn," I said. "I miss him."

I could hear her rolling her eyes through the phone. "Oh, *now* you miss Shawn."

"I miss him all the time. I just be too busy working to come through and see him." Shawn was her 2-year old son.

"*Working?*" she repeated. "You mean robbing."

"C'mon, 'Shaunie. I didn't call to fight with you. I miss you, too," I admitted. "And I wanna come through to give you this money."

"What money?"

"The money you lent me six months ago," I reminded her.

She whistled dramatically. "Shit was so long ago, I damn near forgot."

"So, I can drop it off?"

"Sure. Me and Shawn will be waiting on you," she said before disconnecting the call. I was happy that she didn't mention Profit. I wasn't ready to see that douchebag baby daddy of hers.

After hanging up from her, I rushed to shower and get dressed. The whole time under the spray, I thought about Master and the positive effect he had on my life. Sensation made me wanna stay in the streets. But Master made me wanna stay out of them.

Stepping out of the shower, I toweled myself off and thought about his realtor, Lydia. She was so polished, pristine and professional looking just like his wife Maloni. Maloni was what you called a ghetto snob. She had two degrees but wouldn't hesitate to snatch a bitch bald over her husband. Suddenly, I realized that I didn't dress like either of them.

Does Master like those type of chicks? And has anything ever popped off between him and Lydia?

A dozen thoughts ran through my mind and I quickly began to feel inadequate. Maloni was decent, but Lydia was beautiful enough to instill a sense of insecurity in me. She looked like money. A bag of money. And she and Master seemed pretty close. It wasn't like me to doubt myself but that's how bad and boujee this bitch was.

After throwing on some clothes, I headed to the mall and copped some new threads from Ann Taylor and Macy's. I then went back home and tossed all my old shit down the trash chute. If Master wanted a mature woman, then I would give him just that. I changed into a navy pantsuit, pinned my hair up like Lydia's and sprayed on some Dior.

After checking my reflection, I headed to my sister's place. Thankfully, Master left me his spare car, so I wouldn't have to push mine around the city. I still had yet to take it to the shop to get repaired. And since Master had me riding foreign, it honestly wasn't on my list of things to do.

A'shaunie and Profit lived in a gorgeous 5-bedroom home, located in the Kingwood area. It was a safe, beautiful town, and an awesome place to raise a family. When I reached her front door, I raised my fist and knocked. I waited all of two seconds before she answered the door with a headscarf on. However, it didn't detract from her looks in the slightest. A'shaunie was 2 years older than me, model pretty and thicker than a bowl of cold grits. Growing up, boys always liked her more than me because her boobs were bigger and she didn't have scars. She also had these beautiful greenish-gray eyes. Honestly, it was a wonder that Sensation ended up with me instead of her. I mean, don't get it twisted, I knew I was cute and all. A'shaunie was just far superior when it came to looks.

"'Bout time you got here, bitch," she said. "And why the fuck do you look like a public defender?"

I looked down at my suit and frowned. "You don't like it?"

"I mean...it's cool...if you were thirty years older," she said. "You remind me of the social worker we had as kids."

"Whatever, hoe. Here," I said, pushing the money I owed into her hands.

"How'd you get all this?" she asked, flipping through $2000.

"Where's Shawn?" I asked, ignoring her question.

"In his bedroom."

I was about to walk off when she grabbed my arm. "Seriously, Z. Where'd you get all this? You hit some heavyweight?"

"I didn't rob anyone, if that's what you're asking," I told her.

"Then where'd you get all this money?" she asked. "We both know you're allergic to making an honest living."

"Damn, you nosey, 'Shaunie," I whined.

"Tell meeee," she begged.

I sighed deeply, then took the bobby pins out of my bun since they were bothering me. My hair fell over my shoulders as I raked my fingers through it. "Fine...I'll tell you."

A'shaunie folded her arms and waited on an explanation.

"Is Profit here?" I asked, looking around.

"No...he stepped out, why?"

I grabbed her arm and pulled her into the den. Her baby daddy was gone, but she still had her maids walking around the place and I didn't want them ear-hustling. Hell, I shouldn't have even been telling A'shaunie, but she was my sister and I knew she'd keep her mouth shut.

Closing the French doors behind me, I turned to her and said, "I got it from Master."

"What? Why is Sensation's brother giving *you* money?" A'shaunie asked, confused.

My expression must've said it all because A'shaunie shook her head. "You ain't finesse some heavyweight. You fucking the heavyweight," she said judgmentally.

"*Sshh!*" I scolded her.

"Why? Master's wife ain't here," she teased. "So, is that why you walked in here, looking like Olivia Pope? You trying to compete with the Mrs.—"

"They're not together anymore," I said angrily. I was already regretting telling her. She never could let me have my happiness.

"Is that what he told you?" A'shaunie laughed. "Girl, you just as naïve as ever. They might not be together now, but you don't just walk away from twenty years' worth of marriage. You see, sis, you're what they call a rebound. Just something pretty to pass the time with. Eventually, he'll get bored and run home to his wife. I hate to admit it, but niggas been doin' that shit since the beginning of time."

"Bitch, that's not what this is," I argued.

"That's exactly what it is," she said. "Don't worry. You aren't the first hoe a nigga with some money tricked off on and you damn sure won't be the last. If I were you, I'd stack as much paper as possible. It's only a matter of time before he up and leaves your ass."

"Dammit, 'Shaunie! Why can't you ever let me have some happiness?!" I cried. "You did the same shit when we were kids!"

"All I've ever done since we were kids was tell you the muthafuckin' truth," she said. "Someone has to..."

Shaking my head, I folded my arms and looked away.

"Does Sensation know?" she asked.

"Of course not. If he did, I wouldn't be standing here."

"You better hope he never finds out—"

"He won't," I said indignantly.

A'shaunie shook her head at me. "Have you been to see Ma yet, while you fuckin' on married men?" she added surreptitiously.

"No...I haven't."

"You need to," she said. "Let that be a reminder of what happens when you love the *wrong* nigga."

I thought about bursting her bubble and telling her about Profit's affair, but figured she wasn't even worth stooping to her level. "Can I see my nephew now?" I asked instead.

A'shaunie walked past me, opened the French doors, then led the way to her son's room. He was playing with a Smart-wheels toy garage when I walked in. "Hey, Auntie's Baby!" I sang jovially.

He cracked a smile at me and waved, and I was surprised to see he had all of his teeth. I hadn't seen him in months. Back then, he only had his two front and bottom teeth. Shawn was a perfect combination of A'shaunie and Profit with vanilla skin, blue eyes and black curly hair. I always told my sister that when he grew up he'd be a little lady killer. "Hi Aunnie, No." He always called me No, instead of Nova.

"*Ooohhh*. What are you in here doing?" I asked, walking over to the toy all wide-eyed. "Are you building a car for Auntie?" He smiled and handed me a toy firetruck. "You're making me head of the fire department? Wow! I feel so special."

"Get out his face with your dick breath," A'shaunie teased.

"Screw you," I laughed.

A'shaunie smiled and shook her head at us. "Can you believe it took Profit a week just to put that shit together?" she said.

"What all does it do?"

"It's supposed to play songs and phrases and stuff."

"So, it's like an educational toy?"

"Yeah..." A'shaunie paused. "Nova, I cannot *believe* you fucked Sensation's brother," she blurted out.

I kissed my nephew on the head. I didn't want him overhearing the messy details of my dilemma. Not that he could understand; it just made me uncomfortable. "Auntie will be back to see you soon, okay?" I reached in my oversized Michael Kors bag and pulled out a small box. I'd grabbed him a pet vet playset while at Macy's, shopping for new clothes. Shawn anxiously grabbed the box and started opening it. "Love you."

"Luh you, Aunnie No," he whispered.

Standing to my feet, I left his room with A'shaunie hot on my heels. "So, you're really not gonna say shit to Sensation?"

"Why would I tell him?" I rounded on her.

"Um. I don't know. No big reason, other than the fact that you been with this nigga for years."

"And look where the fuck that's gotten me?" I yelled. "That nigga has my head so far gone, I can't tell up from down. Got me out here doing stupid shit. Do you know I almost *died* last night?"

A'shaunie's eyes grew big with curiosity.

"Sensation put me up on a lick a few years back and I ran into the nigga I robbed in traffic. I'm tired of that shit, 'Shaunie. I'm tired of having to watch my back 24/7. I'm tired of sleepin' with the enemy. With Master, I don't feel like that. I don't feel like I have to do all that shit."

"Yeah. All you have to do is dress like Annalise Keating for him," she said.

I smacked my lips at her. "He didn't tell me to dress like this. I bought these clothes on my own accord. I just wanted to look...mature for him, since he's way older than me," I mumbled the last part.

A'shaunie just shook her head at me. "Say what you want, but you and Sensation got history. And with him, at least you knew what you were getting. You're never gonna be able to replace Master's wife. I'mma just keep it a stack with you. That nigga's using you, Nova. He's using you as a stand-in. And if you don't realize that now, you gone fuck around and wind up hurt."

"Nobody asked for your advice. Look, I have to go, 'Shaunie," I said, walking towards the door. I was done listening to the shit she was spewing. If I didn't leave soon, I might've slapped the shit out of her ass.

"I'm only telling you this shit to spare you the hurt and pain," she said sympathetically.

"I'm a big girl," I tossed over my shoulder. "It won't be the first time a nigga's hurt me or caused pain." I opened the front door, skipped down the steps and headed to my car.

"Don't forget to go see Ma!" she yelled after me.

I quickly hopped in the vehicle and started the car. "Fuck Ma and fuck you," I said under my breath with hot tears in my eyes. A part of me knew she was telling the truth. And as much as I hated to admit it, the truth hurt.

16
A'SHAUNIE

After closing the front door, I walked to the family room and peeked my head inside. It was right next to the den and seated in a taupe-colored leather chair was none other than my baby daddy. He'd never left. I only told Nova's dumb ass that he had.

"You hear that silly ass bitch?" I asked him, smothering a laugh. "Hoe think she poppin'. Bitch a mattress and happy about it," I snickered.

Profit shook his head and rubbed his goatee. "Yeah, I heard. So, she fuckin', Master..." From the expression on his face, this was obviously news to him. "I tell ya, I wouldn't have believed the shit if I didn't hear it myself," he said. "That explains why he ain't want her dancin' at the spot. He tryin' to keep all da action to himself," he laughed.

"Oh, so he made her hang up her stripper heels, huh?"

"Yup, but he played it off like she was causin' problems for him. Ole slick ass."

"Well, I guess he's the problem solver." I tossed him the

$2000 Nova had given me. "That nigga cakin' her and every-thing. Bitch was *actually* able to pay me back for once."

Profit flipped through the money. They were all blue notes. "That shit brazy," he said, shaking his head.

Walking out of the room, I headed to the bathroom so that I could make a private call. I was sure that Sensation would be *very* interested to hear what Nova had been up to.

An evil grin crossed my face. "Once he finds out his brother is stickin' it to his bitch, he's definitely gonna wanna hop on board wit' this plan. I put money on it."

Nova didn't know it, but I was secretly helping Sensation take over Master's business. Why? Because I was secretly in love with him.

One night when they got into it, Nova came to my house crying about him cheating on her with some thot. I told her she should stop going back to him and that bitches didn't want niggas with community dick. She argued that she loved him and that the sex was bomb as fuck. I could still remember laughing and telling her how crazy she was. But she cried and told me that I'd have to fuck him myself to see what she meant. So, I did. And, damn, was Nova right. That dick was A-1. Ever since, I'd been creeping with him.

I knew a guy that knew a guy who had connections to the DEA. If Sensation agreed to working with him, he could get his charges exonerated. I wanted to see him in a position of power, and right now, I was the only one capable of making it happen. But first, I had to get his ass out of prison, and in order to do that, he needed to drop a dime on Master. He'd already been locked up for 2 years, why waste any more time?

I had propositioned Sensation before, but his ass didn't believe in snitching. He claimed that shit was a death-penalty in the hood. However, beggars couldn't be choosers. It was the only way to ensure he got out of prison.

After plopping down on the closed toilet lid, I called the number to Sensation's burn out phone. "Make it quick. I'm in the yard," he answered. "And there's eyes all around me."

"How 'bout this. I'll make it just as quick as the time it took Nova to fuck Master."

Sensation fell silent.

"Fuck is you talm'bout?" he spat into the phone.

"Look, I just wanna keep ya eyes open. Nova left my crib and we had an *interesting* conversation. She claims to be poppin' that poom poom for your brother—"

"Bullshit."

"I'm keepin' it real. This comin' straight from the horse's mouth."

"Yo, you overdosing on the clown sauce. I know my Nova," he said.

"That's the thing, Sensation. She's not *your Nova* anymore. She's Master's," I teased. I just had to fuck with him. Messy always was my middle name. "You know what they say. Once a real nigga treats her better and fucks her better, then that old nigga's a wrap."

"Bitch, where the fuck is you gettin' these facts from? 'Cuz you obviously need to check your source! I know my bitch, inside and out! She wouldn't 'een *think* to do some shit like that!"

"Oh yeah?" I challenged. "Well, evidently, Master knows her insides too."

Click.

Sensation hung up on me and I immediately called back.

"What kinda bullshit you on? Man, you wastin' my mutha-fuckin' minutes."

"If you think I'm lying, just ask Master—since Nova made it clear she won't tell you."

Sensation sucked his teeth.

"I always said you should've picked me. If you were my nigga, I would never have you out here lookin' foolish."

"So *that's* what this shit is about?"

"I mean, what's done is done. You got with her and she got with your brother. It is what it is. But the real question is, what the fuck you gone do about it? I already got the nigga from the DEA on standby. All he need is your testimony, then after you'll walk and we can start putting this plan in motion."

"I told you, I ain't flippin' on no nigga! Fuck I look like snitchin' on my own flesh and blood?"

"Your own *flesh and blood* is stickin' it in your bitch's kidneys! You ain't gone do nothin' about that shit! All the years you talked about knockin' him off, now you sleepin' on the nigga? You ain't gone handle this muthafucka? You just gone let him take your girl?!"

"Bitch, you'll say whatever to get the ball in yo court," he laughed. "You don't get enough of being on my dick, huh."

"You serious? Fuck you, nigga! This ain't about me and you. It's about Nova and Master—"

"Nah, this about you still being salty that I chose her over you. Get over it, dry ass bitch."

Click.

"Damn."

Sitting in the dark on top of the closed toilet seat, I reflected on his words. He was right. I *was* still salty about him picking Nova. I'd had a crush on him ever since I was 14 but instead of choosing me, he chose Nova. Perhaps, he found her easier to mold. That had to be it, because she damn sure didn't look better than me. I was pissed when they started dating and I thought I could make him envious by getting a white boy. Sensation didn't pay me any mind, though. He had his head too far up Nova's ass.

If Profit knew that I was fucking Sensation, there was no

doubt he would kill me. It was a secret that I planned on taking to my grave. Hell, I still remember being scared about Shawn not being his baby. But when he came out of me with blue eyes, I knew that he was Profit's.

"Shit...what the hell am I gonna do now?" I asked myself.

Sensation didn't believe me, which meant I'd have to find some other way to convince him. As long as he was locked up, I couldn't make a single move. I needed Sensation to set this plan of mine into motion.

17
SENSATION

eak ass pussy ass Mitch. On God, if he fucking Z, I'll cut that nigga's dick off and feed it to him myself! I promise that nigga gone feel somethin' awful! If you violate, you get dealt with. Plain and simple. Hell, both they asses gone catch it. I don't give a fuck about Master being my father. A nigga can still get knocked off.

W

I was so full of hate right now, I was going crazy. What I'd just heard had me feeling homicidal. I tried to convince myself that A'shaunie was lying, but she didn't really have much of a reason to. I knew that she wanted me onboard with her plan, but she wasn't desperate enough to just conjure up some bullshit. Besides, Nova *did* break a sweat when I asked if she'd been fucking anyone.

I just saw this bitch the other day. She looked me right in the eyes and told me shit was good.

"Nah, that hoe gotta be cappin'," I said. "Ain't no way. Ain't no muthafuckin' way."

I guess the fact that I was this upset meant that I really did love this girl. If I didn't, I wouldn't be mad about some other nigga knockin' my bitch. Then again, Nova wasn't just any bitch and Master wasn't just any nigga.

Nova and I had been going strong for 8 years. I took this bitch's virginity, gave her her first taste of some dick. Put her in the place we were living in, showed her how to get some real money. There was no way in hell she'd repay me by fucking my father.

"Nah. 'Shaunie full of shit. I know my bitch. I know the shit she's capable of. She don't get down like that. She may do a lot of messed up things, but fuckin' me over ain't one of 'em. Since day one, Nova's always been all about me."

That hoe worshipped the ground I walked on, like I was some sort of deity. If I told the bitch to jump, she'd say how high how. She wouldn't dare fuck up what we had. Not for Master, not for anyone. I refused to believe what A'shaunie had told me. Nova wouldn't cheat on a nigga, period. She damn sure wouldn't cheat on me with my own father. Some shit you just don't do, and that was definitely at the forefront. It was a respect thing. I didn't care if I plugged her sister a few good times. Sleeping with Master was an automatic trip to God's doorstep. Hell, I might even let the whole gang run through her ass before killing her. That's how pissed I'd be if she really did fuck this nigga.

I knew it wouldn't come down to that, though. I knew because Nova wasn't fool enough to sleep with Master. *It's only two niggas in the world that's better than me and I'm both of them.*

Distracted by my thoughts, I didn't notice the Mexican in front of me until I bumped into his ass. In prison, we were segregated. The blacks with the blacks, the whites with the whites, the chinks with the chinks, the Muslims with the Muslims and so forth and so forth. Invading each other's personal space was a no go.

"The fuck?" the 'migo looked me up and down. He was

twice my size and ready to scrap. "Watch where the fuck you goin', dusty ass nigga—"

WHAP!

I knocked his fronts out before the word 'nigga' even left his lips. He dropped to the ground instantly and I went Stallone in '87 on that ass. Before I knew it, I was grabbed by the COs and dragged out of the yard.

18

MASTER

The sun was just beginning to set when Dru and I strolled into *The Exclusive Barbershop* off Farm to Market Road. I wanted to take Nova out tonight so I decided to get a quick cut and trim. Dru, on the other hand, liked to get her edges lined. She'd been rocking thick ass dreads for as long as I could remember. She always wore them up high in a bun, and if she didn't keep that shit maintained, her edges started looking like a patch of pubic hairs. I used to tease her about that shit all the time when we were younger. I wasn't close to my siblings on my father's side, so Dru was the closest thing I had to a brother *and* a sister. And since she was gay, it was like having the best of both worlds. She schooled me to women's wants and needs, taught me how to understand and communicate with them. Hell, she even helped me get through some rough patches with Maloni.

"Big Daaawwwgggg!" Trevor sang jovially as I walked into the shop. He wasn't the owner but he was the coldest barber in the city. He'd been lining my shit for close to a decade now and hadn't once shown up late to an appointment. At 6'6, he was a big man like me but burly in stature. If I didn't hit the gym on the regular, we'd basically be built the same. He knew everything in the hood. All the word play came through his ass. "Long time, no see. Wassup wit' it, mayne?"

"Shit. Same ole'. In these muthafuckin' streets hard-bodied."

"A'ight now. You know the streets play by different rules."

"I know. I wrote 'em," I bragged, laughing the whole time.

Trevor laughed too, as he pulled a cape out and pointed to his chair. "What'chu gettin', Boss Man? The regular?" he asked.

I took a seat and he wrapped the cape around me. "Nah... matter fact, gimme somethin' different. My young boy say I need to get to this new shit so I'm takin' his advice," I told him. Truthfully, I was hoping a different cut would make me look younger. I already looked young as is. But since I was seeing a young chick, I wanted to fit society's mold of what a young man should be like.

"This new shit, huh?" he chuckled. "Don't worry, Big Dawg, I got'chu."

Dru headed for the chair next to mine. She always let the Mexicans cut her hair. She claimed her edges turned out sharper or some shit. "Wuz happenin', Hector?"

"*Hola. Siéntete,*" he said, patting the chair.

That nigga ain't speak no English, but let Dru tell it, could cut the fuck out some hair.

"So...what's poppin' wit' you and the tenderoni?" Dru asked, making idle conversation.

"Oh, Master done got himself a young tender, huh?" Trevor laughed.

"Did he ever? Bitch pussy hairs ain't 'een grown in," Dru cackled.

"Fuck outta here," I laughed. Dru loved to instigate some shit. "You just make sure he line that pussy hair above ya lip," I teased. She looked so much like a man, she was actually growing a mustache.

"Damn, so is she *that* young?" Trevor asked curiously.

"She's legal. That's all that matters," I said vaguely.

"Man, look. You ain't gotta twist my arm, brother. I love a young bitch," he said. "Would probably marry one if I wasn't already."

"Damn, you too," Trev," Dru joked.

"Mayne, you ain't did shit till you fucked a young hoe," he told her.

Hearing him say that gave me instant flashbacks.

"The pussy tighter, hotter, and it got an extra kick to it," he said.

"Not an extra kick," Dru laughed. "This nigga said an extra kick."

"Shit feel like hot potato pie around ya dick."

We all started laughing.

"Master know what I'm talm' 'bout," he said, clapping my shoulder. "That's why he want me to cut his hair like he in kindergarten."

Dru started laughing even harder and all I could do was shake my head. "Ya'll got big jokes today," I said.

"Man, these young bitches ain't on shit," Dru said. "Like, I'll fuck 'em. But I'll never fuck wit' em." She cut her eyes at me. "I still don't see how you do it, man."

I was kinda disappointed to not have her support, but I wasn't trippin'. I fully understood where she was coming from. I was 38, Nova was 20.

"Like what do ya'll have in common?" she asked.

"Other than the need to breathe to survive," Trevor joked.

"We don't need to have shit in common," I told her. "We just got that vibe."

"Nigga, she *got that* pussy," Dru laughed. "That young, hot potato pie pussy."

Trevor laughed but I was actually getting tight about that shit. One joke was permissible, but Dru was getting reckless. Anytime she had a crowd, she got to showing the fuck out. That was the one thing about her ass I couldn't fucking stand. Don't get me wrong, I was all for a good laugh, but not if my bitch was gonna continuously be the punchline.

"Aye, chill."

"Aww, V gettin' in his fee fees. Let me fall the fuck back," Dru said. "Besides, that shit ain't gone last no way."

"Fuck makes you say that?" I asked angrily.

Dru looked at me like *I* was tripping. "Fuck you mean. We just saw the hoe leave the club wit' some nigga the other night. Bitch probably got mo' miles than an '86 Corolla."

Trevor started howling with laughter.

"Plus, you told me she was bat shit crazy. *And* I hear she clip for the chip."

"Damn, she be robbin' niggas?" Trevor was all in the mix.

"That's what I hear," Dru verified.

"So, you pullin' resumes now?" I asked sarcastically.

"If I got to," she said. "This bitch could fuck around and be a liability to all of us. How you know she ain't gone do you like she did the rest?"

"Once a thief, always a thief," Trevor said, instigating. "Say, what this girl name is? I might have heard of the joint. You know all the information from the 'hood comes through the shop."

"Nova," Dru told him, like I gave her ass permission to.

I might not have even wanted this nigga to know her fucking name.

"*Nova?* Lil' mama from South Park?" he asked in disbelief.

"Aww, mayne. Don't tell me you done plugged this bitch, too," Dru said.

"Nah, nah. But a lot of niggas came in here claimin' shawty done hit they pockets," he said. "Dru's right. You might wanna keep an eye on that one, Big Dawg."

"My point exactly!" Dru yelled, in a tone someone would use to shout 'bingo'.

"Man, whatever." I waved them off. "You just let me worry about Nova."

"You my brother, V," Dru said on a serious note. "I'd lose my fuckin' shit if somethin' happened to you, man. I love you. You all the fuckin' family I got," she stressed. "I just don't wanna see you fucked up out here over some bitch, that's all."

"I know what I'm getting into, and it ain't that," I said with confidence. "So just trust me, a'ight."

"Mayne, I trust you *beatin'* them walls loose," Trevor cut in.

We all started laughing again, which alleviated the tension.

Twenty minutes later, he pulled the cape off and handed me a mirror. I couldn't have been happier with the way he cut my shit. There was a line design in the front and the sides were neatly tapered.

"Good lookin', man. This is just what the doctor ordered." I went to pay him but he stopped me.

"Aye, man. Don't worry 'bout it."

"You sure?"

"Real niggas fuck with real niggas," he said.

I dapped him up. "'Preciate it, man. If you need anything, hit my line."

"Fa'sho, and aye, you be careful wit' dat young girl," he warned me. "Remember, mayne. Women are the root of *all* evil."

19
NOVA

I was on my way to my old place to start packing up me and Sensation's shit when Master hit my line out of the blue. A sudden wave of giddy pleasure swept over me. I was like a school girl with a crush and all of my doubts and inhibitions melted the minute I heard his voice.

"Hey..." I answered shyly. I'd been waiting on his call like a welfare queen waiting on the first.

"I'm takin' you out tonight," he said. "Do me a favor and wear heels, a'ight."

I thought about asking him where we were going until I remembered I loved surprises. "If we keep going out together, people gone think we're a thing." I was nervous about being spotted by one of Sensation's homeboys. If word got back to him, there was no doubt he'd put a hit out on me. Sleeping with your boyfriend's sibling was the ultimate no-no.

"Who you think I am? I don't give a fuck what people think," he said.

"I do," I muttered.

"Just wear heels," he said with finality.

Before I could say anything else, he disconnected the call. "Well, I guess his word is final," I said, shaking my head at his abruptness. Putting the pedal to the metal, I rushed to the condo, not knowing there was someone following me.

***

Two hours later, Master called me to meet him at *Uchi* on Westheimer Rd. I googled it on the way over and found out that it was a popular, 4-star restaurant known for having the finest Japanese cuisine. I'd never tried Japanese food before but I had eaten Chinese takeout on several occasions. *Master wasn't lying when he said he'd introduce me to some culture.*

It was 9:30 p.m. when I strolled into the establishment wearing a tailored gray pantsuit and black leather pumps. I'd purchased both at *Ann Taylor* in an attempt to impress Master. After seeing his wife and Lydia, I figured that he was into professional and mature women.

After looking around, I spotted Master sitting at the bar. He must've sensed my presence because he looked over at me and waved. From across the room, I saw a certain radiance emanating from his being. He lightened the mood in the dark corners of my heart, while making me feel like everything would be alright.

I smiled and waved back at him. Rocking a Gucci shirt and black slacks, he was a lot less formal than me. On his feet was a pair of Gucci loafers with the snakes embroidered on the front.

Damn, he's fresh as fuck, I thought to myself. And I smelled him before I even reached him.

"Hey, beautiful," he smiled.

He had me feeling a little tingle in my chest. The sensation traveled to my clit when he stood and hugged me. Ever the gentleman, pulled out my seat for me. He wasn't wearing his grill that day and it was my first time seeing him without it. Usually, he sported a mouthful of sparkly diamonds.

"Hi there...You smell good," I said shyly. I still didn't know how I went from hating him to having intense feelings for him. "How are you today?" I asked.

He looked at me with fondness. "Better now that I got you here," he winked.

"I hope I didn't have you waiting long," I said as he pushed my chair in.

"Nah, not at all. I actually pulled up not too long ago." He dug in his pocket and extracted a small trinket, then stepped behind me. "Here. I got'chu somethin'," he said.

"What's that?" I asked, starry-eyed.

"Just a lil' somethin'," he said plainly.

He swept my hair over my shoulders and secured a diamond solitaire pendant around my neck. "You keep giving me gifts like this, people gone *really* think we're a thing."

"We *are* a thing," he said, kissing the side of my neck. "Besides, a wolf don't concern himself with the opinions of sheep."

His lips on my skin sent chills down my spine and I had to cross my legs just to keep my pussy from throbbing.

This nigga gone fuck around and get me killed. I wasn't ready to proclaim my feelings for him. I wasn't prepared for that level of judgment. People wouldn't have shit nice to say about a bitch who dick-hopped from one brother to the next. We had to keep this shit under wraps until I could handle that degree of scrutiny.

Master took his seat and I did an automatic doubletake when I noticed Bun B and his wife, Queenie, sitting across from us. I was about to fangirl until the bartender came over and introduced himself.

"Evening, my good people. Can I get you started with

drinks?" he asked. He was a white boy with blonde hair and blue eyes, who looked like he surfed in his downtime.

I grabbed the drink menu and was about to order, but Master said something before I could open my mouth. "Sake."

"You got it, Chief. Can I get you two started with any appetizers?"

I went to answer but Master beat me to the punch again. "Let's do the hirame usuzukuri and oysters with watermelon sorbet."

I was about to get in his ass till I looked at the menu and realized I didn't know what any of this shit was. *I'm happy he did order*, I thought to myself.

"I'll get that right in for you," the bartender said before sauntering off.

"You must come here often," I said.

"I've had lunch here several times with a few colleagues of mine. Never been here for dinner, though, so this will be a first."

"Well, I've never eaten Japanese food at all, so this will be a first for me."

"Aye, there's a first for everything." He flashed his spell-binding smile, showing off those dimples.

It was my first time really noticing them. In the past, he'd never smiled at me. He was always scowling and looking like he didn't wanna be bothered. Half the time I saw him, he was handling business. His beautiful smile was infectious and in turn, I smiled and blushed. He had me feeling all warm inside.

"So, what's this?" he asked, pinching the hem of my peplum blazer. "You done switched up the wardrobe on a nigga."

"You don't like it?" I frowned.

Master paused. "I like *you*...and this don't seem like *you*."

"And your haircut don't seem like you," I said pettily. In all honesty, I really did like his haircut but I wanted to hurt his feelings just as much as he had hurt mine.

"Damn, did I offend you?"

"No...I mean, yes. I bought these clothes thinking I'd impress you."

Master chuckled. "You could have a trash bag on and I'd still be fuckin' impressed," he said. "I'm all in, Z. You done already hooked a nigga."

"Oh, I hooked you, huh?" I said, giving him the side eye.

"Like a fish out of water."

Suddenly, our bartender returned with the sake.

"You ever had sake before?" he asked.

"No...what is it?" I was just about to toss it back when he stopped me.

"Hol' up. I gotta teach you how to drink it," he chuckled.

"I just drink it, right?"

"Not quite—"

"What else is there to drinking a beverage?"

"You gone let me talk," he said. "You gotta problem talkin' too much and not listenin'."

I rolled my eyes at him. He was once again sounding like my fucking father. I guess that was the downside of dating an older man. And since I was young, he had no choice but to deal with my stubborn, know-it-all ways. "Yes, Daddy," I said sarcastically.

"A'ight, so you grab the cup and hold it close to your face," he began.

I carefully did as he instructed.

"Then, you take in the aroma and have just a small sip."

Instead of listening, I tossed it back like I was old enough to drink, then twisted my face from the impact. Sake was much stronger than I imagined.

"Yo, you hardheaded as fuck," he said, shaking his head.

I just laughed and kissed his cheek. I knew that I was childish as fuck in some ways but he didn't seem to mind it.

"You know what they say, though. A hard head makes for a soft ass." He smiled and squeezed my thigh.

I watched him sip his sake, swish it around his mouth a little and swallow it. "So, is *this* the culture you bragged on showing me?" I asked him.

"Somethin' like that. But we ain't got to the best part yet."

As if on cue, the bartender approached us with two small plates. One was filled with small, paper thin pieces of fish and the other contained oysters with a red substance on top. *What the hell does this man have me trying*, I wondered.

"The hirame usuzukuri," he said, placing the plate in front of me. "And the oysters with watermelon sorbet." He placed that in front of Master.

"You ever tried oysters before?" Master asked.

"No never. Is there a certain way I should eat that, too?" This time I planned on being serious during his instructions.

"Yes, as a matter of fact there is," he said.

"Okay, what do I do?" I asked eagerly.

"First, you grab your spoon."

I picked up my silverware and held it in front of me.

"You ready for the next step?" he asked.

"Yup!" I said, anticipating the next step.

"Then, holding the spoon lightly, you bring it forward.

A look of confusion swept my face but I did as I was told.

"Next, you bring the spoon close to your face..."

I felt like a fucking fool but I did it, anyway. "Okay..."

"Lastly...you balance it on your nose."

I was just about to do it till I realized he was fucking with me. "You play too much!" I said, playfully shoving him.

"Nah, but on some real shit, ain't nothin' to eatin' oysters. You just pick 'em up and suck 'em down. Like how you did me last night." He whispered the last part and I couldn't help but laugh.

"Like this?" I grabbed the oyster and sucked down the sorbet covered center.

"Yup. How you like it?"

"It's an...um...interesting taste. Not good...not bad...just interesting," I laughed.

"It's an acquired taste," he said, sucking down two.

"Now what's this?" I asked, pointing to the paper-thin slices of fish in front of me.

"Flounder," he said. "Try it." Master grabbed a couple chopsticks then picked up a piece with tiny, orange balls covering it.

My eyebrows pointed upward in an inquisitive fashion. "Um, what's that?" I asked, pointing to the unknown topping.

"Fish eggs," he said plainly.

"Eww, fish eggs??? Seriously??"

"You can barely taste 'em, bay."

I made a disgusted face.

"Go 'head. Try it," he urged.

Against my better judgment, I opened my mouth and let him feed me. Much to my surprise, I actually enjoyed the sliced founder.

"I'm glad to see you willin' to take risks for a nigga," he said.

"What do you mean?" I asked confused.

His face cracked into a big smile. "That wasn't fish eggs," he said. "It was candied quinoa."

My eyes widened when I realized just how much influence he had on me. "Oh my God, Master! You play too damn much!" I laughed, pushing him.

Master just laughed and sucked down another oyster.

"Are you gonna eat some of this?" I asked, pointing to the

plate in front of me. I was ready to devour the flounder. It was so delicious and flavorful.

"Nah. You can kill that."

"Don't mind if I do," I said, gulping down the last four slices.

"I'm happy that I can show you some new shit. I wanna show you even more, dependin' on how you act," he added.

"What all are you gonna show me?" I asked with a big smile on my face.

Master kissed my lips. He tasted like watermelon. "The world," he said confidently.

20
NOVA

To my surprise, I turned out to really love Japanese food. Other than the oysters, I enjoyed the flounder, nigiri and wagyu beef. After our date, Master said that he had to make a quick run. He tossed me his keys on the way out of the restaurant.

"You drivin', I'm too full," he said, patting his abs.

"I'm starting to think that's the only reason you keep me around. So I can drive you around like I'm driving Miss Daisy."

"I'm busted. You caught me," he laughed, pulling me close to him. He wrapped his arm around my shoulder as we neared his old school. This time, he was pushing the Mustang. It was yellow with black stripes down the middle. It looked like a race car and the chrome rims had spikes sticking out of them.

"Your country ass, Master," I laughed. "Do you drive anything *normal*?"

Master just hopped in the passenger seat, reclined and closed his eyes.

"Where are we going?" I asked him.

"Tops and Bottoms," he said, not opening his eyes. He was obviously tipsy off the sake.

"Oh, so I'm allowed back in?"

"Absolutely not," he said. "Yo ass mine now, Z. You better tell dem niggas it's dead. Ain't no more of that strippin' shit."

I shook my head at him as I started up the car. Thankfully, it didn't start leaning from right to left. It did, however, drive incredibly fast. I was glad I only had one cup of sake or else we'd be in the same boat.

Halfway to the club, I glanced over at Master and saw that he was sleeping. The Rollie on his wrist shined brightly, along with his diamond pinky ring. He had boss written all over him. Even when he toned it down, he still screamed millionaire.

Suddenly, my eyes wandered down to the cup holder. Inside was a small handgun, a diamond bracelet and rolled up wad of cash. *Who the fuck just leaves some shit like that in their car*, I wondered incredulously. Niggas obviously knew better than to try a man like Master.

If it was anybody else, I would've stolen that shit...but Master wasn't just anybody. Whether he knew it or not, he inspired me to do better. I was tired of being a fucking thief. Tired of that whole lifestyle. I made a promise to myself right then that I was forever done with that shit.

Twenty minutes later, we arrived at Tops & Bottoms. Master was still asleep and I shook his shoulder softly to wake him. "Damn, we here already? Pull around to the back," he said in a groggy tone. He was tired and all I wanted to do was rub his shoulders till he fell asleep. But he had business to tend to.

"Park right here?" I asked.

"Yeah, this cool. Pop the trunk for me," he instructed. "I'mma make this quick."

I did as I was told while he placed a call on his phone.

"Aye, fool, come out back."

WHEN A GANGSTA WANTS YOU

A few minutes later, I saw Profit walking up to the rear of the car. I had a half a mind to switch gears and run his silly, white ass over.

Master climbed out of the car, grabbed his gun and tucked it in the waistband of his slacks. Walking over to Profit, he dapped him up and they kicked shit. I couldn't hear a word they were saying since they were talking in hushed tones. Several moments later, Master grabbed a duffel bag out the trunk and handed it to him.

"I wouldn't be surprised if he snorted half the product," I seethed. Every time I saw Profit, he had white residue in his nose. I thought about telling Master that shit but he obviously trusted Profit enough to do business with him. Besides, who the hell was I to warn him about someone's ill intentions? Shit, I robbed for a living.

Using the sideview mirror, I watched them dap each other again before Profit walked over to my window. I rolled it down for him—even though I wanted to roll over his damn foot.

"Wassup, P?" I greeted dryly.

"'Sup, Z. Aye look, 'bout the other night. I'm real sorry for what I said. I had no right to disrespect you like that. You family and you ain't deserve that."

"We good," I smiled, resisting the urge to spit on him.

He patted the roof of the car. "Cool. I'm glad we got that squared away. I'll see you around, a'ight." Profit headed towards the club with the duffel bag. I couldn't believe he actually had just apologized to me.

Master climbed back in the car and put his gun in his lap. I was about to pull off but he stopped me and turned in my direction.

"That gun you had the other night," he began. "It is an airsoft, right?"

"Yeah...how do you know?"

He chuckled. "Little girl, I been in these streets a long ass time. Long enough to know the difference between a real choppa and a fake one," he said. "Here..." He handed me the small handgun. "I want you to hold this. Don't worry, it's clean and registered."

I carefully took the weapon from him.

"I know you thuggin' out here," he teased. "So you need to be able to protect yaself at all times. My pops always told me *you gotta learn to swim with the sharks, or don't bother getting in the ocean.*"

"Master...can I ask you a question?"

"Wassup?"

"You don't think I'mma go back to robbing, do you?"

"I don't know what'chu gone do, Z. You full of surprises," he smiled. "But I can say I feel safer knowin' you got some heat on you." He pointed to the gun. "Now you movin' wit' precision."

I turned it over in my hands. It was small but kinda heavy. "Can I ask you one more question?"

"You may as well just interview a nigga," he joked.

"This is the last question, I promise," I said. "Did you tell Profit to apologize to me?"

"I didn't *have* to tell Profit to apologize. He knew he was out of pocket."

"He was," I agreed.

"And so were you," Master added.

I rolled my eyes at him and pouted like a kid.

"We gone work on that attitude of yours," he said.

"Yeah, I hear you..."

"Don't hear me, feel me."

"Yes, Daddy. So, where we headed to now?"

"Pull up your GPS and type in Alley Kat."

Fifteen minutes later, we arrived at a hip bar and lounge

featuring live music on Main St. When we walked in, *"Fallen"* by Mya was playing. As soon as people saw Master, they started treating him like a celebrity guest. The crowd was full of people mostly his age. All the niggas dapped up Master and all the bitches had their eyes on him. They probably would've pounced on him if it wasn't for me being with him. A few hoes looked like they still didn't care but not a naan one dared to try me. The DJ saluted him and the bartenders rushed to get him bottle service on the house.

Damn. Everybody and they mama know this nigga.

For an hour or so, we stayed downstairs while he mingled with folks he knew. He introduced me to everyone as his girl, not giving a damn that I was still technically with his brother. I'd had yet to break things off with Sensation, and to be honest, I didn't know if I had the courage to. At this point, I was definitely feeling Master more.

It took Sensation 8 years to break me down and only 3 days for Master to build me up. Whenever I was with him, I felt so safe and secure. For once, I actually felt like I was with a man and not some little boy. There was an air of humility with him while at the same time authority and menace.

Master was polished, charismatic and well-spoken like a man of the highest society. He was a gentleman in every sense of the word. I also loved that he had some hood in him. Plus, he was a great kisser to both sets of lips.

After chopping it with a few of his colleagues, Master took me upstairs. There was a whole different vibe on the second level. A live band was playing Zydeco music and people were dancing like their souls had been taken over.

"You dance?" I asked Master in surprise. He always seemed so serious. He didn't take me as someone who could get down if he wanted to.

"I do a lil' somethin' somethin," he said casually.

"Show me."

Master grabbed my hand and pulled me to the center of the dance floor. Together, we grinded to the groove and had the time of our lives. As crazy as it was, I just knew that I was falling fast for this man.

***

After dancing till I got blisters on my feet, we headed back to the condo. All I wanted was a hot shower and to get the shit fucked out of me. It'd been a long time since I had fun and I wanted to repay him. To only be 20, I was always stressing about finances, bills, and putting money on Sensation's books. In between all that, I had to keep my head on swivel 24/7. When I was with Master, I didn't think about any of that shit. It was like I only saw him and I didn't sweat the small stuff.

"Did you have a good time?" he asked on the way up to our unit.

The elevator couldn't get to our floor fast enough. The raw power and presence of him made me wet. "I had a great time," I smiled, tugging on his belt. "Now I wanna show you an even better time in the bedroom."

"Oh yeah?" He licked his lips. "Can I get a quick preview?"

I reached down and grabbed the bulge in his pants, then stood on my tiptoes to kiss him. He had to lean down a bit since he was so gotdamn tall.

Things were just about to heat up when the elevator chimed. We'd finally reached the 30th floor. We were halfway to my unit when I noticed a beautiful dark-skinned woman outside my door. I did an automatic doubletake when I realized it was his wife.

"Maloni?" Her name left Master's lips in a surprised whisper. He looked just as shocked as me, if not more.

"Hey, ex-lover," she smiled, walking up to us. She looked from me to Master. "Divorce ain't even finalized yet and you already trying to replace me. Peep how I said '*try*' 'cuz you'll never replace a bitch like me. We been together twenty-one years, which is probably longer than this hoe's life-span."

"*Hoe???*" I popped off on the spot. "I'm sorry but I'm nobody's hoe."

"A whore should never address a queen. Know your place, little girl. This ain't what you want, trust me."

"You don't know me. And all that gum-bumping gone get you fucked up!" I spat.

She tried to get in my face but Master pushed her back gently.

"Fuck is you doin' here, 'Loni?" he asked her.

"No, what the fuck are *you* doing here? Buying bitches condos and shit with our muthafuckin' money—"

"It's my money. You gave up that privilege," he said.

"Your money *is* my money till the ink dries on the papers." Maloni looked at me. "You *did* know he was still married, right?"

"I knew...but I was under the impression that you two were separated."

"And I was under the impression that a married man was a married man. See, that's the problem with you young bitches. Ya'll got no respect for the sanctity of a union," she spat. "Then be acting like you accomplished more than just a couple dollars and a wet ass." She shook her head. "You hoes feel like cum breath is more important than self-respect."

"Look, old bitch, you got one more time to call me out my name—"

Suddenly, she snatched me up by a fistful of my hair. I went to swing on her but Master quickly got the in the way. If it wasn't for him, I would've dragged her ass up and down these fancy halls.

"Aye, ya'll doin' too fuckin' much! Chill!" Master said, grabbing his wife by the arm. Pulling her away from me, he took her around the corner.

"I thought you trained these bitches better than that!" I heard her yell from afar. "You a grown ass man! Nigga, what the fuck you want with a child?!" she hollered, growing more distressed by the moment.

Tears filled my eyes as I looked down at my feet. Did Master really see me as a child? Hell, did he see me as anything at all other than good sex? All of a sudden, I heard A'shaunie's voice in the back of my mind, "you're never gonna be able to replace Master's wife. That nigga's using you as a stand-in."

The fact that he went to console his wife instead of me had me feeling some type of way. *Have I just been a stand-in to him this entire fucking time?*

21

MASTER

Pulling Maloni away from Nova, I backed her up into the wall. I didn't know whether to kiss or smack the hell out of my wife. I wanted to choke her for just showing up out of the blue but I'd be lying if I said I didn't miss her crazy ass. This woman owned every part of me. Hell, we'd spent half our lives together. She knew all my insecurities, downfalls and everything. She held me down and supported me throughout every phase in my life. The memories of us were lodged in my heart and even though we weren't together, I still loved her very much.

Maloni was the purest example of what strength and beauty is and she possessed every quality of a trophy wife. She was beautiful, strong and graceful. Plus, she cooked, cleaned and took care of a nigga. And in the midst of all that, still managed to take care of herself. To be damn near 40, she aged like fine, imported wine. She could easily pass for a bitch in her 20s and she was often carded. I wasn't sure if it was from the time spent apart or not, but she looked even better to me now.

Her skin was milk chocolate, she had gray eyes and naturally long hair that touched the middle of her back.

The smoothness and flawlessness of her skin made me want to caress her. She wasn't super thick like a lot of Texas chicks. On the contrary, she was slim and toned from years of yoga but she still had curves where it mattered. She always had a killer body.

She was wearing the fuck out of the yellow wrap dress she had on. Her long, athletic legs were on full display, which instantly caught my attention. She'd broken into a sweat from trying to fight Nova and the pungent scent of her womanly essence had me harder than a pack of frozen neckbones.

"Why you here cuttin' up?" I asked, caging her between me and the wall. I was afraid to move out of fear that she'd go running after Nova. She had a tendency of fighting women that were attracted to me. Seeing me with Nova had her ready to blow her lid.

"'Cuz I miss you," she confessed. The close proximity made her suddenly turn bashful. "I miss the fuck out of you, Master. But I still can't stand you for making me feel so alone."

"A nigga been missin' you too," I said. I was humble enough to admit that. "I never wanted it to be this way. You chose that route," I reminded her. "I mean, I thought what we had was real—"

"Yeah, *real* fucked up," she retorted.

Using my thumb, I brushed away her tears as they slid down her cheeks.

"You were always busy," she continued. "Always in the streets. I felt forgotten. Neglected."

"I'll take the L for that one," I told her. "But it was always about you. The long hours, the nights you had to sleep without me...it was all for us. I wanted to give you a life you were accustomed to, so I went hard in the paint...maybe a lil' *too* hard," I added. "But it was never nobody over you. It was always about you, 'Loni."

My wife looked up at me and smiled.

"But that was then and this is now," I told her. "A nigga gone always have love for you, baby...but I've moved the fuck on."

Maloni deflated in sadness, but just as quickly that sadness turned into hatred. "Get the fuck away from me, Master!" she said, pushing her way past me.

I hurried after her, thinking she might attack Nova but instead she stormed to the elevator and slapped the button till the doors opened. Once they closed, I turned around to face Nova. Her eyes were red-rimmed and she looked really sad. She must've overheard me and Maloni's conversation.

"My bad 'bout all that," I told her.

There was an awkward silence between us.

"But I think it's best we put this shit on ice," I said, avoiding her intense stare.

"What? What do you mean?" she asked disappointed. "Are you saying you don't wanna fuck with me?"

"I'm sayin' we need to put this on ice. A nigga need time to sort out some shit."

"Why should I suffer just 'cuz *you* need time to clear *your* head?! We were just happy together a minute ago, Master! Now she shows up and suddenly, you wanna put us *on ice*???" she made air quotes.

Suddenly, I flew off the handle. "Dammit, Z! See, this the shit I'm talkin' 'bout!!" I yelled. "All you do is fuckin' talk!! You don't fuckin' listen!! You ain't ready, man. You ain't ready for a nigga like me," I said, pushing her away.

"Don't tell me what I'm ready for!"

"Mayne, I'mma tell you one thing. I ain't the nigga to stand here and argue wit'chu. I'm out."

I went to walk off but she grabbed my arm. "So you just gone walk away from me?" she asked with tears in her eyes. "You just told me earlier that we were together—"

"Well, it was never chipped in stone that we'd be together forever." Snatching my arm away from her, I headed towards the elevator.

"No. It's okay." She pulled out the keys to the condo and tossed them at my feet. "I'll leave." Fuming with rage, she stormed towards the elevator then stopped mid-stride. "You know what?" she said, walking back towards me. "The whole time we were together tonight, I kept telling myself how different you were from Sensation. But now I see...ya'll two of a muthafuckin' kind." She turned and walked to the elevator.

"Like father, like son," I muttered.

Nova stopped again and turned to face me. "What?" she said with an attitude. "What the fuck does that even mean?"

I didn't break eye contact with her this time. "That nigga Sensation's my son," I told her straight and forward.

I didn't even think about it; the shit just came out. But now that the truth was out, I couldn't un-ring that bell. I didn't know why I was pushing Nova away like this. All I knew was that after Maloni's visit, a nigga was conflicted as fuck.

Nova stared at me with a blank look, then opened and closed her mouth several times. She was floored by the news and at a loss for words. "But—Sensation—you—how..." She paused when she realized she couldn't form a complete sentence. She was taken aback and it took her a few seconds to recover. "You know what? I don't even give a fuck anymore," she said, walking to the elevators. Halfway there, she stopped then turn around and ran at me full speed. "YOU A FUCKIN' PIECE OF SHIT!!!" she hollered, punching me in the chest. "YOU A MUTHAFUCKIN' SCUM BAG!!!!" There were tears in her eyes as she hit me with everything she had in her. "YOU

FUCKIN' BITCH!!! YOU *WORSE* THAN SENSATION! YOU AIN'T
SHIT BUT A FUCKIN' LOW LIFE!!!!"

Her words cut like daggers and I said nothing in my
defense.

Suddenly, the neighbors opened their doors to poke their
heads into the hall. They all saw Nova swinging on me like an
Everlast punching bag. She was so small and I was so big that
her hits did very little damage. Still, I stood there and took
them since it obviously made her feel better.

"I fucking hate you, Master," she said after tiring herself
out. "I hate that I ever kissed you! I hate that I ever slept with
you! And I hate that I actually began to catch feelings for your
ass!" Using what little strength she had left, she dragged
herself to the elevator.

I didn't say shit as I watched her smack the down button
impatiently. The elevator doors opened and she quickly
stepped inside. Her shoulders were slumped and she appeared
drained and hurt beyond repair. Right before the elevator
doors closed, she looked at me in sadness.

"I may be fucked up, but I ain't nowhere near as fucked up
as you."

22

NOVA

Storming inside my apartment, I slammed the door behind me in tears. I felt hurt, confused and misled. Not just by Master but by Sensation, as well. We'd been together for eight years and he didn't once mention Master being his father. I didn't understand. But I did sympathize with his hatred for Master.

That nigga treated him like a distant cousin instead of how a dad should treat his son. Then on top of that, he watched him struggle for years, robbing just to get by. I thought I couldn't stand Master before. Now I really despised his ass after finding out this shit.

"I can't believe I fucked this nigga!" I screamed, kicking over a lamp.

Winded from his betrayal, I slid down the wall and cried out wretchedly. *Why would he tell me this right after his wife popped up*, I wondered? *Why couldn't he wait? Why couldn't he have not told me at all?*

We had such a good night, connected in ways that I'd never connected with Sensation. I was actually falling in love with his ass as crazy as it sounded. He charmed me, whispered sweet nothings in my ear, and gave me an entire galaxy when I only expected a single planet. Master was nothing short of amazing. But he could be so fucking cold at the same time.

Snatching the diamond pendant off my neck, I tossed it across the room in anger. "That muthafucka is a real fucking scoundrel!" I hollered.

Staggering to my feet, I went to the kitchen, opened the cabinet under the sink and pulled out a Ziploc bag full of weed. I'd actually stolen it from Marcus the day that I robbed him. I didn't just hit up niggas for money. I stole anything I could make a profit off of.

Dumping a blunts worth on the counter, I lined it up nicely then split a Backwoods with a knife. If Master was anywhere near me, I would've jammed this shit in his heart. Hell, that's exactly what I felt like he just did to me. If telling me we needed time apart wasn't bad enough, he really made it worse with the bomb he dropped on me.

"How the fuck can he be Sensation's father?" I asked myself. "He ain't even that much older...unless he had his ass young." I did the math in my head. Master had to be seventeen or eighteen when Sensation was born. "Why didn't Sensation ever tell me this shit himself?" I rolled the blunt and lit the end. None of this shit was making any sense. Drowning my sorrows in marijuana, I puffed on the Backwoods hoping it would ease my pain.

Leaning against the counter, I hung my head and thought about Master. The way he kissed me, the way we made love and the way he made me smile back at the restaurant. How could he do all these things knowing what he knew? You had to be a soulless person to mislead someone the way he misled me. One thing was for certain, his ass was gonna get what he had coming.

23
MASTER

That night, I stayed in the crib I got for Nova instead of going back home. She'd left all her shit here, including the clothes she brought from the mall today. Smoking a blunt, I rooted through the bags and saw that they were all the same type of attire. Then I thought about her telling me she was only trying to impress me. I knew she was mad at the time but the gesture really did speak volumes to me. To have such a hard shell, she was incredibly soft in the center. Before truly getting to know her, she never took me as the sensitive type. I always figured she was heartless and callous because of the shit she and Sensation did.

Man, why the fuck did I push her away like that, I asked myself.

I really liked Nova. I enjoyed spending time with her. Whenever I was with Nova, a nigga started to feel young again. She was sexy and fun to hang out with and the fact that she, genuinely, could make me laugh was an added bonus. There was an aliveness about her that I craved, which was something my wife began to lack over the duration of our marriage. Nova had that intoxicating blend of lust, risk and uncertainty that kept me begging for more.

You'd think because of our age gap we'd have a hard time connecting but that wasn't the case with us. There was never a shortage of shit to talk about and we even had a few things in common. Our sex drives matched and we shared a healthy sense of humor. To put it short, Nova was everything I'd been missing. Still, a part of me knew that what Dru had said was true.

I couldn't afford to be out here fucked up over some bitch —especially when I clearly had deep-rooted feelings for my wife still. Right now, I wanted to focus on my marriage and decide if it was worth salvaging. I'd given Maloni half my life and I wasn't sure if I was ready to throw that all away.

I wasn't over Maloni yet and I didn't need to drag anyone else into my mess. It wasn't fair to make Nova wait while I tried to make up my mind. Before I could start a new book, I first had to finish the final chapter...and that was only if I was, actually, ready to move on to another novel. Me and my wife might not have had children, but we had history and a lifetime worth of memories. I couldn't just turn my back on that shit.

Tossing the clothes in the closet, I grabbed my cup of lean and sat on the sofa. I still smelled Nova's perfume. Our memories together were imbedded in my mind, as well. As bad as I wanted to call her up and apologize, I figured she was better off without me. I never wanted it to come to a point where I was forced to choose between her and my wife. At the end of the day, Maloni was my other half, and if it came down to it, I'd rock with her. I was almost certain that Nova wouldn't want me anyway after finding out the truth.

Grabbing my iPhone, I reached out to my dawg, Dru. She answered on the third ring with music in the background.

"Wuz good, G?" She must've turned her volume down because the music died down.

"Man, I done had to cut the strings on me and baby girl," I said.

"What?! You broke things off wit' her? Bro, you was just defendin' the broad a few hours ago. What the fuck done happened that quick?"

"Maloni..." I sighed.

"What about her? I thought what ya'll had was over."

"I thought so too, then she appeared out of the blue...A nigga fucked around and got caught up," I admitted. "And I think I wanna make this shit work wit' her."

"Damn, so you just let shawty go?" Dru asked in disbelief.

"Somethin' like that."

"Damn, my nigga. You colder than a baby mama's heart on her way to the child support office."

I laughed despite the conflicted way that I was feeling.

"Don't get yaself down about it, dawg. And don't ever waste ya time on someone who's disposable. What you and 'Loni got, man that shit is *irreplaceable*. She a diamond in a sea of zirconia and she's always had ya back. If you wanna make shit work, I say go for it. In life, we don't get too many do-overs, know what I'm sayin'?"

"Yeah...I feel you," I said with my head hung in shame. "There's somethin' else...I told Z about Sensation..."

Dru's line went silent and for a second, I thought she hung up. "What'chu mean? You told her Sensation's ya kid?"

Dru was my best friend, my ride or die, so of course she knew the truth. "Yeah, and she didn't handle it too well." I rubbed my chest, where Nova had hit me. The spot was still sore and I was surprised that she'd managed to land such an impressive punch.

"Can you blame her?"

"I know, bro. Shit's all fucked up."

I could hear Dru shaking her head through the phone. "Damn, that's all bad."

"I know. Tell me about it. I just didn't want us to part ways without her knowin', you feel me?"

"Yeah, I hear you, dawg. You want me to pull up on you?" she asked. "You sound like you could use some company, and I got a pint of mud wit' me."

"Nah, I'm sippin' as we speak," I said. "I just wanted to let you know you were right...and apologize for gettin' so tight at the shop."

"Aww, man, we family," she laughed. "That's what family does. We square up, then make up. I love you, Big Dawg. Holla at me if you need me."

"One hunnid," I said, hanging up.

Tossing my phone on the couch, I thought about Nova's last words. It hurt like hell to stand there and stomach the shit she was saying. But the ultimate measure of a man wasn't where he stood in the moment of comfort and convenience, but where he stood at the time of challenge and controversy.

Maybe my pops is right. Maybe it's time I be a father.

I didn't know, at the time, that I was too little, too late.

24
SENSATION

I was lying in my bunk, aggressively swiping through Tinder, when a guard opened my cell and told me I had a visitor. On any other occasion, I would've hidden my phone but he was one of the niggas on my payroll. He also made sure I didn't get tossed in the hole after my fight with the Mexican in the yard.

Who the fuck is coming to see me, I wondered. I didn't have any visitations lined up that I knew of. Hopping off the top bunk, I went to walk out of the room but he stopped me.

"Say mayne, I need some of dat white shit," he said, wiping at his nose. "You think you can get one of dem hoes to hook you up?" Some of the COs were bigger junkies than the inmates. I didn't mind since they were all cutting a check.

"Yeah...I got'chu," I said, figuring my visitor was one of my girls.

"'Preciate it, cuh."

The CO led me to the visitation room and I was surprised to find Master waiting for me at a table. *Man, this the last nigga I wanna see right now,* I thought bitterly.

Me and A'shaunie's conversation came to mind but I still had a hard time believing that shit. I'd have to hear it from the horse's mouth. That was the only way I'd know that it was true. "Fuck you doin' here?" I asked, taking a seat. I had a fucking attitude and it was evident in my tone. I really didn't wanna be bothered with this nigga. Hell, it was *his* fault that I was even locked up in the first place.

"I needed to address some shit," he said. "And I wanted to do it in person, like a man."

I snorted at his statement. "A *man? You?* Fuck outta here," I laughed. "You ain't no man. Just a nigga with money and many resources."

"You're entitled to feel that way," he said, without taking offense. "Matter of fact, I don't blame you for feelin' that way at all. I was never there for you the way you needed me to be... and for that, I truly am sorry."

"*You sorry?*" I repeated. "Nineteen years later and you sorry?" I laughed. "Nigga, you know what to do wit' that apology. I ain't 'een gotta say it."

Master cleared his throat and clasped his massive hands together in front of him. "That ain't the only reason I'm here," he said. "The streets talk...and I wanted you to hear it from me before you heard it from someone else..."

I looked up into his eyes. *Don't tell me this nigga gone say what I think he's gonna say...*

Leaning forward, I clasped my hands together and waited. "Fuck was I gone hear?" I asked, when he didn't speak fast enough.

"That shit got crazy between me and ya shawty..."

"Fuck you mean shit got crazy?" I asked, getting hostile.

"Shit got crazy," he said again. "Shawty went the other way."

"The fuck? Yo, is you sayin' you bust my bitch?" Clearly, A'shaunie was telling the truth.

"Shit just happened, it wasn't planned. And it ain't her fault so don't hold it against her. Things just went left. It was a mistake. But I can assure you that shit is done wit'."

"You a real life clown," I said, waving him off. "For nineteen years, you couldn't be a father to me. But it took you no time to knock my bitch," I scoffed. "Nigga, I'm done sittin' here listenin' to this. And don't come back to me wit' dis shit. We done." Standing to my feet, I prepared to walk off—then turned around and stole on his ass out of nowhere. "MAN, YOU A SORRY ASS NIGGA!!!!" I yelled at him. I was ready to go blow for blow.

Unfortunately, the COs rushed to grab me after Master fell to the floor. He grabbed his jaw and looked up at me. His nose was leaking like a running faucet. The nigga was big enough to kill me with a single hit if he wanted to, but he gave no inclination that he planned on retaliating.

"FUCK YOU AND THAT BITCH!" I hollered as the COs restrained me. "THAT'S WHY I'M COMIN' FOR YA SPOT!!! BETTA KEEP YA HEAD ON SWIVEL!" I yelled as they escorted me from the room. "YOU HEAR ME, OLE MAN? I'M COMIN' FOR YA CROWN!!!"

25
MALONI
THREE DAYS LATER

I was on my way in my apartment when Master called me out of the blue. I didn't want Shoota's lazy ass to overhear our conversation, so I backpedaled to my car and climbed inside.

"Hey...I didn't expect to hear from you so soon," I answered. "With everything that happened, I thought you wanted to keep your distance."

"Well, you thought wrong," he said. There was a long pause before he continued. "I feel like what we have is worth fightin' for, 'Loni. I realize how much you've suffered in the past and I know we got some shit to work on. We've said and done some hurtful things out of anger, frustration and despair. I've lied to you and kept secrets from you and betrayed your trust in every aspect," he confessed. "I'm not perfect, 'Loni... but when we married twenty-one years ago, I knew I wanted to spend my life with you. That shit hasn't changed, despite us being apart for a year and a half. I want another chance to make things right and to remind you why you fell in love with me. I'm willing to spend the rest of my life doing it if I have to 'cuz I'm not ready to let you go. It breaks my fuckin' heart that we have no other recourse but to get a divorce. I won't be able to live with myself if I signed those papers. And I'm willing to sacrifice whatever it takes to keep that from happening. With a little work, I know that we can make this marriage last, we just have to set aside our pride and differences. I guess what I'm tryin' to say is...I want you back home with me."

"Oh, Master. I've been so lonely, I don't even want to be with *myself* anymore," I said. "I've missed you, baby, and I promise to be more understanding and appreciative. I listen to my home girls tell me about their husbands all the time. And I'm always grateful that you don't put me through that same type of shit. I realize I've been selfish and unwilling to compromise. I promise to do better," I assured him. "I know I've got a good man and I'll never take you for granted. I'm ready to come back home, Master. I'm ready to make this marriage work."

"That's what I wanna hear," he said. "I guess I'll see you soon."

"I guess you will..." Before he could hang up, I stopped him. "Oh, and Master...we're gonna need to have a sit-down about your son."

Master was so quiet, I thought he hung up till I looked at the phone. He had no idea that I knew about him being Sensation's father.

"Of course, baby. I'll be at home waitin' on you," he said.

"Okay then...I love you."

"Love you too, 'Loni. I'll see you soon, a'ight."

I disconnected the call, wiped my fake tears, then reached out to my partner in crime—and I wasn't talking about Shoota.

They answered on the second ring. "Wuz poppin?"

Shoota didn't know that I was in cahoots with someone else. His ass was so unreliable, I needed outside help from an insider. When I saw Master with that whore, I knew I wanted him six feet under. I was even willing to do it myself, if need be. His little speech was touching and all, but at the end of the day, I wanted the bag.

I'd be damned if I wasted another minute on Master's triflin' ass, let alone another year. We were beyond done and it had never been clearer to me than the other night.

I gave half my life to this nigga, and he turns around and lets some young jump off talk sideways?

I had something for his ass!

"You won't believe who I just got off the phone with?"

"Who?"

"Master's soft ass," I laughed. "And this nigga actually wants me to move back in with him."

"I think you should. That's a good move. Plus, it'll be easier to do our thing."

"I think I wanna do this shit myself," I said.

"I thought you couldn't kill him."

"I know what I said before. But I think I can do it now." I thought about how happy he looked with Nova in the hallway. He looked happier than he'd ever looked with me. I knew that he only wanted to make our marriage work out of obligation and because he was comfortable with me. But no matter how hard we tried, we would never have the same connection. Those days were far behind us now. "Nah. Matter fact, I know I can do it," I said.

"Are you cool wit' killin' the nigga? Do you think you can you live wit' that?

"Trust me, I know I can."

"And Shoota?"

I sucked my teeth. "Man, all that nigga wanna do is sleep, eat and fuck. He more useless than a broken condom. Trust me, he's ran his course. His ass can get knocked off, too."

"You want me to take care of him?"

"Nah, I can handle his ass on my own," I said.

26

A'SHAUNIE

I had just laid Shawn down for the night when I got an unexpected call from Sensation. After tucking my son in, I quietly closed the door behind me and crept into the hallway bathroom. Profit was home and I didn't want him overhearing our conversation. He still didn't know that I cheated on him with Sensation several years ago.

"Hello."

"I'm in," Sensation said. "Just tell me what all I gotta do."

I was shocked to hear him jump on board but relieved, nonetheless. "Right now, you don't have to do shit but wait for my people to call you. They'll put everything together."

"And how soon will I walk?" he asked eagerly.

"As soon as they file your statement. It should take no more than a few weeks."

"A'ight then. Cool."

"So, I take it you found out the truth, huh?" I asked. "Did Nova tell you herself?"

"Nah, the bitch ain't breathe a word about it," he spat. "Master came here himself to tell me the shit."

"Well, I respect his candor," I said.

"Man, fuck that nigga's candor. And fuck that bitch, too. When I get out, both them niggas is dead!"

"Mayne, hol' up now. You do remember that Nova's my sister, right."

"I don't give a fuck."

"Well, I do. If you touch her, the deal is off."

"Fuck it. I won't kill her...but I may knock out her fuckin' teeth."

"*That* I can live with," I smiled. "So, do we have a deal?"

"Yeah, we got a deal," he agreed.

"You may not now, but you will love me when it's all said and done," I told him. I couldn't wait to convince him to kill Profit, so that we could be a modern-day Bonnie and Clyde. Nova couldn't handle Sensation no way. I was what Sensation needed. I had what it took to tame him. "You've been owed this shit for so long. And now you finally get to be in a position of power. No more standing in Master's shadow, waiting on him to feed you breadcrumbs."

"I'm comin' for it all," he said. "And it won't be long till I'm on top of this nigga's city."

27
SENSATION
TWO WEEKS LATER

God bless the justice system. I ended up walking after giving a full testimony to the DEA. It was just the evidence they needed to begin putting together a case to take down Master. I thought about killing him myself, but figured it'd be far more suiting to let him rot. After all, he had no problem letting me rot in prison.

After being processed through outtake, I was given back all of my possessions at the time of my arrest. I was so damn happy to get my hands on my iPhone—even if it was 2 generations behind. A nigga was sick of using the cheap ass Droid I had acquired in prison. Speaking of my Droid, I turned it on and sent a text to all my hoes, letting 'em know Daddy was fresh out in the streets.

Veronica, the most loyal of them all, came to pick me up. She was pushing a white BMW convertible with custom rims, and it looked like she'd recently gotten it washed and waxed. Getting hoes with paper wasn't out of the norm, though. All the bitches I beat had bread, and Veronica was the most successful of them all. She was an accountant at a law firm and

I planned to put her to work once I took over my father's business.

"Hey, baby," she smiled as I climbed in her car. She was decent-looking but nothing to write home about. She damn sure wasn't as bad as Nova. "You looking good now that you fresh out of the box." She went to kiss me but I mushed her in the face.

"You gotta earn that shit," I told her.

Veronica just laughed. She must've thought I was playing.

"Aye, lemme see yo phone," I said, as we pulled out of the penitentiary.

Veronica handed it over and I called Nova's cell. I knew she probably wouldn't answer an out-of-town number, which was exactly what my throwaway phone was. I would've called her on my own shit but my iPhone's battery was long dead.

Nova answered on the first ring, which was a little too fast, if you ask me. She probably thought I was that nigga, Master but she was, sadly, mistaken.

"Hello?"

"Word? That's how we givin' it out?"

"Sensation?"

"Who the fuck you thought it was? Ya lil' knight in shinin' armor?"

"Look, Sensation, I'm not in the mood to fight with you," she said weakly.

"So, wassup wit' you and big fam?" I asked, ignoring her. "That nigga told me he bust you down. That's what'chu on now? Wait till I get locked up, then go behind my back and fuck my fam."

"Sensation—"

"Tell ya lil' boyfriend I got somethin' for that nigga!"

Click.

I hung up on her stupid ass, then told Veronica to drop me

in the hood. The first thing I wanted to do was pay my fellow gang members a visit. I needed to put them niggas up on game and let 'em know what I had going on. I would need a team of killers at my side and who better than the Terror Squad? They were known for bodying niggas anyway, so knocking off Master's workers would be foreplay.

"Oh shit! Is that Sensation?!" Quez yelled, the minute I walked into the trap.

"Yeah, I'm back on these streets," I bragged. "Back on these niggas' heads."

All of them stood and dapped me up.

"Shit, long time no see. Wuz good, fam? How you been?"

"Whippin' and dippin' on these niggas. Same ole," I said.

Quez handed me a blunt and I anxiously fired it up. I'd been smoking nothing but Reggie behind prison walls. My hoes ain't know shit about buying good quality weed. Speaking of my hoes, Mercedes sent me a text. She was a middle school teacher who I met off of Tinder. She never smuggled in drugs for me, but she did put money on my books religiously.

I opened the text and saw that it was a picture of a baby boy. He looked to be about six months old, and in the texts, she claimed he was mine. He had hazel, slanted eyes, which was my family's trademark. I'd fucked her plenty of times in the closet during visitation, so he probably *was* my seed. Either way, I didn't give a fuck. I had more important shit to worry about.

Stuffing the phone in my pocket, I turned to Quez, who was something like my right hand. "I know ya'll niggas ready to make some real money."

"We always ready for that, 'Sei."

"Well, let me put ya'll up on game and let you know how

this shit going down...We gone hit that nigga, Master's trap. Show his ass that these streets ain't nothin' to play wit'."

Quez's mouth fell open in surprise. He had no idea that I planned on going after the biggest boss Houston, Texas had ever seen. "Master?" He repeated in shock. "Master as in yo *people's* Master??"

"That fuck nigga ain't my peoples," I said defiantly. "He ain't shit to me but a meal. Now is you niggas tryin' to eat or nah?"

Everyone in the trap nodded their heads in agreement and Quez rubbed his hands together excitedly. You would've thought he was waiting on the numbers to hit. "Shit, say no more." He pointed to his homies. "I already got the hittaz on standby, and you know dem cats stay ready for the bullshit. Just tell us what you want us to do."

***

In the back of the apartment we trapped out of, kids were jump-roping and playing tag as Pitbulls barked at them from the posts they were chained to. Just another day in the hood and no one seemed to notice or care about the gang of hood-lums dressed in all black from head to toe. We were something like the mob, only scarier.

As soon as we reached an old school Chevy, Quez popped the trunk to show me what we'd be working with. Them niggas kept some heat. I whistled dramatically once I saw the artillery and grenades stashed inside. He had enough weapons and ammunition to blow the whole city apart if he wanted to. We were only killing a couple of niggas, but this muthafucka stayed ready for war. He had *real* guns that did *real* damage. Them young boys were always armed to the teeth.

After grabbing their weapon of choice, everyone started

tying black bandanas around their faces to shield their identities. It didn't matter anyway. Everyone would know that the Terror Squad was responsible because we were the only cats crazy enough to clean out entire traps. We'd been pulling stick-ups for as long as I could remember. Luckily, I was rollin' with some niggas who were with the shits. They were all Bloods and wild as fuck. They were also the type of niggas you *wanted* on your team when it came time to do some crazy shit.

Grabbing an HK, I loaded it with a 30-clip magazine. "We gone push up on that fuck nigga," I said with a sinister smile on my baby face. "Clean 'em out of a house and home. You feel me?"

***

"This the spot?" Quez asked, sitting forward in his seat as we slowly pulled up to Master's trap. It was in the Northside part of Houston and from the looks of it, heavily guarded. There were two niggas stationed in the front of the building and only God knows how many inside. Knowing Master, he kept a few hittaz on standby. I figured there couldn't have been *that* many. Apart from me, no one had ever really tried to rob him so his security measures weren't as tight as they could've been. If it were my trap, I'd have a whole militia guarding my shit.

Shaking my head, I stared at the two young niggas guarding the front. For some odd reason, Master had nothing but young boys working for him. It was fucked up too because most of the cats he employed were my age, so I never understood why he wouldn't just hire me instead. It was fucked up. Pussy ass nigga fed everyone at his table but gave me the fucking breadcrumbs. That's *exactly* why we were in the fucked up predicament we were in now.

"Yeah, this the spot," I said, checking my magazine to make sure that it was full. I planned on cleaning house and claiming every brick inside for myself.

"Any idea on how many are inside?" Quez asked.

"Enough to not waste any ammo," I laughed. I planned on killing all of them hoe ass niggas.

"Fuck it. Say less," Quez smiled, pulling a black ski mask on. Luckily, he was on the same type of shit.

There were six hittaz in the back of our truck all wearing black bandanas and carrying sawed offs and automatics. Today, Master would feel my wrath. Every ounce of agony, betrayal and pain. I planned to make him experience exactly what I felt that day he told me he slept with Nova. After today, he would know that I wasn't the one to be crossed.

"Ya'll niggas ready?" I asked my entourage.

Quez cocked his gun. "Locked and loaded."

"A'ight then. Let's get to this money."

Hopping out of the truck, we stealthily made our way across the street towards the apartment building. Master owned the entire building but he only trapped out of one unit. He must've figured it'd keep suspicions down, but in my opinion, it was just stupid. If it were me, I'd have the whole damn building cooking up crack.

Can't believe I'm finally 'bout to run up in this bitch, I thought to myself.

I'd known where Master's trap was for the longest—even after he relocated it—but I'd never had the courage to actually run up in it till now. Those birds I stole from him in the past were found in his trunk. I'd never had the balls to kick in the doors of his hotspot. But I guess every man had his breaking point and I'd finally reached mine.

As soon as the goons guarding the entrance of the trap saw us, they immediately reached for their weapons.

"The fuck—"

TAT! TAT! TAT! TAT! TAT! TAT! TAT!

Me and my young boys wet 'em up, then stormed the trap like we were SWAT, taking out every dude in the vicinity without the slightest drop of compassion. I didn't give a fuck if they were all young like me. If you were even an associate of Master's, you got an automatic bullet to the head. No explanations and no empathy.

TAT! TAT! TAT! TAT! TAT! TAT! TAT!

Brakka! Brakka! Brakka! Brakka! Brakka! Brakka!

POP! POP! POP! POP! POP! POP! POP! POP!

We took out every nigga in the kitchen and front of the house before they even had a chance to grab their straps. I was just about to body the last cat when he held his hands up in surrender and begged for mercy. He was the only one who didn't reach for his piece when he had the chance.

"Wait! Please don't kill me, dawg! PLEASE!!!!"

"And why the fuck should I spare you?" I sneered.

"Cuz you *need* me, man!" he said. "You *need* me!"

I placed the barrel of my HK against his temple. If I squeezed, his head would be shredded cheese. "How so?" I asked through clenched teeth.

"Man, fuck dis simp ass nigga, man. Put a hole in him!" Quez said impatiently.

"If you do then you won't be able to get the money and drugs from the safe!" The young guy argued with tears in his eyes. "It's not like most safes. It's high tech. Only opens with voice recognition and since ya'll bodied everybody in this bitch, ya'll *need* me to open it!" He cried. "If you kill me, you lose access it."

"He bullshittin'. We can just crack that bitch open ourselves," Quez said dismissively.

"If you try to, it'll alert the authorities. Laws will be all over you before you can even make it out this bitch. You know I'm not lyin'. Master keeps a couple cops on his payroll," the young guy explained. "He set it up that way just in case anybody tried to rob him again. I'm telling you the God's honest truth. On my set, my son, everything. You *need* me to open that safe."

"Why even tell us this shit?" I asked angrily. "You're that scared of getting your ticket punched, pussy nigga?" He definitely knew what he signed up for when agreeing to work for Master. It was pathetic seeing him turn soft so quick, just for the sake of saving his own ass. I couldn't believe these were the type of niggas Master preferred to work with over me. It only made me despise my old man even more.

"I just had a lil' girl, man. I ain't trying to clock out," he cried. "Plus, lately, I been feelin' like 'fuck Master'. Nigga clowned me in front of my peoples and shit. All because the streets were slow and we wanted to chill. Nigga had me hemmed up by my shirt and shit like I was some punk ass bitch. Straight sonned my shit. It was mad disrespectful. Nah'mean?"

I shook my head at this dude. He had no idea that I was Master's son. He'd been feeling like 'fuck Master' lately, but I'd been feeling that way all my life.

"Get the fuck up and take us to this safe!" I demanded, snatching him up by the hood of his sweatshirt. "And if I find out you cappin', I won't hesitate to open you up." I pushed the barrel of my HK into his back for added effect.

Sniffling like a little bitch, he led us to a dimly lit bedroom in the back. The safe was in the closet, only it wasn't an ordinary closet. Master had dropped some serious paper to have it made into a state-of-the-art security room that was accessed by using a fingerprint scanner. After opening the door, we found the safe inside and sure enough a voice scanner had to be used to access it.

"Terror Town," the guy said before its doors opened, granting us access to the kilos and countless stacks of money inside.

"Daaammnnnnn. Good lookin'," Quez said before putting a bullet in his head.

I was actually considering letting the young nigga go, but Quez obviously had other intentions. All of my savages were trigger happy so I couldn't say that I was surprised in the least.

Grabbing all of the chickens for ourselves, we stuffed them into our duffel bags, then collected the money and fled the trap as quickly as we had come, leaving behind a bloody massacre. Now that I had the bricks, all that was left was to secure the plug.

That nigga Master should've put me on when he had the fucking chance, I thought as I hopped back into our truck. *Now, it won't be long before I'm the king of moving weight.*

28
NOVA

After hanging up from Sensation, I rushed to the toilet to throw up. A tiny roach scurried past me as I dropped to my knees and heaved. I wasn't sure how my life changed so drastically, then changed back in a matter of days. One minute, I was in a high-rise condo and the next, I was back in this dump. I kept telling myself this wasn't how it was supposed to be. I was supposed to be laid up next to Master while he fed me crackers and rubbed my belly. After all, I was carrying *his* baby.

Unfortunately, I never got around to telling him because every time I tried to call, I hung up in mid-dial. We hadn't talked since that night in the condo, and Master didn't make a single effort to come and see me.

I felt weak as fuck and I hated myself for not having the strength to just talk to him. I missed him so much it hurt. But I also despised him for misleading me the way that he did. And the way he dropped me...that shit was just heartless.

I didn't care if we'd only spent a few days with each other. It was long enough to leave a powerful impact on me. It felt like a rug had been snatched from underneath me. We were over but our emotional business was unfinished. Master was still with me, still in my heart and mind. Every time a love song came on, I thought about him, and every single moment seemed to remind me of his presence.

His absence was fucking killing me. That and the fact that he didn't even know I was pregnant. *Maybe I should wait till the baby's born to announce it,* I thought. Nah, that's just silly and tactless.

Wiping the saliva from my lips, I stood and squashed the roach. I felt hurt, alone and confused. And I still didn't understand why Master did me the way he did. Then to add insult to injury, he drops an earthshattering bomb on me. It was like he *wanted* to hurt me, like he *wanted* to push me away.

Swallowing my pride, I walked into my living room and grabbed my phone off the coffee table. Gathering what little dignity I had left, I punched his number in, then stopped at the last digit.

"No...I can't do it..."

A tear rolled down my cheek.

You have to, my conscience whispered.

Master deserved to know the truth, even if he didn't want to support it. At least, I'd feel better with whatever course of action I took. Punching in the digit, I pressed the green button and waited for him to pick up.

"Yeah?" he answered dryly.

"Um...can I talk to you?" I asked timidly.

"Spin it," he said in a voice so cold I hardly recognized him.

"Um, well...I hope everything's been going good for you." I didn't know how to come out and say I was pregnant so I stalled. "I, uh, miss you..."

"Lemme stop you before you take it left," he said. "I'm back wit' my wife, Z."

I paused as another tear rolled down my cheek. This was the hardest shit I'd ever had to deal with in my life. Even harder than almost being burned alive. Why was Master dissing me like this? What the hell did I ever do?

"It's prolly best if you just forget about me," he said.

"I can't forget about you," I cried. "I fell really fucking hard, really fucking fast."

There was a brief pause on Master's end. I thought he would say something comforting. Hell, anything would've sufficed. But he just said he had to go, then hung up on my shit.

***

Feeling lost and abandoned, I did the one thing I hadn't done in months. I went to see my mother in the psychiatric ward she lived in. The reason my mom had been clean for so many years was because she checked herself in but never checked out. The house fire had driven her to a state of insanity, but she still had the mental aptitude to communicate like a normal person—from time to time. Other times, she talked like a little baby...or like she was my dad. The hospital diagnosed her with PTSD and multiple personality disorder.

After checking in at the front desk, I was led to a quiet and sterile visitation room. My mother was the only one present and she waved at me from her wheelchair when she saw me. She was burned on over 75% of her body and hardly recognizable. She looked like one of those women on an ID show, who got acid thrown on them by a crazy boyfriend. Her skin was hues of dark brown, tan, beige and pink. Her eyes were sunken in and she was still bald from the incident. Her entire scalp had caught on fire at the time of the house fire.

A'shaunie came to visit her often, but it was always hard

for me to see her this way. I guess I wasn't as strong as A'shaunie. She, obviously, had a will of steel. "Hey, mama," I said, taking a seat next to her.

"Hey, 'Shaunie," she smiled.

"No, Mama, it's me, Nova."

"Oh...Nova," she looked at me with a dreamy stare. "You're getting so big now, you look just like your sister."

"Everyone says that," I laughed. "So, how are you feeling?"

"As well as can be expected..."

I was relieved that she was in a good mood and in her right frame of mind. I couldn't stand seeing her when she switched up her personalities. I told myself that one day I'd start a nonprofit for black mental illnesses. I, honestly, didn't think enough people knew how staggering the number of black mental illness patients there were.

"How are you?" she asked, jarring me from my thoughts.

"I'm okay," I said sadly.

"You don't sound okay," she said. "I can tell that something's wrong." She grabbed my left hand and ran her burned fingers over my scar. "What's going on, baby? Talk to me."

Since she was in her right mind for once, I decided to vent to her. "I ended up meeting a guy who swept me off my feet. I thought I'd get a Cinderella ending...but that wasn't the case." Instead my story seemed to end the same way hers had started.

"Niggas ain't shit. There's plenty other fish in the sea," she said cynically.

I pulled my hand away from her and shook my head in disagreement. "No, Mama, Master wasn't like all men. He was special and charming and—"

"Master," she cut in. "Did you say his name was Master?"

"Yeah, Mama, why?"

She grabbed my hand and sank her nails deep into my skin,

drawing blood. "You promise me you'll stay away from him!" she yelled. "You promise me right now!"

"Ow, Mama! You're hurting me!" I had flashbacks to when I was a child and she wouldn't let me go so my clothes caught on fire.

"Not until you promise me!" she screamed.

The nurses came in and my mother abruptly let me go.

"Is everything alright in here?" one of them asked.

"Everything's fine," I lied. They walked back out of the room to give us some privacy and I turned towards my mother. "Why do you want me to stay away from him?" I asked her.

Her eyes teared up and she looked down at her hands. "I told your father we shouldn't have done it. We shouldn't have robbed his trap in Gunspoint but we couldn't afford the dope."

"Who's trap? What are you talking about?"

"We didn't think he'd retaliate the way he did. We didn't think Master would actually have our house set on fire."

"What?" My eyes teared up, as well. "Master burned down our house? No...no...that doesn't make any sense."

"We couldn't afford the dope," my mother repeated over and over.

I went to say something but nothing came out. I was stunned and at a loss for words.

"Master had our house set on fire?" I asked again.

"Torched our house and killed your father," she said, shaking her head vehemently. She was hugging her body and her eyes were shut tight, almost like she was reliving that horrific moment.

"*Killed my father?*" I repeated, voice shaking with emotion. "Daddy's dead?" I hadn't seen him in ages but I didn't think it was because he was dead. "Master killed Daddy?"

"Since he was an addict, the news didn't bother covering the story," Mama said. "They just buried him quietly, while letting Master continue to poison our communities. It's sad how shameless people can be when money's involved. Master paid them to keep that shit under wraps *and* they covered up the fire."

"Mama," I croaked out. "Why haven't you told me this before?" I squeezed her knee. "Does A'shaunie know?" I asked her. "Did you tell her Daddy's dead?"

My mother looked up at me with wide, confused eyes. "*Owwww*, Mommy, that hurts," she said in a baby's voice. "I'm gonna tell Daddy on you! I'm gonna tell Daddy what you did!"

I released her and stood from my seat.

"I'm gonna tell Daddy on you!" she continued to say in a child-like voice.

I looked down at my mother in sadness, hating Master for what he did to my family. Hell, what he did to me! How could he fuck me knowing the shit he was responsible for? He sat in my face and let me share memories of my father, knowing that he was the cause of his death? How heartless could one mutha-fucka be? That shit was downright inhumane!

"I'm sorry," I said before turning to leave. I couldn't stand to be there a second longer.

As soon as I walked out of the building, I sucked in a lungful of air and cried. It took me five whole minutes to compose myself, then after I pulled out my phone. I was just about to order an Uber when I was struck from behind with a heavy object.

Dropping like a bag of bricks, I fell and hit my head on the concrete. The impact left me dazed and confused and before I knew it, I was being dragged by my hair through the parking lot. I thought about grabbing my gun till I remembered that I dropped my purse after they hit me.

When we reached a green drop top, I suddenly realized who my captor was. Before I could say anything in my defense,

Marcus popped the trunk and tossed me inside. He was the same nigga I robbed and stole the pounds of weed from. He was also the same crazy ass muthafucka who tried to kill me in traffic.

Fearing for my life, I attempted to hop out of the trunk. He shoved me back in, then accidentally slammed the lid down on my hands.

"HEL—"

Without warning, he jabbed me twice in the face, shattering my nose and busting my lip. "Shut the fuck up, bitch! Lay yo muthafuckin' ass down!"

"GET THE FUCK OFF OF ME!" I screamed. "Nigga, I'm preg—"

Before I could say I was with child, he pistol-whipped me into a state of unconsciousness.

***

I awoke to a throbbing sensation in my head and the taste of blood in my mouth. Looking around, I took in the unfamiliar sight of my dark and dank surroundings. If I was dead, surely this was hell.

I tried to say something but my mouth was covered in duct tape. *What the fuck? What type of Alfred Hitchcock shit is this?* Alarmed, I tried to move but quickly discovered that my hands were tied behind me to the chair. *What the hell is this shit?*

Starting to panic, I looked around frantically. I was confined in a basement of some sort, bound to a chair with little recollection of the events that led up to this very moment.

Where the fuck am I, I asked myself.

The sudden sound of a door being opened jarred me out of my thoughts. Immediately, I felt the hairs on the nape of my neck stand as I listened to the sound of someone descending the short flight of stairs. Seconds later, Marcus appeared and it was then that I remembered everything.

Shit.

Why the fuck did I let Sensation talk me into robbing him?

No.

Sensation didn't talk me into it.

I talked myself into it.

He might've led me to water but he didn't force me to drink it. I chose this life. And the consequences chose me.

"Hey there, sleepy head," Marcus smiled, like he hadn't tried to pistol whip me to death earlier. My mouth was still bleeding and it felt like my nose had been shattered. I could hardly breathe through it. He had really fucked me up.

"*Mmmmmmmm*!!!" I tried to curse him to hell but because of the tape, my rants came out muffled.

Walking over to me, he snatched the duct tape off, taking the top layer of my skin off with it—or so, that's what it felt like.

"Somethin' you wanna say? Like for starters, where the fuck my money is?" He crossed his hands together in front of him and waited on a response.

That shit was good and spent, but honestly, I was too afraid to tell him that for fear of what he might do. I did have a generous amount of weed left over still, but I doubted that he would accept that alone. He wanted his paper and who could blame him?

"I...Just give me time, Marcus," I stammered. "I swear, I can get it all back to you plus interest."

"You doin' a whole lot of talkin' but you still ain't sayin' much!" He smacked me upside the head like a father would do his disobedient son. "Do you have my fuckin' money or not??!" He growled.

"No, but I swear, Marcus—I swear to you, I can get it all back! All I need is time!"

"You ran out of time! And I ran out of energy!" He yelled. "So, if you don't have my money…" he reached behind him and grabbed the pistol out of his waist. "Then ain't no use in letting you continue to breathe."

"MARCUS, PLEASE!!!" I cried out, snot pouring down my lips. "I'm pregnant!!!" I told him. "I know that I fucked up! But please, if you have any compassion in your heart, you won't let my baby suffer for my fuck up."

Marcus paused and lowered his gun and for a second, I thought he would spare me till he raised his gun again and aimed it at my head.

"Why the fuck do you think I care 'bout you bein' pregnant?? I ain't help make that muthafucka," he spat. "Fuck you and that bitch ass baby."

POW!

Marcus shot me in the stomach at point blank range, without a drop of sympathy for me or my unborn child.

The impact of the gunshot caused me to jerk in my seat, and because of the fear, panic and adrenaline coursing through my body, I didn't feel the pain immediately. I was more shocked that he actually shot me, if anything.

"Now I'mma ask you one more time, 'cuz I don't believe your ass ran through fifty G's that fast." He pointed his gun at my chest as I, profusely, bled all over the chair. "Where the fuck is my money at, bitch???" He said through clenched teeth.

I, instantly, saw my life flash before my eyes and I started crying hysterically at the thought of it ending prematurely. I never even got to tell Master that I was pregnant. Hell, I never even got to tell him that I loved him.

"Marcus, please," I cried. "Please…give me…time," I struggled to say through the pain that finally showed up out of nowhere.

Marcus sighed, ran a hand over his brush waves and looked as if he were actually considering my offer. "Nah," he said, much to my dismay. "Ya time is up."

He was just about to pull the trigger when I kicked him in the knee, throwing him all out of whack. His stupid ass made the fatal mistake of not tying up my legs. As soon as he dropped the gun, he went down to pick it up and that's when I sent my foot sailing into his forehead.

WHAP!

He dropped to the ground and I kicked the gun far away from his reach, then focused on freeing myself from the chair. When I finally realized that I couldn't, I tried to stand but toppled over.

CRACK!

My head smacked the filthy floor of the basement, leaving me dazed and confused. Unfortunately, Marcus gathered his bearings well before I had time to get to my feet. "I'mma make you fuckin' regret that shit," he said, rushing towards the gun.

Since it was halfway across the room, I had just enough time to limp to my feet and sprint up the stairs. Halfway to the top, I paused and grabbed the stair rail since it felt like I was about to faint. I was losing blood and at an *incredibly* fatal rate. If I didn't get to a hospital soon, surely, I would bleed out.

God, I know I don't come to you often, but please...please don't let me die down here, I prayed. *Don't let me die like this.*

POP! POP! POP! POP! POP!

Marcus started firing shots at me, determined to make sure that I died in the confines of his basement. One of the stray bullets grazed my shoulder, but by the grace of God, I was able to make it out of there alive. He'd obviously answered my prayers. When I finally reached the top of the stairs, I collapsed onto the tiled floor of the kitchen. I was in such a panicked state, that it took my brain several seconds to realize I was in his home.

I remembered coming here after meeting him at the club. I told him to shower and get ready for me, playing it off like I was about to fuck him. By the time he got out, I was long gone and so was his drugs and money. It was one of my biggest scores to date.

Suddenly, I heard the thunderous sounds of his footsteps as he ran up the stairs after me. Mustering up what little strength I had, I slammed the door to the basement then pushed the back of the chair I was tied to up against it, trapping him inside.

BOOM! BOOM!

Marcus slammed his shoulder against it twice. "YOU CAN RUN BUT YOU CAN'T HIDE FROM KARMA, BITCH!"

BOOM! BOOM!

As he hollered and called me every name in the book, I struggled to free my hands of the duct tape wrapped around my wrists. Thankfully, I had abnormally small wrists because of my small stature and it didn't take much to wiggle my hands out of its confines. Once I was finally free of the chair that held me hostage, I took off running towards the front of the house —but collapsed halfway there.

I barely had enough energy to walk let alone run, yet I refused to die a fucked up way and in a fucked up place like this. I didn't care if I *was* the one who'd robbed Marcus in the first place. I didn't deserve to be killed like this. There was still so much I wanted to do—like getting my life together and starting the fuck over.

Picking myself up off the hardwood floors, I half-ran, half-limped to the front door and yanked it open, revealing salvation. The smell of fresh air smacked me in the face and in the distance, I heard the unmistakable sound of the basement door exploding off the hinges. Marcus had obviously gotten out.

"Shit! Shit! Shit!" I cursed in fear.

I took off running up the street, then made a sharp left on the boulevard. Thankfully, it was daytime and there was crazy rush hour traffic. Usually, I hated Houston traffic but I had never been more grateful for it till now. I knew Marcus wouldn't shoot me in front of hundreds of witnesses—or at least, I hoped he wouldn't. Then again, this was the same crazy ass nigga who unloaded on me *in* traffic.

Speaking of Marcus, I looked behind me to see if he was following me but I didn't see him anywhere. I did, however, see a trail of blood left behind from my wound. Clutching my stomach, I continued to limp up the boulevard until my legs suddenly gave out. Dropping to the pavement, I held my midsection and rolled over to look up at the pale blue sky. It was a beautiful sunny day in Houston, contrary to everything that had happened to me. Too beautiful of a day to die on.

I didn't wanna die.

Not like this.

But hey, I'd made my bed and I had no real regrets...other than not telling Master how much the time we spent together meant to me.

Succumbing to my injuries, I closed my eyes and accepted my fate.

29
MASTER

I felt bad for cutting Nova off the way that I did, but I figured she was better off without a nigga. It wasn't fair to keep her waiting on me, knowing that I wasn't ready to leave my marriage. I liked Nova, but what we had was a fling at best. The shit me and 'Loni had would last a lifetime. I couldn't give that up, not for Nova, not for anybody.

"Dinner's ready!" Maloni sang.

I strolled into the dining room and was met with a sight that could've been plucked from a royal banquet. The table groaned under the weight of 'Loni's culinary creations, each dish a masterpiece in its own right. Despite my countless offers to hire a chef, she remained steadfast in her insistence on cooking everything from scratch. For her, it wasn't just about the food—it was a ritual, a way to channel her love and care into every bite. She often said it made her feel more like a wife, harkening back to a time when the kitchen was the heart of the home. And as I took my seat at the table, surrounded by the aromas of her cooking, I couldn't help but marvel at her dedication and the way she poured her soul into every dish.

I expected Maloni to join me, but instead she kneeled in front of me and undid my jeans. "What'chu on?" I chuckled. I wasn't used to her moving like this.

She took my dick into her mouth and my balls into her hand. The familiar feel of her mouth on me had me groaning like a bitch. Bobbing her head up and down, she savagely sucked my dick. Unlike most women, she could tickle the tip of my dick with her tonsils.

"Damn, 'Loni," I said, grabbing a handful of her hair. She said she'd make sure I didn't go unappreciated and she wasn't lying, either. She didn't know it but I needed this shit. I was stressed as fuck after my visit with Sensation. Not only that, but I got a call from one of my guys, letting me know the nigga got out a few hours ago. I didn't know what his next move was gonna be, but I was prepared for it, either way.

"You like that, baby?" she asked, smacking my dick against her cheek.

"I love it, baby."

Maloni greedily shoved my hard meat into her mouth, her strong fingers jacking the base of it. I grinded against her face, then dropped my head back when I felt myself cum. "Shit, bay," I groaned.

Maloni swallowed all of my seeds, then wiped her lips and burped.

"Now that's how you keep your man," she said, proudly standing to her feet.

I spanked her ass as she walked away, then grabbed my fork and cut into the steak on my plate.

Maloni sat down across from me and placed a napkin in her lap.

"I was thinkin' 'bout takin' you to Paris this weekend," I said, with a mouthful of barbecue simmered beef. I wanted to repay her for being so understanding about the whole Sensation situation. She could've left me after finding out he was my son but she stayed down for me. I had to do something special for her in return. "Do some shoppin' and sight-seeing. How that sound?" I asked her.

Maloni took a sip of her wine and smiled at me.

"Is that a yes or a no?"

"I'd love to go to Paris. Just not with your ass," she said coldly.

I was about to say something when I felt a sharp pain shoot through me. Dropping my fork, I leaned forward in agony.

Maloni stayed seated as she watched me choke on the food. "I had to test it out on my lil' side nigga to make sure that the shit worked," she said. "His ass died in less than ten minutes. Let's hope it doesn't take that long for you."

Hell nah!

This bitch poisoned me!

I went to grab her but was too weak to move. Clutching the tablecloth, I fell over, dragging all the food and silverware with me.

Maloni quickly stood to her feet with her glass of wine still in hand. "Oh, I just remembered you don't know who my side nigga is. I guess I should tell you since you're about to die, anyway."

Maloni walked over to me and kneeled down so that we were eye level. I tried to reach up and grab her but I was paralyzed from the neck down. All I could do was lay there and listen to her talk shit.

"You remember that night you were shot, right? He's the one who pulled the trigger," she smiled. "The reason you be checking closets and shit like you looking for the Boogeyman."

I tried to say something but ended up spitting up a glob of blood.

"Don't fight it, baby. That'll only make it worse," she said.

Suddenly, I heard someone else walk into the room.

"Is he dead yet?" Dru asked, kicking me in the side.

"Not yet...but he will be soon."

A tear rolled down the side of my face. My own wife betraying me was bad enough. But knowing Dru was in on this shit too really fucked me up. I thought back to what Trevor had said in the shop. Women really were the root of all evil.

"I'm proud of you, bay," Dru said before kissing my wife. "I knew you had it in you."

I was guess this was the meaning of you reap what you sow.

"Grab his legs. I'll get the duct tape." That was the last thing I heard Maloni say before I blacked out.

***

When I finally came to, I noticed that it was dusk and I was being dragged through the woods by my wife and right hand. I just knew I was as good as dead after consuming whatever poison she'd put in my food but, apparently, the effects didn't kick in as soon as she thought it would.

I considered making my move while their backs were turned but figured it'd be better to wait it out. Besides, I didn't know if I had enough strength to take them both on at once, so I continued to play possum while they talked shit, unaware that I was conscious.

"How much further?" Dru asked, breathing heavy. "This big ass nigga heavy as fuck."

"You don't think I know that?" Maloni huffed. She was far smaller than Dru, so pulling my dead weight must've been tough on her body. "Anyway, not much further. We'll bury him with Shoota. Ain't no sense in digging two ditches."

"I feel you but I don't remember burying Shoota this far out," Dru complained.

"That's cuz you be high on that lean you love to sip so much," Maloni laughed. "I keep telling your ass to leave that shit alone, baby. It effects your memory."

"Nah, fuck that. My memory is just fine," Dru argued. "And I know for a fact we ain't come this far to bury that nigga Shoota. You sure we ain't lost, bitch?" She asked Maloni.

Suddenly, my wife stopped and released my legs. "I don't know. Now that you mention it, it does feel like we've been walking forever."

Dru let my legs go too, then looked around to make sure they weren't off track. "Look!" She pointed towards a huge oak tree with upwardly diagonal branches that was surrounded by shrubbery with white flowers. Next to it was a shovel. "Over there! *That's* where we put the fuck nigga," she said matter-of-factly.

"You're right," Maloni smiled and nodded her head. "I guess your memory *is* perfectly intact," she agreed. "What would I do without you, babes?"

Babes was the nickname she used for me. Just hearing her say that shit made me sick to my damn stomach. How long had they been fucking with each other? Were they having an affair while Maloni and I were still together? How long had they been planning this shit?

Closing my eyes, I allowed the weight of her betrayal to sink in. I didn't lose a friend. I just realized I never had one. My pops used to always say 'some people are willing to betray years of friendship just to get a little bit of the spotlight.' That shit spoke to me on so many levels now.

"Yeah, yeah. Just grab his legs," Dru said with a hint of laughter.

I didn't see a damn thing funny, though.

I'd trusted this bitch with every secret and insecurity I had, only for her to pull some shit like this. Hell, I even made her my second in command and lieutenant even though my own son begged for the position. Suddenly, I felt like shit. I'd been riding for everybody *except* the people I *should've* been riding for.

I promised myself that if I made it out of this alive, I'd mend the broken relationship I had with my son and teach him everything I knew about the game. Better yet, I'd groom him to take over my spot. I was tired of the game anyway. It was beyond time for some new blood.

Maloni grabbed my legs, snapping me out of my thoughts, as she and Dru continued to drag me through the woods.

A sharp twig lying in the grass sliced me on the face, drawing blood instantly. Under any other circumstances, I would've made a sound. But I wanted their bitch asses to think that I was dead until it came time to make my move...whatever that move may be.

"Right here," Dru said minutes later. "Put him right here." Dru paused and scratched her head. "This is where we buried Shoota, right? Yeah." She answered her own question. "We buried Shoota right here."

"I can clearly see that...but where the fuck is he?" Maloni asked, visibly shaken up.

Dru peered into the ditch they'd buried and put Shoota's body inside of. Then, she turned to Maloni, face pale as a ghost.

"He's not here..."

"Duh, bitch! That's what the fuck I just said!" Maloni snapped.

Dru looked around frantically, then grabbed and pulled at her dreads. "Man, where the fuck is he, man?! We buried the fuck nigga right here! I KNOW I'M NOT TRIPPIN'!"

"Just calm down! He couldn't have gone far!"

"Bitch, he wasn't supposed to go *nowhere*! You told me the fuck nigga was dead!" Dru argued.

"He was! Or at least, he looked dead," Maloni said doubtfully.

"Bitch, don't tell me you ain't check the nigga's pulse! How fucking stupid can you be???"

"Why would I??? He ate the poisoned food I made him! I assumed he was dead!"

"Hoe, that obviously wasn't no poison," Dru argued. "Where the fuck did you get that shit anyway???"

"Some nigga in Ridgemont."

Dru sucked her teeth aggressively. "Bitch, they obviously scammed your dumb ass!"

"Keep calling me out of my name and I'mma bury *your* ass in these woods!" Maloni threatened.

Suddenly, Dru snatched Maloni up by her hair. "Black ass bitch, I'd like to see you try!"

The old me would've rushed to my wife's rescue but that was *before* she tried to kill me. As they argued over Shoota's whereabouts, I slowly felt my strength returning to me. Dru was right about one thing. Maloni had *obviously* been scammed.

"Get the fuck off of me!" Maloni screamed, pushing Dru away. "You got all this energy, you oughta be helping me look for the nigga!"

"Bitch, that nigga is as good as gone!" Dru reached for the gun tucked in her waist and I assumed she was about to use it on Maloni till she pointed it at me—and noticed that my eyes were wide open.

Before she could pull the trigger, Shoota cracked her in the head from behind with the shovel. She dropped to the floor in a heap in front of me and I saw that her shit had been split, exposing her skull. She was, without a doubt, dead to the world. It was a damn shame, too. I really loved that girl like she was my own family. Shit, I even put her over my own family in some instances.

"Shoota!" Maloni gasped, taking a step back.

"You look surprised to see a nigga," he said, advancing on her with the bloodstained shovel. "You ain't really think a fucked up ass meal was gonna take me out of the game, did you?"

"What do you want from me, Shoota?" She cried. "I got sick of you making me wait. I wanted my husband dead and you just couldn't make that shit happen! I got impatient! I got tired of fucking waiting!"

"So, you tried to kill a nigga 'cuz of it? What the fuck type of fucked up ass logic is that?!" He yelled.

"Shoota, please! I'm sorry! I love you!" She cried hysterically. "We were supposed to get married, take the money and live in South America, remember? That was our plan, baby! That can *still* be our plan!" she pleaded. "I love you, baby! Don't do this!"

"Nah, you don't love me. You don't love nobody. You only love what people can do for your ass."

"I swear on everything, Shoota, I do love you! I love you so fucking much, you have no idea," Maloni cried, continuing to back away. "Please, don't do this, Shoota."

Suddenly, and without warning, I stood to my feet and pushed her into the ditch she'd buried for me and Shoota. Instead of attacking me with the shovel, he stood off to the side and let me do my thing. We had no beef with each other. We were merely pawns in Maloni's messed up game.

"He's right. You don't love any fuckin' body but yaself," I spat.

"Master, that's not true, baby!" She cried from the ditch. "I love you, baby! I made a mistake! I was just so angry about that bitch I saw you with! And I was upset with you for lying to me about who Sensation really was! I swear, baby! I wasn't gonna kill you! You have to believe me!"

Maloni would say damn near anything to save her own ass.

"But you just told *this* nigga you loved him," I argued. "Pick a side. You can't play both sides of the field."

"Fuck Shoota! I love you, Master! I've always loved you!" She said in desperation.

Shoota scoffed and shook his head at her antics. My wife was un-fucking-believable.

I gave Maloni a pitiful look. Before today, I never even knew she could be this malicious. I felt like I'd been sleeping with a total stranger for 21 years. Who was this bitch? Surely, this wasn't the same girl I fell hard for in high school. No. This woman was a monster. A savage.

"Some people will love you as much as they can use you. Their loyalty ends where the benefits stops," I told her.

Maloni opened and closed her mouth several times. She couldn't even come up with a sufficient enough rebuttal in her defense. Turning my back on her, I grabbed Dru's gun off the ground.

"Master, please! Please, Master! Don't do this!" She sobbed hysterically. "Master, I'm sorry!"

I thought about putting a slug in her skull but I couldn't bring myself to do it, so instead I tucked the burner in my waist. Maloni breathed a sigh of relief, thinking I was going to spare her but that was before I kicked Dru's lifeless body into the ditch, causing her to land on top of Maloni. She was twice as big as Maloni so the weight of her body crushed my wife.

"*Mastteeerrrr*!!!!" She cried out in a muffled voice. "Master, please!!! Have mercy, nigga! For God's sake, I'm your fucking wife!!!!"

"And I'm your husband, yet you had no mercy for my ass," I said, snatching the shovel from Shoota.

"Master, I'm sorry!!!" she begged.

"I know you are," I said. "And you'll spend the last few minutes of your life reflecting on just how sorry you truly fuckin' are."

With nothing left to say, I started covering up her and Dru's body with the pile of dirt beside the ditch. They'd come here thinking they were going to bury me and Shoota but we quickly turned the tables on their asses.

Karma was a bitch.

After burying Maloni alive, I turned towards Shoota who was still standing idly by. He was the same cat who'd popped out of the closet and shot me some years back, and I had a half a mind to dig a ditch for him as well.

"I loved her, man. That's the only reason I did the shit," he explained.

"I loved her, too," I admitted. "That's why I gotta do this."

WHAP!

I cracked him in the face with the shovel, knocking him out cold. I could've killed him but I just decided to give him a taste of his own fucking medicine. Besides, my beef wasn't with him.

After leaving Shoota sprawled out in the middle of the woods, I tossed the shovel at his feet and made my way back to civilization. Now that I'd been given a second chance at life, I planned on doing right by everyone I'd ever wronged, starting with Nova.

30
NOVA

The steady beeps from my heart monitor let me know that I was still alive when my eyes finally cracked open. Instinctively, the first thing I did was reach for my stomach. It was never that big in the first place because I was only a few weeks pregnant, but still, I welcomed the idea of being a new mom. I figured it was just what I needed to calm my wild ass down. But now that opportunity had been taken from me by a coldblooded murderer.

Fuck my life.

If it ain't one thing it's another.

First Master dumps me, now this.

I was on the verge of crying when my doctor suddenly walked in my room, followed by A'shaunie and her white ass boyfriend Profit. *Why did she even bring him,* I thought to myself? She acted like she couldn't make a single move without him, and all he did was make moves without her. Hell, she still didn't know that he was smashing the dancers at the club he managed.

"I was just checking to see if you were finally awake. As you can see, you have visitors," my doctor said. He was an elder black man with salt and pepper hair who reminded me of Morgan Freeman.

"Oh, Nova," A'shaunie said, shaking her head in disappointment. "What have you gotten yourself into?"

"What *hasn't* she gotten herself into?" Profit remarked, as if anyone asked him for his fucking opinion. I swear, he was always talking shit with his stankin' ass.

Ignoring their questions, I turned to my doctor. "My—my baby," I stammered with tears in my eyes. "What happened to my baby?"

The doctor smiled at me reassuringly. "The baby's fine," he said. "He has a strong heartbeat and so do you, despite the amount of blood you've lost. Thankfully, the bullet only grazed your abdomen before going clean through your hip," he explained. "Another inch or so, and you and the baby might not have been so lucky."

I closed my eyes and allowed the good news to wash over me. I really needed some good news after everything I'd been through. "Who brought me here???" I asked him. I desperately wanted to thank them, personally.

"A couple found you on the side of the road. They actually left not too long ago but I practically had to beg them to," he chuckled. "They refused to go anywhere without first making sure you and the baby were okay."

I touched my stomach again, relieved that I still had a chance at motherhood. It was a blessing from God. I knew I was young and probably not ready for it. But I couldn't help feeling like the life inside of me was just what I needed to save my life.

"Thank you, doctor. Thank you so much. I can't tell you how grateful I am." I cried like he'd just told me I'd won the lottery. Honestly, this was *much* better news. "Thank you so very much, Doc." I was too distracted by my own gratitude to make an effort to read the name on his name tag.

"Yes, thank you so much, Doctor Montgomery," A'shaunie cut in. I didn't know why her gratitude sounded fake. Maybe because *she* was.

"We don't know what we would've done if we'd lost her," Profit added.

We?

This dude had a lot of damn nerve talking 'bout some *'we'*. As if he really gave a fuck about me and my state of health. He didn't even like me.

"Don't thank me. It's my job," Doctor Montgomery said humbly. "Now I *do* wanna inform you that the police may be coming by soon to take your statement," he advised me.

I nodded my head in agreement. "I understand." I couldn't wait to throw Marcus's crazy ass under the bus. Usually, I didn't believe in snitching but that bastard had tried to kill me and my unborn baby in coldblood.

Fuck ethics and street codes! I was tattle-telling like hell!

That muthafucka was going to con college!!! And I prayed they kept his ass in prison for a long ass time!

"Well, I'll give you all some privacy," my doctor said. "In an hour or so, the nurse will be here to check your vitals. Let me know if you need anything."

"Thank you," I smiled weakly.

He left the room and A'shaunie and Profit immediately laid into me.

"Bitch, what the fuck have you gotten yourself into?!" My sister hollered.

"Who the fuck shot you?" Profit demanded to know, as if he would actually do something about it. His scary ass was as soft and white as Charmin tissue.

"Was it a nigga you robbed?" A'shaunie asked.

"Did you meet him at my club?"

"I'm not in the mood to be interviewed," I complained.

"Why? The police are gonna do that anyway?" A'shaunie smartly replied.

"You ain't really gonna rat to the laws, are you?" Profit asked with a hint of disappointment in his tone.

"Why wouldn't I? That son of a bitch deserves to rot in a cell!"

"Yeah but you ain't 'posed to rat," Profit said, shaking his head. "Just tell us who he is. Me and Master will put numbers on that muthafucka's head! I can guaran-damn-tee that!"

"I don't want you or Master doing a gotdamn thing for me!"

"But I thought Master was ya mans," Profit said confused.

"He ain't shit to me but an afterthought," I spat. "Matter fact, don't even tell him what happened to me. I don't want shit to do with him."

"Even if I don't tell him, he'll find out somehow. You know that muthafucka is the king of Houston," he said slyly.

"More like the king of lies," I muttered.

"What happened between you and Master?" A'shaunie asked. She was floored at the foul way I was speaking about him. "Does he have anything to do with why you're here?"

"No..."

"Well, what happened?"

"I don't wanna talk about it," I said, turning my head away from her. "Besides, don't act like you care about us now. You ain't wanna see me with the nigga no way."

"I didn't wanna see you hurt," A'shaunie stated boldly. "But from the looks of things, it still happened."

"Don't start with me right now, 'Shaunie. I'm not in the fucking mood."

"Does he know you're carrying his seed?" She asked, ignoring my statement.

"*Is* it his seed?" Profit asked with uncertainty in his eyes.

I was exhausted from their presence *and* incessant questions. "Can ya'll please get the fuck out of my room!" I yelled. "Like seriously, get the fuck out!"

"Sis, we're only trying to—"

"GET THE FUCK OUT!!!" I screamed at the top of my lungs, tearing my stitches in the process.

"Fine. We're leaving," A'shaunie said defeated. "Just call me when you're ready to talk."

I turned my head away from her and folded my arms in disgust. I wouldn't call her if she paid me to.

When they finally left, I breathed a sigh of relief then laid in my bed and stared at the sterile white walls of my room. I didn't wanna talk about Master. Hell, I didn't even wanna *think* about him. He had hurt me so bad. I wanted to forget about the last conversation we had but it constantly replayed over and over in my head. Master was so cold with me. I hated the way he confessed to being Sensation's father. Then on top of that, I find out he killed mine.

How could that muthafucka do this to me, I asked myself. *I cared about him! I was fully invested in him, as well as our future! How could he play me for a fool?*

I would never forget how he flipped the script on me after a perfect night on the town. We'd had such a wonderful date. Shit, come to think of it, it was my first ever date. Sensation never took me on romantic outings. He wasn't the romantic type at all. His definition of being romantic was popping some popcorn and watching Netflix. Hell, he'd never even told me that he loved me. But Master wasn't like that at all. He had no problem showing me his tender side. He was passionate. Perfect...all up until that night. I still couldn't believe the way he did me. I wasn't a saint by far but I still didn't think I deserved that level of disrespect. I wasn't just some fling as much as he wanted to believe that. I was special. What we had was special. I knew it and so did he. He was just fronting for whatever reason.

Sniffling, I wiped my tears as I thought about him telling me he'd gone back to his wife. He wasn't even trying to hear anything that I was saying on the phone. I wanted to tell him that I was pregnant but I never even got the chance to. That's how much he wasn't fucking with me.

I then thought about A'shaunie telling me how I'd never be able to compete with her. As much as I hated to admit it, she was right. Even if he did choose me, he'd always compare me to her. I'd probably never be enough for him. There was no telling the type of sacrifices she'd made as his better half. Probably shit I could never even fathom doing and I'd done lots of shit for Sensation.

Shaking my head, I despised myself for falling for him as fast and as unexpected as I did. I guess it was true what they say; love really is pain.

31
MASTER

Instead of going back to the home I shared with Maloni, I went to my penthouse in the city to relax and clear my head. I was still a bit nauseous from ingesting whatever bullshit Maloni had put in my food but I'd survive, nonetheless.

After walking into my apartment, the first thing I did was check the closets, then after I poured all the lean I had down the kitchen sink. I was giving that shit up for good, along with some other bad habits I had inherited over the years. I wouldn't squander this second chance at life. Not after I was so close to losing it.

Suddenly, my phone rang and I immediately answered it since it was my business line. "Wuz happenin' wit' it, mayne?"

"Boss, I've got some good news and some bad news," Trae said into the receiver.

Sighing deeply, I ran my hand over my fade. After everything I'd been through, the last thing I wanted to hear was bad news.

"Which one you want me to give you first?" He asked.

I blew out air and shook my head. "Mayne...hit me with the good news first. That way, I can brace myself for the bad."

"Nova was shot and she's in intensive care right now."

I squeezed my phone so hard the screen cracked. "What?!" I yelled angrily. "Which hospital is she in??? And who the fuck is responsible?!"

"She's at the West Houston Medical Center. And I'm not sure about that other part but you know I'm keepin' my ear to the streets. As soon as I find out, you'll be the first to know."

"Find out man," I stated with authority. "I want a price on dat nigga's head and his fuckin' family!!! You hear what I'm sayin'?"

"I hear you loud and clear, Boss."

Nova being shot wasn't good news at all and I feared knowing what the bad news was. "What else did you have to tell me?" I asked.

Trae paused, and I just knew it was a mouthful he was about to say. "The hot spot's been hit," he said in a low tone.

It was bad, but nowhere near as bad as Nova being shot. "I need you to get on top of that, too," I told him. "Find out who—"

"We already know who was responsible," he interrupted. "The cameras we installed caught everything."

"Well? Who was it? Lemme guess. Dem niggas from South-side?" I said. They'd been pushing stepped on coke in my turf for the longest. But instead of doing anything about it, I let 'em be. They weren't making any money anyway and the only people buying that dirt were crackheads, who couldn't afford my product. After all, I dealt with nothing but top paying customers.

"Are you sure you wanna know?" Trae asked, stalling for whatever fucking reason.

"Spin it, mayne."

Trae paused for a long time before he answered. "....It was Sensation..."

***

I could've gone and dealt with Sensation myself but for now, his ass would have to wait. Our issues were placed on the back burner since I had more pressing shit to tend to, like checking up on Nova and making sure she was good. I didn't give a fuck about that trap nor the lives that were lost in it when it came to her. She was my main priority so I enlisted Trae and his men to clean up that situation for me and pay off the cops to keep it from airing on the news. I needed it to be swept up under the rug because me and my business couldn't afford that type of publicity.

It was a little after 6 a.m. when I stormed into the medical center, demanding to know where Nova was located. They tried to give me the runaround at first since it was before visiting hours but I put up a fight until they had no choice but to cave into my demands. Shortly after, I was escorted to her room by a nurse.

When I walked in and saw her hooked up to machines, I damn near lost my shit. "What happened?" I asked the nurse, ready to lift her off of her feet till I got my answers.

"I'm not sure. I work in the pediatric unit but I can find her doctor for you if you'd like—"

"Please, Nurse Mancini," I said, reading her nametag. "I'd really appreciate it."

"No problem. I'll be back shortly," she said, hurrying out of the room.

After she left us alone, I slowly walked over to Nova and leaned down so that we were level before brushing a kiss over her forehead. She was sleeping still but she stirred a little when she felt my presence.

"I'm sorry, baby," I whispered in her hair. "I'm sorry that a nigga wasn't there to protect you."

Nova was so bruised and battered, she hardly looked like herself. She was completely unrecognizable. In that moment, I promised to make whomever was responsible suffer. Matter fact, I'd cut his fucking hands off myself.

Suddenly, Master's doctor walked into the room. He was a tall and broad elderly black man with black and silver hair. "Good morning. I'm Doctor Montgomery," he said, extending his hand.

I shook it with a firm grip then turned my attention back to Nova. "What happened here?" I asked with my back to him.

"Unfortunately, I'm unable to provide that type of confidential information. I hope you can understand."

I turned around to look at him sideways. I was just about to say some slick shit when Nova, suddenly, interrupted me.

"It's not his business to understand. As a matter of fact, it's not his business period," she said in a nasty tone. "Doctor Montgomery, I'd like this man to be escorted from my room immediately."

"Nova...about what happened...about the shit I said—"

"I don't give a fuck, Master! I don't wanna hear your weak ass excuses! Now unless you wanna end up in a room next to mine, I suggest you get the fuck out!"

Doctor Montgomery slyly dipped out of the room and I assumed it was to get the security.

"Nova, let me explain—"

"Nigga, there ain't shit to explain! You lied to me! You played me for a fucking fool!" She held up her burned hand. "YOU DID *THIS* TO ME!!!! You..." she paused as tears flowed down her cheeks. "You killed my father, Master," she said in a low, broken voice. "There ain't shit to explain. Now go...just go..."

Instead of saying anything in my defense, I stood there speechless for several moments. I had no idea that she knew I was responsible for the house fire. Honestly, it was something I planned on taking to my grave. I never knew I'd fall for this girl the way that I did, so before then, I never felt a need to tell her. Hell, I didn't even like her up until recently. I didn't think it was important for Sensation to know either because this happened well before he even met Nova.

Now that we were involved, I chose not to tell her because I didn't want to hurt her. How could she understand that I was only acting out of anger and retaliation? Her parents had stolen from me. Thievery was not something that I tolerated and it definitely wasn't something that could go unpunished. If I didn't do anything, niggas would only continue to try me. I had to make an example out of their asses. That's just the way this street shit went. It was nothing against her. It was simply hood ethics. You stole, you suffered the consequences. Plain and simple.

I had no idea that I'd end up falling in love with the same girl whose life I'd ruined. If I'd known that, I would've never gone through with the shit. It didn't matter, though. Nova knew the truth now and I was sure that she hated me even more than me telling her I was Sensation's dad. The damage was done.

"Nova...You don't understand. You were too young to understand—"

"I understand that you're a lying, manipulative ass piece of shit just like your son! Now get the fuck out of my room, Master! I'm done looking at you. I'm done talking to you. Shit, I'm done breathing in the same air as you!"

"But baby—"

"GO!!!" she screamed.

"Nova—"

Suddenly, she jumped out of the bed so fast, she tore her stitches, causing her wound to bleed through the nightgown, soaking the front of it.

"I said get the fuck out of my room!" She yelled, swinging on me. "I could fucking kill your ass!" WHAP! WHAP! She punched me in the chest over and over again until she exhausted herself. "After every fucking thing I told you! After everything you did to me—after everything you took from me, you bring your sorry ass here?!!" She hollered. "Bitch nigga, I got five words for you! DIE IN A HOUSE FIRE!"

Suddenly, security rushed in and grabbed me. "Sir, we're gonna have to ask you to leave."

"Get the fuck off of me!" I spat. But the more I put up a fight, the more aggressive they got. Soon, a swarm of police officers were dragging me out in cuffs and it took every single one of their asses to escort me from the room. The shit was embarrassing but nothing was worse than not being able to tell Nova the truth. That I didn't kill her father.

32
NOVA

As soon as security carried Master's goofy ass out of my room, the first thing I did was look at my reflection in the mirror above the sink. Well, to be honest, it actually looked at me. The moment I saw myself, I assumed someone else was standing in the room. I didn't even look like Nova anymore. The knots on my head had me looking like an alien, like I wasn't even human. Marcus had really done a number on my ass. Beat the shit out of me like I was a grown ass man instead of a petite girl who was only 5"1 and 130 pounds soaking wet.

It's all good. That hoe gone get what's coming to him. Him and that bitch ass nigga Master, I thought bitterly. *Karma is a mutha! I'mma just sit back and let her do her thing.*

Walking over to the mirror, I touched the largest knot on my head. "To hell with all these niggas. They all ain't shit," I told myself.

Before today, I was so certain that I wanted to see Master—even after the horrific truth my mother revealed to me. I was so sure of the things I planned to say to him. But when I saw him,

I saw nothing but red. I couldn't even bring myself to tell him about the baby because I was too fucking mad about everything else.

How could Master lie to me for as long as he did? How could he fuck me knowing the shit he knew? He wasn't as bad as Sensation—he was worse!

I couldn't believe he even had the gall to show his fucking face here. He'd better be lucky nothing sharp was around me because I might've tried to stab his bitch ass! That's how fucking furious I was!

CLACK!

I kicked the machine that my tubes were connected to. I had to hit him something since I couldn't hit him.

Damn him!

Damn him for getting in my head and heart! As pissed as I was at his treacherous ass, I couldn't deny the feelings that I had for him. However, beneath all of that, I was also harboring hatred.

33
SENSATION

"*Shoot*" by BlocBoy JB was pouring through the speakers of Onyx Gentlemen's Club as me and my hittaz made it rain on some tatted yellow bone on stage. She'd been givin' a young nigga the eye ever since I walked in this bitch. She was cute and all, and I thought about taking her down but right now, my mind was on some other shit. Besides, I had so many bitches, pussy didn't even excite me like it used to. Still, I chose to come to a strip club to commemorate the lick we just hit. We should've been thinking of ways to invest the money we'd stolen from Master but instead we were blowing it in the club, celebrating our come up.

We ain't give a fuck if we looked hot. We were just young and having fun and now that I'd robbed Master twice, I was feeling like the man. Only this time I wouldn't get knocked because of it. As soon as I got the product in my hands, I passed it off to my young boys to distribute in all of hoods his drugs hadn't touched.

The almighty Master ain't like to sell his shit to the little people. He felt like his filth was too good for them but that's where he was wrong. A fiend was a fiend at the end of the door. Whether you were rich or poor, your money was still green.

To be the self-proclaimed Boss Hogg of H-Town, Master had a fucked up outlook about a lot of street shit. That's why I felt like I was a better man for his position. He'd had his reign in the 90s and 2000s. Now it was time for some new blood and some fresh ideas. Master was hustling backwards. And I would prove it by securing every customer that he'd ever missed out on.

I'm fucking on Betty, her head got me steady...
I call her Lil Caesars, that bitch hot and ready...

Some of my niggas were so leaned out, they were in this bitch doing the Shoot Dance better than BlocBoy JB himself! We were all under 21, so we were just doing shit that niggas our age did—even if the old heads disagreed. At the end of the fucking day, we were just living life.

Suddenly, my burnout phone started ringing and I looked at the caller ID and saw that it was Mercedes. She'd been blowing me the fuck up about that lil' nigga she claimed was mine. I didn't know if he was or not; I mean, he looked like me. But either way, I wasn't losing sleep over it. If she wanted money, she'd have to take a nigga to court first. I was just a kid my damn self. I wasn't on that fucking fatherhood shit. Blame my own dad for that mind state. The shit just wasn't in me.

After ignoring her call for the hundredth time, I took a sip from my double cup and looked around the club. "Fuck is this nigga, Quez, at?" I asked.

He got a call not too long ago then dipped off and hadn't come back since.

Suddenly, as if on cue, he appeared through the thick of the crowd and urgently made his way back to our section. There was a frown on his face. *What the fuck is wrong with this nigga*, I thought. *Don't tell me some shit done popped off.*

"Aye, fam. I just got off the phone with my peoples. They say Nova got hit and she's in ICU."

"What?" I made a face like I didn't believe him. "Nova got shot? By who?" I asked.

"I don't know the details, fam. All I know is she in West Houston Medical Center now."

I frowned then took a sip of my deuce. "Why should I give a fuck?" I asked stubbornly. Deep down inside, I cared. I just didn't wanna show the shit. A pimp was a master of love. Never a slave to it.

"'Cuz that nigga Master just left there not too long ago."

Suddenly, my cheeks flushed with anger. I was consumed by jealousy and rage, so much so that I snatched Quez up by the collar of his shirt like he was some fuck nigga. "And? What the fuck of it? You sayin' that shit like it's 'posed to mean somethin'."

"Obviously it does. Look how the fuck you comin'," he said, snatching away from me. "Besides, I figured somethin' was up when you ain't reach out or even mention the bitch. When my home girl said the nigga pulled up to the hospital, I started putting two and two together."

I shook my head in misery. I was so busy celebrating our successful robbery that I didn't think about the very reason we had to rob this nigga in the first fucking place. He had piped my bitch while I was on lockdown. As much as I claimed I didn't love the hoe, I really took that shit to heart. I guess I really did have feelings for the bitch after all.

"Which fuckin' hospital is she in, man?" I was ready to finally pay her trifling ass a visit. And maybe even strangle her with the tubes she was hooked up to.

"West Houston Medical Center," he said. "You need me to ride wit'chu?"

"Nah, I need you to do somethin' else for me," I told him.

"Find out where the fuck nigga lay his head. I'm finally ready to put that bitch down. Nah'm sayin'?"

"Shit, say no more. I'm all over that."

Grabbing my jacket off the chair of the sofa behind me, I walked out of the VIP section and headed for Quez's car. He let me hold it since I was fresh out in the streets and didn't have my own set of wheels.

Let me go see what this bitch is on, I told myself. I'd heard everyone else's side of the story *but* hers. After being with each other for 8 years, I owed it to her and I owed it to myself.

34
NOVA

After Master and I fucked in the shower, we toweled off then threw on some clothes and he took me to Snooze, an A.M. Eatery. For the first time in my life, I had pineapple upside down pancakes and egg scrambles with hash browns. The food was so good, I found myself eating like a starved scavenger.

"Oh my God," I laughed after a chive dropped into my lap. "I'm sorry you have to see me eat like a Neanderthal. But this shit is too fucking good," I said, not hiding my love for fine cuisine. I was tearing that shit up like I hadn't ate a decent meal in years.

"You ain't been here before?" Master asked, cutting into his pancakes. For him to know about this place, he was a fat boy at heart. Luckily for me, he didn't look like it one bit. He must've hit the gym on the regular.

"No. Never. Honestly, I've never even heard of this place before," I admitted.

"Sensation never brought you here?" he asked curiously. He was talking like Snooze was one of the best restaurants in Houston.

I rolled my eyes at his question. "Please. Sensation feeds me frozen Jimmy Dean sandwiches for breakfast." That nigga didn't *know the first thing about fine dining. Hell, he didn't even know what Yelp was for that matter.*

Master had to cover his mouth to keep from laughing and spitting food all over the place. He knew I wasn't lying. Sensation was hood as fuck and he didn't believe in romantic shit, especially taking women out to breakfast.

"Damn, bay...that's all bad. Don't worry. We gone change all that shit," Master said confidently. It was like he already saw us having a future together.

"What's your favorite food?" I asked, out of nowhere. Thinking about our future made me nervous because I had yet to break things off with Sensation. I didn't even wanna think about how he'd react once he found out I fucked Master.

"Um..." Master rubbed his chin and thought about it. "To be real, I don't even think I have one. All I know is you the best thing I've eaten so far," he said, licking his lips.

My clit jumped with excitement, but I shook my head at him to mask my lustful thoughts. "Real clever. So, you don't have a favorite food?" I asked him.

"I like all foods. I always say I'd rather eat well than sleep well," he laughed.

"So not a one?" I pressed.

"I do enjoy sushi," he confessed.

"Really? Never had it before," I said.

"I see a nigga gone have to introduce you to some culture."

"Blame your brother," I smiled. "Besides, I don't have the money to be eating all fancy like you," I shot back.

"Aye, as long as I got it, you got it," he told me. "You my baby. We locked and loaded."

A single tear rolled down my cheek as I slowly drifted back to reality. I was laying in my hospital bed, staring at the walls like they could talk to me and tell me everything was going to be okay. It would have been nice to have someone tell me that. Anybody.

But my sister was fake as fuck, my mama was clinically crazy, and my father was six feet under. Honestly, I'd never felt more alone in my life until now.

I touched my belly and forced a weak smile.

Well, at least I still have you...

Suddenly, the last person I expected to see strolled inside my room like he had a personal invite. The moment I saw Sensation, all of the color rushed from my face. It was like I was seeing a ghost. How the hell did he get out so early? *When* the hell did he get out? And why didn't I hear about it?

Just fucking great, I thought. *As if my life could get anymore fucked up.*

"What's wrong?" He asked with a sinister smile on his face. "Were you expectin' someone else?"

I knew that he was referring to Master. It was all in his tone.

"I sure as hell wasn't expecting you," I retorted.

Seeing Sensation was almost as bad as seeing Master. They were two peas in a pod and I didn't know how I'd ever missed the possibility of him being his son. They might not have favored one another, but they acted just like each other. The only difference being, Master was a far better actor.

"You ain't miss me?" Sensation asked, with a sneaky smirk on his face.

"Can't say that I have," I said dryly. "I damn sure don't miss giving you my last. You were selfish, inconsiderate, disrespectful and—"

"I love you," he suddenly said, out of nowhere.

His words, immediately, interrupted my breathless rant.

"Would you believe me if I told you, you the reason I'm here now?" He asked.

I couldn't answer because I was still floored and at a loss for words. "Wh—what did you just say?" I asked, totally disregarding his last statement. Of the eight years we'd been together, he had never *once* told me that he loved me.

It seemed silly holding Sensation down for all of these years like I did without him ever telling me how he felt about me. But what could I say? I loved him. I loved him well before he even realized that he loved me too.

Sensation slowly made his way over to me and took a seat on the edge of my bed. Cupping my chin in his hand, he pulled my face close to his. I knew I shouldn't have kissed him. Not with the conflicted way I was feeling but that still wasn't enough to stop me from pressing my lips against his.

If there was any doubt that this was a dream before, it all vanished when his tongue invaded my mouth. Sensation wasn't even the kissing type and yet he was giving all of himself to me. Telling me things that I had only dreamed of him saying.

"Wait," I said, breaking away. "Where is all this coming from? And when did you get ou—"

Sensation placed his index finger against my lips, silencing me. "Do you love me?" He asked in a soft and tender tone.

I didn't miss a beat. "Yes," I admitted.

"Do you wanna be wit' a nigga?"

"Yes," I said, hypnotized. "I mean, no," I quickly backtracked. "I mean...I don't know. You can't expect me to just drop everything for you now that you're out."

"So, it's hard for you to drop a nigga you only been fuckin' wit' a few weeks?" He asked offended.

"I'm not talking about Master."

"Well, we should be since we on that topic," he said, turning back to the coldblooded Sensation I always knew. "When the fuck did ya'll get to that level anyway? And why didn't you mention it the last time you came to see me? I got every fuckin' right to choke the shit out of your ass! You know that, right?"

"Nigga, I'm in the hospital. I've just been shot and you wanna talk about some shit like that?!" I yelled. "How 'bout you talk to ya daddy about it!"

Sensation's mouth fell open in shock. He had no idea that I knew about his little secret.

"Oh, so ya'll muthafuckas done had time to cover a lot of ground, huh?" He asked.

Before I could answer my nurse walked in. "Sorry to intrude. I just came by to check on you and the baby's vitals," she said.

"*Baby*?!" Sensation spat out the word like it was venom. "You let this nigga put a baby up in you?!" He yelled, snatching me up by my throat.

The nurse shrieked and ran out of my room to fetch security for the second time that day.

"ANSWER ME, BITCH!!! You let that faggot ass nigga knock you up??!!"

"Sensation, I...can't...breathe," I struggled to say through his tight grip on my neck.

In a fit of rage, he released me then jumped to his feet. "You ain't shit, hoe! You'll never be shit! And you wanna know what the most fucked up part about it all is? I actually was being real wit' you when I said that I loved you." He shook his head at me in disappointment. "But I guess we all capable of lovin' the wrong person, huh?" Once again, he was referencing Master. "It's all good, though. You hoes belong together." Sensation headed for the door just as the security guards walked in. He made a move to leave but then he stopped and turned back around to face me. "Oh, by the way, I fucked ya sister...so I guess we even," he said before leaving.

35
MASTER

I was cruisin' down I-10, reflecting on me and Nova's final moments together before everything came crashing down around us. Our dinner date at *Uchi* was truly a night to remember. We had such a good time together. We laughed, talked shit, and Nova even tried a few different dishes for me.

From the corner of my eye, I noticed Nova watching me sip my sake. She had never tried it before so I wanted to teach her how it should be enjoyed. Swishing it around my mouth a little, I swallowed it and Nova looked on in awe like an eager son watching his dad do an oil change.

"So, is this the culture you bragged on showing me?" she asked.

"Somethin' like that. But we ain't got to the best part yet."

As if on cue, the bartender approached us with two small plates. One was filled with small, paper thin pieces of fish and the other contained oysters with a red substance on top. Nova looked confused and I could tell she was skeptical about trying it.

"The hirame usuzukuri," he said, placing the plate in front of

her. *"And the oysters with watermelon sorbet."* He placed that in front of me.

"You ever tried oysters before?" I asked.

"No never. Is there a certain way I should eat that, too?"

"Yes, as a matter of fact there is," I said pointedly.

"Okay, what do I do?" she asked excited.

"First, you grab your spoon."

She picked up the silverware and held it in front of her.

"You ready for the next step?" I asked.

"Yup!" she said, anticipating the next move.

"Then, holding the spoon lightly, you bring it forward."

A look of confusion swept her face but she did as she was told.

"Next, you bring the spoon close to your face..."

"Okay..."

"Lastly...you balance it on your nose," I teased.

Nova was just about to do it till she realized I was fucking with her. *"You play too much!"* she laughed before playfully shoving me.

"Nah, but on some real shit, ain't nothin' to eatin' oysters. You just pick 'em up and suck 'em down. Like how you did me last night." I whispered the last part and she couldn't help but laugh.

"Like this?" She grabbed the oyster and sucked down the sorbet covered center.

"Yup. How you like it?"

"It's an...um...interesting taste. Not good...not bad...just interesting," she laughed.

"It's an acquired taste," I said, sucking down two.

"Now what's this?" she asked, pointing to the paper-thin slices of fish in front of her.

"Flounder," I said. *"Try it."* I grabbed a couple chopsticks then picked up a piece with tiny, orange balls covering it.

Her eyebrows pointed upward in an inquisitive fashion. *"Um, what's that?"* she asked, pointing to the unknown topping.

"Fish eggs," I said plainly.

"Eww, fish eggs??? Seriously??"

"You can barely taste 'em, bay."

She made a disgusted face.

"Go 'head. Try it," I urged.

Against her better judgment, she opened my mouth and allowed me to feed it to her. "I'm glad to see you willin' to take risks for a nigga," I said, holding back laughter.

"What do you mean?" she asked confused.

My face cracked into a big smile. "That wasn't fish eggs," I said. "It was candied quinoa."

Her eyes widened when she realized just how much influence I had on her. "Oh my God, Master! You play too damn much!" she laughed, pushing me again. "Are you gonna eat some of this?" she asked, pointing to the plate in front of her. She seemed to really enjoy the flounder.

"Nah. You can kill that."

"Don't mind if I do," she said, gulping down the last four slices.

"I'm happy that I can show you some new shit. I wanna show you even more, dependin' on how you act," I added.

"What all are you gonna show me?" she asked with a big smile on her face.

I kissed her lips. "The world," I said confidently.

I had so many plans for me and Nova before Maloni came and put a halt to all of that. I got so wrapped up in my back-stabbing ass wife, I didn't think twice about ditching Z. I knew I did her foul, but I was only acting out of the loyalty and devotion I had to my wife.

It wasn't fair to make her wait around while me and Maloni sorted out our issues. I was only doing what I thought was right, but in the process, I didn't think about it being wrong. Now it was too late.

Flying down the freeway, I headed to my pops' crib on the opposite side of town. I needed someone to talk to. Someone I could confide in that wouldn't try to poison me or bury me in the woods. And who better to talk to than the wisest pimp I knew?

Twenty minutes later, I pulled into the gated building my father lived in. By then, I was feeling strong again and back to my old self. Whatever Maloni had tried to poison me with had finally worn off. I prayed there were no side effects but for now, I felt fine.

After having valet collect my car, I headed up to my father's unit, which was on the top floor of the high-rise building. Essentially, it was something like a nursing home but it was the flyest assisted living building in Houston.

"Pops?" I called out after letting myself in. "Pops, you in here?"

"Where the hell else would my old ass be?" He shot back.

I walked into the living room and found him on the sofa watching a documentary about exotic birds.

"What are you doin'?" I asked confused.

"What's it look like? I'm watching a show about birds."

"Pops, you can look out the window and see that shit," I chuckled.

My dad tore his eyes off the TV screen to look at me sideways. "Now I know you ain't drive all the way over here just to critique my taste in television."

I plopped down on the sofa next to him. "Nah. I actually dropped by to chop game wit'chu."

"Last time we did that, you got offended."

"Sometimes the truth hurts," I admitted. "But you were right. I should've been there for Sensation like you were there for me." I looked at the TV, where a red bellied bird was soaring across the sky. "Unfortunately, I think it's too late to right my wrongs."

"Son, it's never too late to right your wrongs," he said.

Sighing deeply, I ran a hand over my fade. There was still dried up blood on the side of my face since I had yet to clean the wound. My father saw it but he wouldn't dare speak on it because he knew the type of life I lived. He lived a similar life-style back when he was pimping. "I wanna believe that's true," I said.

"Just remember to do what is right. Not what is easy."

Easier said than done, I thought.

I was sure that Sensation wanted nothing to do with me and who could blame him? I'd denied him for nineteen years, then turned around and took his bitch. Righting that wrong wouldn't be a simple task. And there was no guarantee that Sensation would even forgive me. If the shoe was on the other foot, I damn sure wouldn't.

Suddenly, my phone rang. It was Trae. One of my foot soldiers. I immediately took the call and he updated me on the latest happenings. Apparently, Sensation had gone to see Nova. He explained that things had gotten out of hand and Sensation had to be escorted out by security—much like myself.

"'Preciate the update."

With Sensation being so temperamental and reckless, I made sure to have a couple shooters on standby at the hospital. You never did know when he might fly off the handle. Sensation was so damn unpredictable and hot-headed. I was kind of like that at his age. Only I was smarter.

"Oh. One more thing, I need you to handle the funeral arrangements," I said before he hung up. All of the men who Sensation had brutally murdered needed to be buried, and their families compensated. "I *would* do it but...My mind ain't right to handle that shit right now," I admitted.

"Nah, I feel you, my G. Don't worry 'bout it. I'm on top of it."

After he hung up, I turned my attention back to my father. He was shaking his head at me after hearing the tail end of my conversation. "Sounds like you're knee deep in some shit," he said.

"When am I not?" I sighed.

Like I said before, I was really starting to get tired of the game. This shit was a young nigga's sport. I was getting too old for all of this mess.

"Son...It's time you start cleaning up your shit," my dad said.

Honestly, I couldn't have agreed more.

36
MASTER

The Cromwell Center for Mental Health was where I ended up next, and no, I wasn't there to check myself in. After calling in a few favors, I found out that Nova's mother was currently being cared for here. Evidently, the doctors had diagnosed her with PTSD and multiple personality disorder.

To be honest, I was shocked that she ended up checking herself into a psychiatric ward to begin with, but after what I did to her I couldn't fault her. One tragic night had changed her entire life.

After paying off the employees at the concierge desk, I was led to small visitation room and told to wait while they fetched her mom. She wasn't expecting any visitors, so they had to get her dressed and make sure she was in her "right frame of mind". Their words, not mine.

"Damn," I muttered, as I sat there waiting for her to appear. I felt like pure and utter shit. I couldn't believe that I'd pushed this woman to the brink of insanity. And what's more, I couldn't believe that I'd set her house ablaze with her children inside.

Was this really what the game had turned me into? A fucking ruthless, black-hearted monster? What type of man did some shit like that?

No man at all, that's who.

Moments later, the doors to the visitation room opened and a nurse strolled inside, pushing a tiny woman in a wheelchair. She was badly burned on over 75% of her body, and her skin was hues of dark brown, tan, beige and pink. Her eyes were sunken in and she was still bald from her scalp catching fire during the incident. Regardless of her scars and hyper-pigmentation, Nova's mom was hard to mistake. They had the same hazel eyes and they were eyes that I would never forget for as long as I lived.

"Noooo!" she cried out as soon as she saw me. "Take me back! TAKE ME BACK! He's here to kill me!"

"Relax, Zelda," the nurse said with a gentle smile. "No one's come to cause any harm to you. I promise."

"No! No! You don't understand!" Zelda argued. "You don't understand! TAKE ME BACK!"

To the nurse, she sounded like a crazy old bat off her meds but to me, she made perfect sense. I was the reason she was even in here. She probably thought I came back to finish the job, but my intentions were the total opposite.

"Do you want an extra dose of your meds?" The nurse asked in the same condescending tone a parent would use when speaking to their disobedient child.

"No," Zelda squeaked out.

"Then I suggest you settle down and act like you're happy to have a visitor. You know some of the other patients here aren't as lucky as you. They haven't had anyone come to see them in years."

Zelda looked over at me and her bottom lip trembled in fear. It was like she was looking the Boogeyman dead in the eyes.

"Now I'll be right outside if you need me," her nurse informed her before leaving us alone.

As soon as the metal doors closed, Zelda started fidgeting with her burned fingers. "I'm sorry," she cried. "I'm so sorry that I didn't have the money to pay you. I'm sorry that I stole your drugs all those years ago. Please...don't kill me," she begged.

Reaching over, I took her hands in mine in order to get her to stop fidgeting. Zelda paused, then looked down at the contact in shock.

"I'm not here to kill you," I said calmly. "I'm here to talk to you."

Zelda snatched her hands away from me like I had Ebola. "What do you *possibly* want to talk to me about after all of these years?"

I didn't blink or break eye contact when I said, "your husband."

Zelda slowly met my gaze. "What about him? You killed him," she spat.

"I didn't."

"Bullshit! You killed him and covered it up!"

"Okay. That's what you believe. Now can I tell you what I *know*."

Zelda settled down. "What do you know?" she asked in a small voice.

Suddenly, my mind drifted back to the night I *tried* to kill him.

"Aye, V! Look, who the fuck I bumped into," Dru said, shoving a drunken and delirious Max into the kitchen of my trap in Guns-

point. It was the same trap Max and his bitch ran up in not too long ago.

After they robbed me, I tried to take every single one of their asses out the game by torching their house, but word quickly got back to me that all of them had survived. I didn't really care, though. I was sure after that scare they would never try me again anyway.

Hell, no one would.

I considered letting bygones be bygones, and not going after them to finish the job, but that was before Dru brought his sorry ass here. Now I had no choice but to finish what I had started.

"Where the fuck did you find him?" I asked, snorting up a line of coke. Back then, I had no problem dipping into my own product, but luckily that habit died down as I got older. Now, I didn't fuck with drugs at all, other than a lil' weed here and there.

"Stumbling around the liquor store in south side," she said. "The owner was just 'bout to call the cops when I offered to take him instead," she explained. "I figured you wanted to get your hands on him way more than the cops," she smiled.

Standing to my feet, I walked up to a cowering Max and slammed my fist into his stomach.

"Bitch nigga, I know you ain't waste my hard-earned money on booze and backwoods!!" I yelled.

Max keeled over and vomited on my Jordans. "I—I'm sorry," He slurred. "I—I promise if you give me some time I can get it all back to you!"

"Don't ever promise more than you can deliver," I said, grabbing my gun.

Suddenly, and without warning, Max shoved Dru and took off running towards the door.

"GET THAT SNAKE ASS NIGGA!" I yelled. "Don't let his bitch ass see the light of day!"

Dru grabbed her piece and started firing at him but only managed to clip his shoulder.

POP! POP! POP! POP!

Max tore out of the trap at breakneck speed with his life still intact, and after that he became a ghost. No one had seen him or heard from him in ages.

"Well? What do you know?" Zelda asked again, pulling me from the brief flashback.

I took her hands in mine and this time, she didn't put a fight as I stared into her sunken in eyes. "That Max is still alive."

Zelda looked like she didn't believe me.

"He's alive and I can prove it," I told her.

"No, no, no," she said, shaking her head in denial. "It can't be!"

"Listen to me, Zelda. He's alive. You've just...made up some crazy conspiracy in your head to atone for his absence." I squeezed her hands gently. "But I can assure you he's still out here."

A tear rolled down Zelda's cheek. "If he's alive, why hasn't he come back?" She croaked out, voice hoarse with emotion.

"I don't know. Maybe out of fear. Maybe out of guilt. Only Max knows the answer to that," I said.

Zelda closed her eyes tightly. "I've always wanted to believe he was still alive," she said. "But I guess, over time, it just became easier to accept that he was dead..."

I brushed her tear away with my thumb. "Listen to me...I promise, I'm gonna find him. I give you my word."

I slowly stood to my feet, but Zelda grabbed my wrist out of nowhere. To be a fragile, crazy old woman she was actually strong as fuck.

"Is it true?" She asked. "Is it true you started dating my daughter?"

"Zelda...we're well past dating," I told her. "I love your daughter...with everything in me. And I know you and I have had our differences, and I am *truly* sorry for what I've done, but Zelda. I ain't that same nigga."

"I know," she whispered. "I know you aren't."

I placed a hand on her shoulder and made unwavering eye contact. "I promise I'm gonna find him, Z. I'm gonna find your husband and bring him home."

"If you do," she began. "Maybe...just maybe...I'll consider accepting your apology."

37
A'SHAUNIE

I had just laid down Shawn for the night and fucked Profit's ass to sleep, when I crept into the hallway bathroom to call Sensation. Unlike his whores, he actually picked up for me. He had no choice but to. If it wasn't for me, he'd still be playing tickle booty in prison.

"Whaddup?" He answered dryly. It sounded like something was eating at him.

"What's wrong, bay?"

"Don't wanna talk about it," he said. "Wassup though? What'chu need?"

"You know what I need...you," I whispered into the receiver.

Sensation paused and sighed into the receiver. "Shaunie...shit's complicated right now."

"Well then let's *un*complicate shit together," I told him. "Kill my baby daddy and we can take over this drug game. You'll never have to worry or stress again. I'll be right by your side helping you make all of the right decisions. All you need is a good woman in your corner to help keep you at the top."

I expected Sensation to say some slick shit, but I was surprised when he replied, "sounds good."

I smiled into the phone because I was slowly but surely breaking him down. Nova didn't know it, but her betrayal had pushed him right into my arms.

"Like I said before, Sensation...one day, you gone love me."

Suddenly, the bathroom door flew open. "Well, it ain't gone be today, bitch!" Profit sneered.

"P—Profit!" I stuttered, dumbfounded by his presence.

"Gimme the muthafuckin' phone!" He snatched the cell out of my hands and placed it to his ear. "Pussy nigga, if you want this bitch you gone have to pry her from my cold, dead fingers!"

I could hear Sensation laughing through the receiver. "Mayne, it ain't that deep," he said. "Ya bitch chose up. Don't be mad at the kid about it."

"Come say that shit to my face, young punk!"

"Profit, just stop! It's not what you think!" I said, reaching for the phone.

Profit shoved me so hard, I hit my head on the side of the bathtub. "Get the fuck out of my face, bitch!" He yelled. "How long you been pillow talking with this nigga?!"

When I didn't answer fast enough, he launched the phone at my head, cracking me in the skull with it.

"Huh?! Answer me, bitch!" he screamed.

"Profit, please!" I cried, backing up in fear. I was so afraid that I pissed myself a little. Most of the time, Profit was mellow and laid back as fuck. But my baby daddy had a vicious temper whenever he got himself worked up.

"And did I just hear you tell this mufucka to kill me???!!!"

"No! No, baby! Why the hell would I say something like that?!" I asked. I could already feel a knot forming on my head.

"You're lying!" he shouted.

"On my mama, I'm telling the God's honest truth!"

"Stupid bitch, do you really take me for a fuckin' fool!" He hollered. "How dumb do you think I am? You clearly told this nigga to kill me!!!"

"I didn't, Profit!" I cried.

But Profit wasn't trying to hear any of that shit as he snatched me up by my long hair. "You wanna kill me?!" He yelled, dragging me towards the bedroom.

The carpet burned my legs, rubbing off patches of skin as I was unmercifully dragged by my hair. Once we reached the room, he tossed me into the dresser, causing me to hit my head again. After today, I knew I would have a concussion.

"You wanna kill me so mufuckin' bad?" He snatched his gun out of the top drawer and I shrieked in fear because I just *knew* he was about to body my shit. "Then do it yourself!!!" He demanded. "Go ahead!" He grabbed my hands and forced the small handgun into them. "Pull the fucking trigger, bitch!"

"Profit, please stop! You're gonna wake up our son!"

"*Is* he my son?!" He spat. "Cuz right now, I'm havin' doubts! You got more secrets than a call girl!"

"Don't be ridiculous! Of course, he's yours! He looks just like you!" I cried.

WHAP!

Apparently, that was the wrong answer because Profit slapped the shit out of me and I went flying halfway across the room. "For some reason, I have a hard ass time believing that." He picked the gat up off the floor. "Silly ass bitch, that's why I been pluggin' almost all the hoes at the strip club. I come home every night just to make you suck the pussy juices off my dick, dumb bitch!"

My mouth fell open in shock. I had no idea that while I was doing my dirt, he was doing his.

Profit looked down at the gun in his hands and smiled.

"Since you won't use this bitch, I guess I will." Cocking the gun, he aimed it at my head.

"PROFIT, NO!"

POW!

Blood and brain matter splattered all over me after Sensation blew a hole through the back of his head with a suppressed gun. The sound was so light, it didn't even wake up my 2-year old son, Shawn. Profit's body hit the floor like a bag of bricks and I looked up at Sensation standing in the doorway with teary eyes. I just knew my baby daddy was about to kill my ass. My mama always told me to leave that white boy alone. She claimed they were crazy as fuck.

"Sensation," I whispered in disbelief.

"Good thing I was on this side of town," he smiled.

Without warning, I ran up to him and threw my arms around his neck. He was my savior. My hero. Hell, if it wasn't for him, the bedroom walls would be painted in my blood instead of Profit's.

"Thank you, baby! Thank you! Thank you!" I kissed Sensation all over his face and lips and he didn't dare stop me. His dick did get hard, though.

"You ain't think I was really 'bout to let this fool put his hands on you, did you," he said.

"I didn't know what to think," I said, face buried in the crook of his neck. "All I know is when he pointed that gun at me, I saw my life flash before my eyes."

Sensation looked down at Profit's dead body. "Too bad he didn't see his."

It was crazy how I'd saved Sensation's life, only for him to turn around and save mine. We were really in sync like that.

"Thank you, Sensation."

"If you really wanna thank me, spread dem legs," he said.

He didn't have to tell me twice and I wasted no time

climbing into the bed and undressing. I didn't give a fuck about my baby daddy's dead body being on the floor. His spirit could watch us fuck for all I cared.

Sensation crawled onto the mattress and I anxiously undid his jeans before pulling them down to his knees. Grabbing his tool, I started sucking his dick like a damn vacuum cleaner. I was so grateful to him for saving my life that it showed in my enthusiasm as my head bobbed up and down his length.

"Shit, 'Shaunie. Shit," he breathed, grabbing a handful of my hair. He damn near shouted, it was so fucking good.

I knew Nova couldn't suck his dick like it needed to be sucked. She was inexperienced at everything in life, including how to keep her nigga satisfied. Luckily, Sensation had me now and I planned to suck his dick, enthusiastically, every morning.

His dick got harder and harder inside of my hungry, suctioning mouth. Lines of spit ran down my chin, but I kept on sucking like my life depended on it. Pulling my lips from his rod, I wrapped my hands around it and resorted to licking his balls while I jacked him off at the same time. Profit always said I had that 'porn star head.'

"Gotdamn, 'Shaunie," Sensation moaned.

Profit's body was getting cold on the floor, but that fact wasn't enough to stop me from giving Sensation the BJ of a lifetime. Thrusting my mouth back onto his dick, I sucked and slobbered, getting him nice and lubricated for his entrance.

Sensation pushed me back onto the mattress and I eagerly spread my pussy lips for him. "Fuck me, Daddy," I said seductively.

Sensation guided his throbbing meat towards my soaking pussy and crammed his cock deep inside of my slippery pink fortress. "Unhhhh!" I moaned in ecstasy. He felt so damn good inside of me.

I gasped as his ten inches penetrated me like a sword to a

sheath. He thrusted into my slit all the way to his fat nuts, filling me up whole. To be so short and skinny, the nigga was packing some serious wood. Nova didn't know what to do with all of this, but fortunately, I did. Hooking my knees over his shoulders, I squeezed his ass tightly as he drove deep into me, causing our skin to slap.

"Yeah," he groaned. "Hold that pussy right there. Don't move that muthafucka."

Now that he had better leverage, he plunged into my twat as deeply as he possibly could. "Oh shit, Sensation!" I cried out. If I didn't know any better, I'd think this nigga was trying to put a baby up in me.

I began cumming almost immediately, my spewing hole becoming slicker than snot.

"Damn, baby. Yeahhh," he moaned. "Cum all over this big dick."

"Don't stop fucking me," I pleaded. "Fuck me like you want to! Fuck me like I'm one of your whores!" I cried out.

He plunged in and out of my pussy like a freight train, the noise of our pelvises slapping together. "Yes, Daddy, get that shit!" I screamed as he hammered into my cunt over and over again. "Damn, I'm 'bout to cum again!" I bellowed as he rabbited in and out of my juicy pussy, causing it to make slurping and squelching sounds.

"Cum as many times as you want," he whispered.

Now I understood why all of his hoes wanted to give him their money. His dick was so good that it should've been illegal to fuck for free. Hell, I was on the verge of paying him my damn self!

"Damn, Sensation! I love you!" I cried out. "Yesssss! Babbyyyyyyy!" I was cumming so hard, there were tears rolling down my cheeks. "Fuck me with that big ass dick! Dick me gooood!" I screamed.

Sensation grunted like an animal as he filled me up with his hot semen. There was so much of it, that some of his cum spilled out of my canal. "Damn, bitch," he groaned. "I should've been fuckin' *you* all these years."

I tried to kiss him but he moved away. He was obviously still in his feelings about Nova's bitch ass. Pulling out of me, he grabbed his jeans and started getting dressed.

"Where you going?" I asked disappointed. I was more than ready for an encore.

"Where you think?" He pointed at Profit's body. "To clean up this mess. Unless you *want* this nigga to sit here and rot."

I licked my lips and smiled. "If that means that I can ride you all night, then fuck it, let 'em rot."

Sensation chuckled. "Bitch, you wildin'. The dick ain't goin' nowhere," he said. "Let me call up my young boys to help me make this body disappear. Then after, I'm all yours."

I laid back on the bed and started rubbing my clit, then I hit him with his own line. "Sounds good."

38
MASTER

Puffing on a Backwood, I flipped through the photos of an old album filled with pictures of me and Dru over the years. I still couldn't believe that she was actually gone. I think I was more in denial about that than I was about her actual betrayal. Regardless of that bullshit, she was my best fucking friend, my right hand, my A-1 day-1. She knew everything about me. My flaws, my insecurities. She was like family to me. Even closer to me than my own siblings.

Every time I closed my eyes, I thought about the sound of the shovel connecting with her skull. "Dammit, Dru!" I yelled at thin air. "All you had to do was stay down! That's all the fuck you had to do!" I wanted to cry over her death but I refused to shed a single tear for a wolf in sheepskin.

I'd been nothing short of fair and generous to Dru, only for her to stab me in the back. Sadly, because she was dead, I would never get the answers I needed. Like how long she'd been laying that plastic wood to my wife. And if she loved her. I knew that it was too late now but it still mattered. I guess, knowing would've served as closure for me. After all, I'd been with Maloni for 21 years.

Blowing smoke through my nostrils, I took another toke from my Backwood. It would've been great if it were paired with some promethazine but I was done sippin' lean. That shit fucked with my focus big time. Maybe if I wasn't always drinking that shit, I would've saw their betrayal coming a mile away.

"Damn."

Closing the photo album, I ashed the 'Wood. I was just about to lay down to try to get some sleep when my phone rang. It was Trae so I immediately answered. He'd been acting as something sort of like a lieutenant to me, now that Dru was dead. I promised myself to promote him later on, because he was the only cat helping me keep my shit together. I wanted to fall apart after the shit Maloni and Dru pulled, but somehow, he was able to keep me level-headed.

"Yo, whaddup, bro?"

"Shit, shit. You good dawg? You kinda sound like you out of it."

"Shit, I kinda am. But you know the comeback always stronger than the setback," I said.

"Aye, I feel that," he said. "I just called 'cuz I wanted to keep ya eyes open. Nova just checked herself out of the hospital."

I quickly sat up in high alert. "Oh yeah?"

"Yeah. My homeboy works up there in reception. He said she just signed her early release papers," he explained.

I ran a veined hand over my weary face. Nova just couldn't stay put for shit. When she was in the hospital, it was easier to keep tabs on her. When she wasn't, it was easy for her to get into all sorts of trouble.

"And it's one more thing, dawg."

"What's that?" I asked.

"My homeboy pulled her file after she left," Trae paused. "He say she's pregnant..."

39
NOVA

I knew that I should've stayed in the hospital. I knew that I shouldn't have checked myself out, if not for my sake, for the sake and welfare of my unborn child. But I just couldn't sit back and do nothing after knowing what I now knew.

I couldn't believe that Miss High and Mighty A'shaunie had actually slept with Sensation! Just thinking about the way she berated me for sleeping with a married man had me ready to snatch all of that bitch's edges out! This bitch was always acting like her shit didn't stink. Come to find out she was no better than me.

Nah.

As a matter of fact, she was ten times worse than me!

People could say what they wanted about me but I never crossed the ones I loved and cared about. Shit, it never even crossed my mind to sleep with Profit! Knowing she had stabbed me in the back in such a fucked up way had propelled me to check myself out early despite my doctor's protests just to check her ass about it. I couldn't sit on that shit no matter how hard I tried to. I had to tell her about herself.

Thankfully, I had money in my bra, so I used some of it to hail a cab to A'shaunie's place. I spent sixty dollars on that fucking trip but I planned to make sure it was worth every penny. After tipping the cabbie, I promptly made my way to the front door of A'shaunie's home. It was a quarter after 3 am but the lights in her hallway and foyer were on.

BOOM!

BOOM!

BOOM!

I pounded on her door like I was a court martial about to serve a warrant.

"A'shaunie, it's me! Open the door!" I demanded.

There was a long period of silence before I suddenly heard the sound of footsteps. Shortly after, the door swung open and my sister appeared wearing nothing but a satin robe. There were beads of sweat on her face and chest and her hair was all messy like she'd just got through fucking.

I told myself that I was only hear to talk, but seeing her made me forget about all that shit.

"Nova?" She said with a surprised look on her face. "What the fuck are you doing here so la—"

WHAP!

I stole her right in the fucking face, knocking the wind out of her. From the corner of my eye, I noticed bloody footprints on the floor but no body, and more importantly, no Profit. I didn't stop to ask about it as I attacked my sister like a rabid animal with rabies.

"BITCH! Why the fuck do you think I'm here?!" I screamed, snatching her up by her long hair. "Trifling ass hoe! You my sister! I trusted you!" I screamed, pummeling her skull repeatedly.

A'shaunie screamed and I heard my nephew start to cry in the distance but it didn't deter me from beating the dog shit out of my backstabbing ass sister.

WHAP! WHAP! WHAP!

I pounded my fist into her head over and over again and when she tried to reach for my hair, I slung her bitch ass to the floor by her hair like a fucking rag doll. "Bitch! Bitch! Fucking bitch!" I yelled, punching her in the head and face. Her legs flailed wildly and she kicked the nearby accent table, knocking over a vase, in the process.

In the background, Shawn started screaming even louder. I had obviously woken him up with my antics. But this beatdown couldn't wait. A'shaunie was getting just what she had coming and if it wasn't for her being my sister, she would've gotten much worse. Shit, I might've even killed her ass.

"Get the fuck off me!" She screamed, nearly kicking me in the stomach.

"Hoe, you gone kick me in the stomach knowing I'm pregnant?!" I hollered. "BITCH!" I struck her in the mouth, busting her shit wide open and her nose started bleeding simultaneously. "Don't fucking play with me, bitch! Don't fucking play!" I cracked her one good last time, then climbed off of her. I was just about to leave till this silly hoe decided to run up on me.

WHAM!

I drew my leg back and kicked the shit out of her ass and she went flying across the foyer.

Crack!

She hit her head against the accent table but leapt back to her feet at lightning speed. She then took off running after me again, determined to get a few licks in.

I kicked her ass back again, not realizing I had torn my stitches a second time. My hip was on fire but I was hellbent on showing her ass that I wasn't the same little Nova who would always take her shit.

"You fucking bitch!" She hollered, running at me again.

I kick-pushed her back, and before she could stand, I kicked her in the fucking face. I was just finna hop on top of her when I suddenly felt someone grab me from behind. I thought it was Profit till I peeped the gang-related tattoos on his forearms.

Sensation?

Lifting me like a feather, he carried me to the front door then tossed me out on my ass like I was a piece of trash.

"You fried, bitch! If you ever bring your dusty ass 'round here again, I'll kill you my fucking self!"

Now I understood why A'shaunie was all sweaty when she answered the door. She'd been fucking Sensation like a bitch in heat.

"Fuck both of ya'll trifling, dirty ass! I hope you give each other AIDS!" I screamed, not caring that I didn't make any sense. I was so fucking mad, I couldn't think straight. I couldn't fucking believe their asses but at least, now I knew how he felt when he found out I fucked his father.

"Nah, you fucked yaself!" He spat. "You had a real nigga. Now you lost him!"

"You were never real! You used and abused me at every turn!" I screamed at him. "So fuck you! You belong with that bum ass bitch anyway! Ya'll can rot in Hell together for all I give a fuck!"

Instead of arguing with me, Sensation slammed the door right in my face. If I had a gun I might've killed their asses but I was glad that I didn't. They weren't worth the trouble. Like I said before, they belonged together—in hell.

40
MASTER

I was going over the speed limit as I raced to Nova's crib. I knew that she didn't want to see me and that was cool and all, but I at least had to make sure she was good. If she was carrying my seed then it was my duty. On the way there, I thought about the very first time we'd ever gotten into a heated argument.

"The fuck happened to yo ride?" I asked once I saw her wrecked vehicle.

"None of your fucking business!" she spat with an attitude. She always had an attitude whenever she dealt with me.

I grabbed my elbow and whirled her around to face me. "You are my fuckin' business," I told her.

She snatched her arm away from me. "Just 'cuz we fucked don't make me your business," she said, stepping inside of her apartment.

I walked in too, then slammed the door behind me. "I won't even combat ignorance with ignorance," I said.

"Whatever," she waved me off. "Then don't." She sounded childish as fuck but what could I expect from a 20-year old?

"You might as well tell me what happened. Shit, I'mma find out either way," I said.

"What happened was you!" she yelled. There was a simmering storm of hatred and rage inside of me. And beneath all that was sadness *"If I'd been at the fucking club, then none of this shit would've happened!"*

"Trouble seems to follow yo ass wherever you go. That shit has nothin' to do with me," I argued.

"What the fuck is you talkin' 'bout?! It has everything to do with you!" she screamed. *"Why couldn't you just give Sensation a shot?! Why couldn't he work for you??? Nigga, I wouldn't even be out here like this if he was making some decent paper!!! Look how the fuck we livin'!"* she said, pointing to her surroundings. *"But yet you call this nigga your family!"* She shook her head at me. *"You act like you're the man, like you're some big-time hot shot, but in reality, you ain't shit! You're nothing but a selfish, self-absorbed, fucked up cocktail of a human being! Just another loser in a long list of poor choices I've made."*

Her words cut like daggers but I knew she was only speaking out of anger. Ever so slowly, I approached her and slowly backed her up against the wall. *"Cut it out. You know you don't feel that damn way, girl."*

"That's exactly how I feel. Now get the fuck out of my house," she said stubbornly, knowing damn well she didn't want me to leave.

"Cut it out, Z," I smiled. *"I don't wanna hear dat shit 'cuz I know you don't mean it. You wanna know how I know?"* I asked, sarcastically but with a tone of honest intent. *"When I hold you in my arms, it feels natural,"* I admitted. *"I know you feel it too. Hell, you feelin' it right now,"* I said. *"A nigga need that, Nova. I been missin' that shit so much in my life."*

Nova paused. *"But Master...you're married,"* she reminded me. *"And have you forgotten that I'm with Sensation."* I could see the guilt all in her beautiful, hazel eyes.

I didn't think twice when I said, "Fuck that nigga. You wit' me now."

When I finally made it to Nova's crib, I was disappointed to discover she wasn't there. All of the lights were off and I assumed that she hadn't returned since her departure from the hospital.

"Where the hell is this chick?" I asked myself for the dozenth time. I even tried calling her phone but the shit went straight to voicemail. I figured she didn't have it on her. Either that, or she was just ignoring my shit.

After pulling out of the lot, I headed for my second destination. There was something else I wanted to do for Zelda in addition to finding her husband.

***

That afternoon, I met up with Lydia to have her show me some of the finest, luxury assisted living facilities in Texas. She'd found one for my dad so I knew she could find one for Zelda, in spite of her mental issues. I knew that her mental and physical well-being couldn't go ignored, so I planned to hire a 24-hour health care team to look after her, cook gourmet meals and make sure she had everything that she needed. Cromwell was cool and all, but I wanted her to be somewhere nicer. Somewhere she could feel more at home, and the place Lydia and I ended up settling on was just that.

"It's a modern Victorian apartment," she said on our way up to the unit. "And it's fully furnished and wheelchair accessible, including the bathrooms. It was recently renovated and all of the appliances are state of the art. She's really gonna love this, Master," Lydia smiled. "I promise."

When we walked inside of the apartment, I told myself that she would. It was so much better than Cromwell but regardless of my opinion, it was ultimately Zelda's decision. I wasn't gonna force her to move.

"Yeah." I nodded my head in agreement. "This is the one," I said. "I'll take it."

"Excellent. I'll talk to the property managers and start drafting up the paperwork right away."

Lydia was just about to walk off when I grabbed her by the arm and slammed her against the wall of the hallway entrance. I got so close to her that I could smell the pussy on her breath.

"It's something else I wanna address, 'cuz somebody's been running their mouth like they're in a fuckin' marathon."

"Master—"

"You told Maloni about the condo. And don't stand in my fucking face and lie to me 'cuz I know you did. You were the only one that knew about it."

"Master, we were at the nail shop. It just slipped out," she lied.

I twisted her wrist, damn near coming close to snapping it and she cried out in pain. I wasn't gonna break it, though. I just wanted her to know I wasn't the one to fuck with. Not today. Not tomorrow.

"I don't give a fuck," I spat. "If you ever speak ill on me again, I'll cut out that cum coated tongue of yours. Do I make myself clear?"

"Y—Yes," she stuttered.

"Good." I finally let her go. "Now get the fuck out of my sight!" That bitch smelled like a cat factory.

Holding her sore wrist, Lydia fled the apartment, not knowing that she was this close to losing her life. I almost lost my shit but somehow, I managed to hold it altogether. I was just tired of everyone close to me crossing me.

One thing was for certain. I knew Nova never would.

***

"Where are you taking me?" Zelda asked as I wheeled her out of Cromwell that evening.

"You'll see when we get there," I said plainly.

Zelda huffed and puffed, sounding just like Nova. "Well, where ever you're taking me, Max had *better* be there," she said defiantly.

Ignoring her protests, I wheeled her to the parking lot and stopped once we reached my Escalade. It was actually Trae's but I had to borrow it to load her wheelchair in the back. It was pretty damn big for such a small woman. Then again, it was supplied by the facility. Maybe one day I'd replace that as well, if she didn't mind.

Before lugging the ancient wheelchair into the truck, I lifted her fragile body and placed her into the backseat. Once the chair was secure in the trunk, I climbed in, started the car and embarked on the long drive to her new home.

"What is this place?" Zelda asked as soon as we pulled up to the Victorian building. I had Lydia close the deal on it while I ran to pick up Zelda and since we were paying cash money, the office sped up the paperwork process. "Is Max here?" She asked curiously.

"No, not yet," I answered truthfully. "I'm still workin' on that."

"Well, why the hell am I here?" She asked, sounding just like Nova again.

I killed the engine and turned around to face her. "Because I still feel fucked up about what I did after all these years," I admitted. "And I wanna do right by the people I wronged, so I decided to start with you. I wanna handle your living and medical expenses and whatever else you need."

Zelda pursed her lips and folded her arms. "You *should* feel bad," she said snidely. "And will I get a stipend with all of these new perks?"

I smiled at her. "Of course. But no drugs," I added.

"I'll have you know I've been clean for over ten years!"

"Good. Let's keep it that way."

After helping her out of the truck, I wheeled her up to the apartment unit. She seemed pleased and even thanked me for getting her out of that hell hole, as she called it.

"Do you think Max will like it, too?" She asked, rolling herself around her new apartment.

"No."

She cut her eyes at me and I smiled. "I think he'll love it."

41
MASTER

After getting Zelda settled into her new place, I swung by Nova's crib again in hopes that she'd be home. The lights were on so I figured she was. "Lemme see what this chick on," I said, killing the engine.

We hadn't seen each other since the hospital and judging by the way she acted then, I knew she still waon't ready to. But she'd just have to deal with it. Because if what Trae had said was true and she really was carrying my seed, then she had to put up with a nigga whether she wanted to or not.

After hitting my alarm, I briskly made my way to her door and knocked before patiently waiting on her to answer. Seconds later, I heard shuffling on the other end and what sounded like Nova looking out of the peephole. I imagined her standing on her tiptoes. The girl was so damn short.

When she didn't open the door for me, I pressed my head against the surface. "I know you in there, baby. Open the door and talk to me," I pleaded. I twisted the knob but she had it locked.

"There ain't nothing to talk about," she stated.

"Bullshit...you carryin' my seed..."

There was a long pause before Nova finally opened the door for me, but based on her expression, it was unwillingly. "How did you find out?" she asked with an attitude.

"You have my baby in you...you really think I wasn't gone find out?" With no invitation, I let myself inside and closed the door behind me.

"Well, you know...Now what?" She asked, propping a hand on her hip.

"What'chu mean *now what*? I wanna be there for mine."

"Oh, so *now* you wanna be a daddy," she said snidely. "What about Sensation—"

"You let me worry about Sensation," I said harshly.

"He damn sure ain't worried about you," she muttered.

I wasn't sure what that meant. "Right now, my focus is on you and this baby. I'll deal with Sensation," I told her.

"Master...I don't even know if I'm keeping this baby," she said stubbornly.

I knew she was just bullshitting to get under my skin and it worked. "Don't fuck with me," I told her. "Don't fuck with me 'bout some shit like that. You know damn well you keepin' my baby."

"Why are you here, Master? You know I got a half a mind to stab you in the fucking face after everything you did to my family—"

"I know. And I know you'll have a hard time forgiving me, but I swear, if it takes the rest of my life, I will spend it on trying to make it up to you." I took Nova's hands in mine. "You need to know, though...I didn't kill your father."

"Why should I believe you?" she shot back.

"Why shouldn't you? I've never lied to you!"

"Um...did you forget you had me believing Sensation was your son!"

"That was different!" I argued.

"But my mom—"

"Fuck what ya moms said. He's alive...but only 'cuz I failed to kill him when I had the chance," I added. "Listen to me. He's out here somewhere and I'm gonna prove it to you."

"Well, you'd better. Because I know what the fuck my mother said, Master!"

I thought about telling her that I'd recently reacquainted myself with her mother but I held back on that bit of info for now.

"Now that I told you that, I need you to tell me somethin'," I said.

"What's that?" She asked.

"Who in the fuck was fool enough to shoot my woman?"

Nova sighed, then shook her head at me. "This nigga named Marcus. He sells weed and pills and shit on the west side of Houston." She folded her arms. "There...you have your answer? Now, is that all?"

"Nah...There's one last thing."

Before she could ask what that thing was, I grabbed her and crushed my lips against hers. Nova didn't struggle or bother to put up a fight, regardless of the shit she was spewing a second ago. Moaning, our tongues dueled with each other as I held her small frame in my arms.

Lifting her off of her feet, I carried Nova to her bedroom, kissing the whole way there. Once we were inside, I gently laid her down on the mattress and didn't bother checking the closet next since I trusted her. She bit her lip and pulled off her clothes and I wasted no time undressing at rapid speed. I needed to feel her insides like I needed oxygen to survive. Her side was bandaged, so I told myself I would take it easy on her just this *one* time.

Flipping her over onto her stomach, I spread her legs a

little. Nova stuck her pussy out for me, then glanced over her shoulder with a sexy, little smirk on her face. I eagerly directed my hard dick towards her opening. I was so excited, I struggled to get it into her hole, but she adjusted herself to help me. When I found it, I slowly slid my dick into her vagina just an inch or so before pulling it back out. I did that several times, getting her good and wet as I probed her hole repeatedly. Her pussy was so moist that it produced wet, sloshing sounds.

"*Mmmhmm*, Master. Don't play with me, Daddy. Put it in," she begged.

"*You* put it in," I teased.

Nova grabbed the base of my dick and guided it into her opening, and I groaned, overwhelmed by her tightness and wetness. Nova grabbed a handful of the sheets as I locked onto a fistful of her hair and slid deep inside.

With my other hand, I grabbed her waist and slid my dick all the way into her pussy, causing her ass cheeks to tighten around me. Nova moaned as I pulled out before thrusting in a second time just as deep. I did it again a third and fourth time and before I knew it, I was bodying them cheeks.

"*Oooooohhhhh*, shit!" Nova moaned as I picked up pace. "Ooh, shit, Master! Gotdamn, I missed you, baby!"

The feeling was electrifying and I could barely hold onto my rhythm. I was so enraptured by the sensation and her moans of pleasure that I could hardly keep myself from cumming too fast.

"Yessssss! Master! Fuck me, baby! Fuck this pussy, it's yours! It's all yours!"

I kissed the back of her shoulder. "Don't say some shit you don't mean."

"Noooo," she bellowed. "I mean, it baby! I swear, I mean it!"

"This pussy mine?" I asked, speeding up my pace.

"Yes! Yes!" she cried out.

"You mine?" I asked next.

"Yes, baby! Yes! I'm yours forever."

This good dick would make her lil' ass say anything.

I chuckled softly as I finally slowed down, then grabbed her chin, turned her face towards me and kissed her. "Turn your pretty ass over. I wanna look at you," I said.

Nova maneuvered onto her back and I swiftly slid between her legs. Reaching for my dick, she grabbed it, then lined it up with her super wet snatch. "Damn, Master. I've missed you so much," she whispered. "Please...put it in," she begged.

I slowly pushed the head of my dick inside of her. "Oh yeah? You missed me, or you missed this dick?"

Nova let out a long moan. "Both."

Pushing myself in inch by inch, I went slow, savoring the way her tunnel of delight felt. "I missed you too, baby," I whispered. I never thought I'd get to feel this slippery goodness again, and now that I was buried inside of her, I never wanted to leave.

Once I was seated all the way in her, her pussy muscles contracted around my swollen 10 inches of steel. I deep-dicked her a few good times before pulling out and climbing down at her waist. She grabbed my head as I started lapping at her clit, then drove my tongue in as far as it would go. I wanted to taste her nectar because I'd been missing that too. When I slipped two fingers in and found that glorious spot, she really started to lose her mind. Using my lips, I latched onto her clit and started sucking it at the same time for dear life.

"Shit, Master, you eat pussy so good! Make me cum, baby!" she begged.

I'd always prided myself on my ability to bring a woman to orgasm with my tongue. It took years of practice to gain these skills. Burying my face even deeper, I sucked and licked and licked and sucked until she lost it and moaned that she was cumming.

"Oh god! Oh fuck!" she said over and over as her orgasm took over her body.

Climbing back up, I slid my dick into her slippery folds and leaned in to kiss her. When I pulled back, her lips were sparkling with her own juices. The sight of it really turned me the fuck on.

"Yessss, baby! That feels so fucking good!" she moaned as I made love to her. "I'm 'bout to cum again."

"Cum all over this dick, baby. I'mma cum wit'chu." And I did, deep inside of her honey pot.

Winded and fatigued, I rolled over and pulled her into my arms. In less than 10 minutes, Nova was knocked out. "I love you," I whispered. "And I will *always* protect you."

42

SENSATION

The sun was just beginning to peak over the horizon when my cellphone rang on the nightstand. I'd been fucking A'shaunie all night and well into the morning. You'd think the bitch was celebrating the death of her baby daddy with sex but I wasn't complaining. A'shaunie stirred a little but remained asleep. I had obviously dicked her into a coma.

Reaching over, I grabbed my phone and looked at the caller ID. It was Veronica, the same bitch who'd picked me up from prison. I hadn't seen or talked to her since I got out and honestly, I had no intentions to. I was on now, I didn't need her ass anymore. But if I did in the future, I had no issue reaching out.

"Why the fuck is this bitch blowing me up so gotdamn early?" I huffed.

These hoes got a lil' taste of dick then went wild with their shit. Just because I fucked 'em didn't mean I was obligated to any of them. Truthfully, the only bitch that I felt like I owed was A'shaunie for getting me out of lockdown. She showed she was down, unlike her nasty, burnt ass sister.

I swear, I got more hoes than I know what to do with, I thought. Maybe it was officially time for me to give up my player ways and settle down with someone real. I looked over at A'shaunie as she slept.

Hitting the ignore button, I placed it back on the night-stand—but suddenly, it started ringing again. "I know this bitch ain't calling me again," I complained, picking up the phone. I looked at the caller ID and was surprised to see Quez's name instead. I assumed whatever reason he was calling me for must've been important. "Whaddup, bro?" I answered.

"Aye, mayne, I just got word that Nova checked herself out—"

"Man, I already know that. You a little too late with the heads up."

"Also, I found out where the nigga Master lives, but when I pulled up to his spot he wasn't there."

Never send a boy to do a man's job, I thought to myself.

"Don't worry 'bout it, bro. I'll deal with the fuck nigga myself."

43
MASTER

Sunlight pierced through the bedroom curtains with such intensity it caused me to slowly stir awake. I then looked to my left where Nova was still sleeping like a baby. For someone who claimed they hated me so much, she had no problem laying up under me. I wasn't complaining though because I loved it. I wanted to wake up next to her every morning, for the rest of my life.

Smiling, I brushed my thumb over her baby hairs, then grabbed her hand where she'd been burned and lightly kissed her scar.

Nova slowly came to.

"Morning, baby." I went to kiss her but she quickly stopped me.

"Nooooo! You know I haven't brushed my teeth yet," she whined.

"I don't give a fuck," I said, tonguing her down anyway. "Now hop up on this dick," I told her, squeezing all on her ass.

"I'm tired," she said.

"Nah. You lazy," I said, rolling over on top of her.

Nova happily spread her legs, grateful that I was once again doing all of the work. I swear, I had her ass spoiled in the bedroom.

Positioning myself at her opening, I pushed into her, causing Nova to let out a shrill moan of ecstasy. Rocking back and forth, I started filling her small stature with deep, powerful thrusts. Her pussy was still somewhat swollen from the beating she took last night and her pussy lips, puffy. But she took every inch of me like a big girl. I was just getting into a good rhythm when my phone suddenly rang.

"Don't answer it," she begged.

I thought about Trae and how he'd been cleaning up *my* mess for the past 48 hours, so I figured I had to. "Just gimme one minute," I said, pulling out of her. "This'll only take a second."

Nova pouted like a big baby. Too distracted by her shenanigans, I failed to look at the caller ID first before answering my phone. "Yo, yo, whaddup, bro?"

"Whaddup, ole man," Sensation said with a hint of laughter in his tone. "Where you at right now?" he asked. "Lemme guess. Somewhere balls deep in my bitch," he cackled. "Shit, judging by the way you breathin', I wouldn't be surprised if you were in her guts right now."

"What's the *real* reason you called me Sensation?" I asked him.

Nova quickly sat up in bed at the mention of her ex-boyfriend. You would've thought he was about to walk into the bedroom at any minute.

"We need to talk," he simply said. "In person."

"Where?"

"Why don't you meet me at the warehouse you just purchased," he said.

"How you know 'bout dat?" I asked him.

"Nigga, you ain't the only one capable of clockin' moves," he laughed. "I'll be there in an hour," he said before hanging up.

"What did he want?" Nova asked after I disconnected the call.

"He wants me to meet him," I told her.

"Don't! It's a set-up!"

"It may be...but I just can't ignore the nigga. He's my son. Plus, we *do* have some unfinished business to deal with," I said, thinking about the trap he'd recently ran up in. He had killed all of my soldiers and that shit couldn't go unaddressed.

"Well, you can't just let yourself get killed either," she said with tears in her eyes.

"I doubt it'll come to all of that," I said, only halfway believing it.

"Well, then you don't know Sensation!" she argued. "He's vindictive as fuck—"

"He's my son, Nova," I said firmly. "I know *exactly* who he is."

"Master—"

"Just trust me," I said before placing a soft kiss on her forehead.

Nova closed her eyes and savored the way my lips felt on her skin. "I love you, Master."

"I love you, too," I said, relishing the fact that the shit sounded like music to my ears.

"Take care of yourself," she said.

I touched her stomach. "You take care of my baby," I told her.

Nova smiled but there was doubt all in her eyes. I could tell that she was afraid of me not coming back. And honestly, so was I.

***

I made it to the warehouse in twenty minutes top and found Sensation's car parked out front. There was only one outside, so I assumed he was alone. When dealing with a nigga like Sensation, it was never safe to assume but I did anyway. I just prayed he didn't surprise me with some shit I wasn't expecting.

After parking, I turned off the engine, climbed out and slowly made my way towards the warehouse. "How the fuck did this nigga even find out about this place?" I wondered. "And if he's known about it this long, why hasn't he tried to run up in it too?"

With all the people crossing me lately, there was really no telling how he got the info. When I walked inside, I found him seated on top of a table with his legs dangling over the edge. He looked unbothered and unfazed. Like he hadn't recently murdered seven of my best men.

"I was beginning to think you wouldn't show," he said. "You know...with you being balls deep in my bitch and all."

"Are we here to talk about bitches? Or are we here to talk about business?"

"I finally got you where I want you so we might as well talk about both." Sensation smirked. "So...How is it?" He asked. "She got that splash or what?"

My jaw tightened in irritation. He'd obviously called me here to play mind games. Something I clearly didn't feel like doing.

"That shit A-1, ain't it?" He cackled. "Mouth kinda trash though but the pussy makes up for it."

"Enough of the bullshit!" I roared.

Sensation looked shocked that I flew off the handle so fast.

Then he suddenly erupted with laughter. "Damn, my nigga. Somebody got tight quick. You must really love this girl, huh?"

"I think you know that," I said. "Now tell me, son. What did you *really* call me here to discuss?"

"You know... I really hate it when you call me son." Sensation reached behind him and grabbed his gun, and I made no move at all to grab my own.

Deep down inside, I already knew what he had planned. But I wasn't some pussy nigga and I wasn't gonna avoid or run from my demons. I was gonna face them head on like a man and whatever happened, happened.

"You were never a father to me," he said. "Hell, you were never even there for me! And when I needed you the most, you turned your back on me! Left me to rot while you fucked on my girl!" He yelled. "Then I wonder why I'm so fucked up." He shook his head. "It's because you made me this way," he said with tears in his eyes. "You made me the nigga I am today!"

"Son, put the gun down and let's talk like men," I said calmly.

"Don't fucking call me that shit!" He yelled through clenched teeth. "Do not fucking call me that shit! I'm not your fucking son! And you're not a man. Just a nigga who's far outlived his usefulness," he said.

"Sensation..." I slowly approached him. "Sylvester." I called him by his God-given name. "If you pull that trigger, it won't change the past nineteen years."

"I don't give a fuck! At the very least, it'll make me feel better." His finger hovered over the trigger and I expected him to squeeze at any given moment but he faltered. Evidently, he was struggling with his *own* inner demons.

"Give me the gun," I whispered. "You don't wanna do this—"

"Don't tell me what the fuck I don't wanna do! I've been dreaming about this moment!" He seethed.

"Sensation...if you pull that trigger, you'll regret it for the rest of your life."

"Pussy nigga, fuck you!" He spat. "You abandoned me! Denied me! Disrespected me for the last fucking time and I'm sick of it! I could fucking kill you!" He hollered. In spite of his threats, he didn't pull the trigger. "I could fucking kill your bitch ass!"

I cautiously continued to make my way towards him and when the gun was finally within my reach, I slowly grabbed the barrel and lowered it.

"I could fucking kill you," he said weakly.

For the first time ever, I didn't see a ruthless and reckless gang banger who couldn't control his temper. I saw a boy who *desperately* needed his father in his life.

Stepping forward, I took the gun from him and that's when he broke down crying hysterically. Pulling him into my arms, I held him like I should've held him a long, long time ago. If I'd been in his life the way I should have, he would've never turned out this way. He was right. I had made him into the man he was today. And I knew that it'd take a lot of work to groom him into the man he was *meant* to be. After all, children learn more from what you are than what you teach.

"I know, son. I know," I said, cradling his head. "And I'm sorry. I'm so, so sorry." I held him tightly as he sobbed into my chest and I promised myself that I would never take him for granted again. "There's still time though," I told him. "There's still time for me to do things the right way and I want to, son. I wanna be there for you. I want us to have a bond. I wanna teach you the game and I want you to have it all, son. You *deserve* to have it all."

44

NOVA

I thought about Master and if I'd ever see him again, following his departure. I didn't care what he said. I knew Sensation and how treacherous he could be. He'd go to the ends of the earth if that meant getting his revenge. He never let shit go. Ever. He was as vindictive as they came.

I pray he's okay.

I pray nothing happens to him.

I thought about following Master to the warehouse, but I didn't wanna risk Sensation seeing me and potentially making the situation worse. Although I only wanted to help, I knew that I might end up fanning the flames in the process. It was best for me to just stay out of it and let them hash out their differences. I only hoped they could come to a resolution that *didn't* involve death.

I couldn't imagine raising Master's child alone. I knew I was talking big shit last night but I had no intentions of getting an abortion. As a matter of fact, I welcomed the idea of being a new mom and I was excited about Master being a part of this child's life.

"Please, Sensation. Please don't do anything stupid," I prayed.

Climbing out of the bed, I showered, dressed then headed to the kitchen to fetch the weed I'd stolen from under the sink. I desperately needed a smoke. When I remembered that I was pregnant, I quickly backtracked and started making breakfast instead. Master would probably flip if I even inhaled the scent of marijuana while carrying his baby. He was already so over-protective of it.

"I'll just cook a meal for when he gets back," I said. I told myself that if I was optimistic enough, he would return. And if I had doubts, he wouldn't.

Opening the cabinets above the sink, I grabbed the pancake batter and cooking grease. Suddenly, out of nowhere, I felt something cold and hard press into the back of my head. It took my brain several seconds to realize that it was a gun.

Oh shit!

Marcus found me!

45
MASTER

When I finally made it back to Nova's crib, I could smell the scent applewood smoked bacon pouring from underneath her door before I even opened it. I smiled because this was the first time Nova had ever cooked for me.

I knocked on the door, but when she didn't answer, I twisted the knob and let myself in. Much to my surprise, it was Maloni in the kitchen cooking while Nova lay hogtied on the living room floor with a sock in her mouth. Her head was leaking and her lip was busted.

"Bitch, what the f—" I went to advance on my wife but she quickly pointed her gun at me.

"Unh, unh, unh. I wouldn't do that if I were you," she said condescendingly. "I might slip up and squeeze the trigger on this bitch," she said, pointing her gun at Nova.

"Maloni...don't do this," I begged.

"Funny...I recall saying the same thing before you buried me alive with a dead fucking body."

"Bitch, you tried to kill me!" I screamed.

"Well, now we're even," she smiled, stirring the bacon in the skillet like she was at our crib and not in the confines of someone else's home.

"Maloni...who the fuck are you?" I asked In a low tone. "You used to be my best fucking friend, my partner in crime. Now I feel like I don't even know you. Who was I married to for twenty-one years? Have I been blind that whole time?"

Maloni turned off the stove, then slowly put the bacon on a plate covered in paper towels to catch the grease. "I wasn't always this way, you know. Once upon a time, I really did love you. I loved you so fucking much, you don't even know," she said. "If I had a choice between going to heaven or sucking your dick, I would've gladly given you head in hell. That's how crazy I was about you. But all of that shit changed. Something died inside of you. Or maybe it was me," she said. "Maybe something died inside of me because one day I just woke up and realized that I wasn't in love with you anymore. You didn't make me feel happy or fulfilled anymore and I needed that, Master. I needed it and I thought I found it in Dru..."

My eyes welled up with tears. At least now, I had my answers. She really did love Dru.

"But Shoota took her from me," she said in a weak voice as a single tear slid down her cheek. "He took her from me and now I'm out here lost and fucked up."

"So that makes it okay to do what you doin'?" I hollered. "'Loni, you trippin' man, gimme the fuckin' gun!"

I thought I could use the same tactics on her that I'd used with Sensation but I was wrong. Instead of listening, she pointed the gun at me and pulled the trigger.

POW!

She blew a hole clean through my chest, near my shoulder

blade. She almost hit me in the heart and I wasn't sure or not if she meant to.

Nova screamed a muffled cry and I slowly staggered backwards from the impact.

"I don't wanna hear shit you have to say!" She spat. "Now sit down, eat this breakfast I've slaved over and shut the fuck up!"

"I'm not eating shit," I told her. Last time I did that, I ended up spitting up my insides.

Without warning, Maloni launched the plate of food at me. The plates were porcelain and I ducked in just the nick of time before they crashed into the wall behind me.

"You never did appreciate shit I did for your ass!" She yelled. "I held you down in school, in the military, even when you got in the drug game but what about me? Huh? What about me? You just continued to put me last on your list of priorities!" She pointed her gun at Nova. "But this young bitch comes around and you treat her like the sun rises out of her ass! Tell me! What number is she on your list of priorities?"

"Maloni—"

"Answer me, nigga! What fucking number is she on your list of priorities?!"

I looked over at Nova. There were tears pouring out of her eyes and a look on her face that begged me to tell Maloni what she wanted to hear. But instead, I told her the truth.

"She's number one in my life. She always will be."

A single tear rolled down Maloni's cheek as she slowly lowered the gun. "I was afraid you were gonna say that." Suddenly, she pointed the gun at Nova and pulled the trigger.

"NOOOOO!!!"

Everything thereafter happened in the blink of an eye. I launched my body in front of Nova's taking the bullet in her place and that time, it did pierce me in the heart.

Before Maloni could squeeze a second time, the police stormed the premises with their guns drawn and pointed directly at Maloni. Usually, I hated five-oh but I don't think I was happier to see them. I knew I was on my way out but at least i got to make sure Nova was okay.

"Put down the fucking weapon!" One of the officers screamed as another rushed to me and Nova's aid. When Maloni didn't move fast enough, he yelled at her in a harsher tone. "I said put down the fucking weapon or else I'll be forced to shoot!"

Maloni tossed the gun at her feet, then placed her hands above her head. Two cops quickly rushed to detain her, while the others tended to me. Someone had obviously reported the gunshots because there were more than two cops present, which was unusual. Then again, we were in one of the deadliest neighborhoods in Houston. They probably figured it was better to be safe than sorry. All types of crazy shit went on in Texas.

By the time they got the sock out of Nova's mouth, I was already feeling the effects of having my life taken from me. As a matter of fact, I could even see a white light.

"Master!!!" Nova screamed. "No! Don't you do this to me! Don't you fucking do this to me! I love you, baby!" She said, cradling my head. "What about our child?" She cried.

"We need EMTs!!!!" An officer shouted, checking my pulse. "This one's losing blood fast!" Blood was pouring out of my chest and he applied pressure on my lung to try and stem the blood flow.

I was going into shock and drifting in and out of consciousness but I could still hear Nova as she continued to sob hysterically.

"Master, please don't do this," she cried. "Please baby. Don't leave me alone."

I went to tell her that I loved her and that she'd never be alone but I couldn't even muster up the strength to utter the words. Thankfully, she was the last face I saw before I closed my eyes and prayed that I did enough good deeds to make it to heaven.

46
NOVA

By the grace of God, Master miraculously survived the gunshot wound to his heart. Hell, the doctors were even surprised. They said that this was one of the rarest cases they'd ever seen.

The bullet had torn through his arm and into his heart and lung. They claimed that even though he was shot in the heart, it was his arm that saved him. But deep down inside, I knew that it was my love.

When Master was finally wheeled out of surgery, I sat by his bed the entire time until he finally cracked his eyes open the next day. As soon as I heard him make the faintest movement, I jumped to his aid.

"Baby...you're up," I smiled. "How do you feel?"

He groaned in pain. "Like I have a hole in my heart," he struggled to laugh.

"It's a little too soon to be making jokes," I said before kissing his cheek.

"I thought I was done."

WHEN A GANGSTA WANTS YOU 271

"I thought you were too...but God had other plans," I smiled.

"*God's plan...God's plan*," he teased, mimicking the Drake song.

"Boy bye," I laughed with tears in my eyes. I was so happy that he was still with me, I promised to start going to church every Sunday just to thank the Lord.

"Knock, knock," Trae said before coming into the room with a few of Master's closest friends. "You up and at em, bro?" he asked sarcastically.

"Nigga, what's it look like?" Master chuckled.

Suddenly, the last person I expected to see walked into the room next, followed by my sister, A'shaunie.

Oh my God.

Is Sensation really here to wish his dad well wishes or am I dreaming, I asked myself.

"Hey, Son," Master smiled at him weakly.

Sensation didn't smile back at him. Instead he folded his arms and looked on with an attitude like the unruly son that he was. "Hey," He spat. "I just came to make sure you weren't really dead. So don't get shit twisted. I still don't fuck wit' you like that, old man."

Master guffawed. "That's good enough for me," he said.

A'shaunie and I made eye contact and I quickly looked away. I didn't know if I could forgive her as easily as Sensation had forgiven Master, but I could try.

"So, is it true that you got shot in the heart?" Trae asked. Master nodded.

"How the fuck did you survive that?" Trae asked surprised.

"He don't have a heart. That's how," Sensation answered.

Everyone laughed, including me.

Even though we'd all had our fair share of differences, it felt so good to come together during these trying times. Maloni was charged with attempted murder and it'd be a long ass time before she ever saw the light of day. Sensation seemed happy with my sister and I guess, at the end of the day, I couldn't really be mad about that. I was damn sure happy with Master and I couldn't wait to raise a family with him.

"He does have a heart." I kissed the back of Master's hand. "It's just in my possession."

EPILOGUE
NOVA

Six months after the incident with Maloni, I ended up seeing a news report about a man's body drenched out of a local river. It was Marcus. I knew that Master had everything to do with his death but I wouldn't dare ask him about. At least, not before our big day.

Master had popped the question right after he was released from the hospital and while I had doubts about marrying a recently-divorced man, I knew that he would put those doubts to rest the moment I said I do.

I was as a big as a house when Trae picked me up the evening before our ceremony for my fitting. I had no home girls so he had to be something like my bridesmaid. I still hadn't made amends with my sister, even after all the time that she and Sensation had been together. He stayed committed to her, gave up his player ways and even put a baby in her. Something he'd never done for me before so I kinda felt some type of way about it. But hey. At least, I had a happy home of my own. And it was a home I cherished with immense appreciation and gratitude.

Master moved me out of the dump I was living in into a big, beautiful mansion on the outskirts of Austin, Texas. I couldn't have been happier too because as much as I loved Houston, there was so many bad memories that I wanted to leave behind.

Twenty minutes into the ride, I realized we weren't going to the bridal store. "Um, Trae? Where are you taking me?" I asked him.

Trae didn't answer. He just smiled and kept on driving. Fifteen minutes later, we arrived at a private helipad near the city.

"What's this?" I asked him.

"You'll see," he said.

After parking the car, he hopped out and opened my door for me. He then led me a helicopter that was already whirring its rotor blades. My hair blew in the wind. I was just about to ask him where my fiancé was when I spotted him standing near the helicopter.

"Hey, baby." Master smiled and took my hand. "You ready to be my wife?"

"I thought the ceremony was tomorrow!" I shouted over the sound of the spinning rotor blades.

"What can I say? I always been the spontaneous type." He helped me board the aircraft.

"Master, this shit is crazy! I've never been on a helicopter before," I said somewhat nervous.

"What did I tell you in the past?" he asked. "I told you I would show you the world and I plan to do just that."

"Are you even licensed to drive one of these things?" I asked, looking around for the pilot. There was no pilot; only Trae waiting patiently to see us off.

"No. But just know you in good hands youngin'," he teased.

I believed him for some reason.

Master climbed into the aircraft. After securing his seat-belt, he reached for the controls, and pulled the collective control stick upwards. The rotor blades pushed into the wind, generating enough lift to get the chopper off the ground and rising. I looked nervous at first, and he told me to trust him.

"Where are we going?" I asked. I couldn't mask the over-whelming excitement in my voice.

"To our ceremony," he smiled. "Everyone's waiting on us."

Two hours later, we arrived at the shoreline of a private island in Cancun. Master lowered the helicopter onto the sand, and that's when I saw the bridal set-up and a small group of people awaiting our arrival, including my mother and...

"Daddy?"

As soon as I saw him, I took off running and threw my arms around his neck. Master said that he would find him and he kept his word.

"Hey, baby girl," he smiled, hugging me and kissing my hair.

"Oh, Daddy, I missed you!" I cried into his chest.

"I missed you too, baby girl. And I'm sorry that I stayed away for so long."

"That doesn't matter. All that matters is you're here now."

"You know I wouldn't miss this day for anything in the world," he said, taking my hand in his as he led me down the aisle in typical bridal fashion.

Each and every one of our guests were seated in a white chair and dressed in formal white attire. Lanterns were placed near each chair, and a rose-sprinkled path led to the elegant pavilion, where a pastor stood, waiting to join us in holy matri-mony. The special day I had been waiting on had finally arrived.

I felt so unprepared but I knew that, ultimately, this was what I wanted.

There were tears in my mother's eyes as she watched me take the stand. Master joined me shortly after. She looked so happy for us, despite our past and everything we'd been through and I couldn't have been happier myself. Now that I had the man of my dreams, I never wanted to let him go. I planned on spending the rest of my life with him.

"I love you, Master. Thank you so much for making this all possible," I said before the pastor started his sermon.

He took my hands in his. "You're welcome, my queen. Anything to see you smile."

We were finally making this shit official, and there was nothing or no one that could ever come between us.

THE END

Made in the USA
Columbia, SC
19 September 2024

42614254R00171